GA
STRANDS

Love's Tangled Tapestries Trilogy

Veronica Bennetts

'The web of our life is of a mingled yarn, good and ill'

'All's Well That Ends Well' William Shakespeare

In memory of lovely friends

'Love's Tangled Tapestries' *(No.3)*

GATHERED STRANDS

Chapter 1

1989

The body remained submerged for several hours, gradually distending with water and beginning its relentless journey of putrefaction. When it finally rose to the surface, its face bloated, discoloured, and distorted, it drifted slowly from the vicinity of Southwark downstream on the Thames. As the current became strong and the wind blew up, it was tossed and buffeted towards Greenwich. The foggy night had given way to a light misty morning, and the pale grey smoke-like veil lingered eerily above the surface of the river, reminiscent of a Turner painting. The body lodged itself in thick detritus by the river bank, where it remained half submerged in murky water, its face bobbing up and down to the surface weirdly as it drifted backwards and forwards to the rhythm of the current. A woman of indeterminate age had, for reasons unknown as yet, ended her days in a watery grave.

A police patrol boat had been out during the early hours of the morning, its fog horn sounding and its bright searchlight penetrating the thick grey. It was on look-out patrol and sounding a warning to hapless risk-takers who were defying the weather and out on some dangerous joyride or other. Now that the fog had changed to a light mist, the naval police officer turned down both search light and horn and chugged slowly along, hugging the bank of the river. It was then that both men saw the body in the water. They were relatively unphased by it. There were about fifty drownings a year along the Thames stretch that ran through the city. Most were recorded as suicides, but only the river itself knew the secret of exactly where and when a body might resurface and what the circumstances had been.

Leaning out of the vessel to look at the drowned body more closely, one of the men remarked that the victim was hardly a modern-day Ophelia. He took in almost immediately that her hands, visible on the surface of the water, displayed red fingernails, which were badly chipped and cracked. What looked like a cheap nail varnish had started, the small hungry scavengers of the Thames were in the process of finishing off. Strangely, the woman had one emerald green stiletto shoe still tightly rammed into her foot. The other had obviously been swept away by the Thames's current of death.

One of the naval patrol officers contacted the local police station by radio, and within minutes, the body was lifted out of the water, examined, and subsequently removed from the scene. The drowned woman's watery grave was replaced by the cold steel slab of the autopsy table.

xxxxx

Meanwhile, the warden at the church army hostel was aware that Pearl Johnson had been missing for two days. One or two of his residents occasionally wandered off for twenty-four hours and then reappeared, finding the comparative comfort of the sleeping arrangements at the Church Army hostel preferable to a hard pavement. Pearl had signed herself into the residents' book three mornings previously around mid-day. This was her routine when arriving back from the local cafe, where she normally had her daily breakfast cup of tea, into which she always poured the contents of a stolen miniature bottle of whisky.

She had not signed herself in or out for the following forty-eight hours. Now, Hughie concluded, she would have to be declared a missing person. Pearl's son Gary had moved into the church army hostel with her after being well cared for temporarily by the Lockwood family at the vicarage in Southwark. Under the influence of their loving kindness, Gary had begun to see the error of his ways. He was already wanted by the law for several rapes and a serious knife crime and had spent his life dodging the police, at which he had become exceptionally skilled. His desire was to stay in the locality as he had a small daughter who was actually the result of one of his vicious rapes. The baby's mother, Hope O'Neill, although shocked and angry beyond words by her terrifying gang rape experience, had nevertheless allowed Gary to see the baby occasionally. This supreme act of kindness was dictated to her both by the kindness in her heart and the requirements of her Christian faith. Gary's life now revolved around having occasional glimpses of his young daughter Lucy.

The warden of the hostel realised that Gary was missing, as well as his mother Pearl, but he also knew that Gary was prone to disappear overnight to try to see his daughter, so he was not unduly concerned. Hughie Penrose, the warden, was a nice enough fellow. He was divorced and lonely, which was why he had applied for the advertised post at the church army fourteen years ago when he was fifty, and he had remained there ever since. Originally set up as a 'Home for Tramps and Inebriates,' the noble church army hostel had cared for hundreds of people over the years. Hughie had always housed under his roof his fair share of folk who struggled with alcohol and drug addiction, which was why alcohol was banned from the premises. Drugs remained the preserve of the crafty, dishonest, needy, and fragile, who somehow managed to keep feeding their addiction by methods unknown to Hughie.

Hughie knew that Gary was a wanted man, but within the walls of the church army, he was temporarily safe. When he first arrived, Gary presented as a surprisingly law-abiding youth, thanks to the recent influence of The Rev'd Oliver and Mrs. Connie Lockwood. Three weeks later, however, worn down, irritated, and angry by his fawning and adoring mother, Pearl, he seemed to be reverting to his truculent and aggressive self. To see his mother Pearl's obsequiousness to her son was obnoxious, and to see Gary's cruel responses to his mother was alarming. The more Gary abused her verbally, the more she cringed and fawned around him.

After a few days, Hughie contacted the police and reported Pearl Johnson as a missing person. The police were familiar with the area's deprived 'down-and-outs' vanishing into thin air in London only to turn up at a later date involved in some illicit activity or other. For every case of genuine hardship—and these were heart-rending—Hughie reckoned there were half a dozen who were used to playing the system. Gary Johnson was in great need on a number of levels, but he was also as wily as a fox when it came to deception, lies, and avoidance of ever being caught by the law. Hughie wouldn't put anything past him. He spelt danger. Hughie shrugged inwardly. Oh well, he himself was coming up to retirement age, so he would leave it to the police. They were largely and understandably ineffectual when it came to missing persons in London. It was like looking for a needle in a haystack.

Chapter 2

Two Days Previously

Gary had committed several heinous crimes, but the worst of them involved Pearl Johnson, his mother. He congratulated himself on picking the perfect night to execute his daring and dangerous plan. Steering his inebriated and stupefied mother through the thick fog of the Southwark streets of London and down the pier at Bankside beach, he had somehow lifted her off the jetty and into a sturdy rowing boat he had previously moored there.

He assumed he went undetected, and anyway, even if there was someone watching from the beach, they could not have seen Gary and his mother at the end of the jetty, so thick was the fog. He put the oars into the rowlocks and began to row strongly and silently through the murky night into the centre of the River Thames. No-one could possibly have seen him, Gary thought to himself. The visibility was that poor.

There, he had tipped his drunken mother into the Thames, seen her bob up to the surface briefly with terrified eyes, then disappear into the blackness of the water. Gary knew he had no option but to hide from the law for the rest of his life. This was murder. He mourned the loss of contact with the Lockwoods, the family that had begun to mean a lot to him, but he knew that if he was caught, he would be banged up for life.

He moored the boat further downstream, having negotiated from memory the areas he was passing. Gary was very familiar with London and knew every tide and every tunnel. He arrived at Rotherhithe, cleared the boat of any telltale evidence such as whisky and gin bottles, and then abandoned it, leaving it to drift to some unknown destination decided by the strong currents of the Thames. Gary pulled himself onto the bank and moved stealthily towards Rotherhithe tunnel. It was one of his many hiding places in London. He often slept there during the night, always aware that the deeper in he went, the more car fumes he had to cope with, but it was a small price to pay for such an anonymous hiding place.

He knew the tunnel was nearly a mile long and slowly made his way to the centre. He was immensely weary from the exhausting row downstream against the current, combined with the emotional numbness that had set in from the enormity of what he had done. It was only rarely that he ever met another person in the tunnel. It had been designated by the police an unsafe place to walk, and on a night like this, no-one would be out, let alone travelling from one end of the cave-like tunnel to the other. It was eerie in the half-gloom, and the thick fog that surrounded the outside of the tunnel hung inside anaemically, reminiscent of puffs of mist erratically pumped from some theatrical smoke machine. The narrow pavement was not designed for pedestrians but for horse-drawn carriages. The unusual curves in the tunnel originally ensured that horses did not bolt from the sudden daylight they encountered as they were faced with it at its end. This suited Gary well. On this night, he would be unseen at every stage of the tunnel. Running his hand along the tiled wall as he slowly inched further in, he suddenly stopped.

A scruffy, half-starved dog cringed his way up to Gary, its belly scraping the ground, its tail flickering a small, apprehensive wag between its legs.

'Hey, boy? Watcha doing in here, then? Get lost or somefink?'

The dog, made braver by Gary's uncharacteristically gentle tone of voice, cringed further up to him and licked his hand, grateful for the slight hint of salt on it from the brackish Thames.

'I know what's 'appened to you, boy. You got lost in the fog, ain't ya?

The dog bravely wagged his tail a little more.

'Oh, you're a nice fella! Homeless, I should't wonder. Come on, then, you and me belong together. Rejects, us'.

Gary pulled the stolen leather belt from his jeans and fixed it round the dog's neck. The dog did not resist but was clearly grateful for the attention and was already visibly growing in trust.

'Now, what we gonna call you, fella?'

The dog was a black and white border collie type, immensely thin and undernourished, with matted fur and weeping eyes; a pathetic specimen of total neglect and life on the run.

'You're a handsome boy, in't ya? And I bet you can have a temper on you when you try'.

The dog wagged a little more.

'Think I'll call you Wolf. Like that? Yeh, that's a good name. Bet you can be fierce when you like. You can guard me; yes, you can. Let's start practising'.

Gary called him several times.

'Wolf! Wolf! Wolfie *sit*! I said *sit!'*.

The dog cringed and wagged and licked and eventually sat.

'There y'are. You knows your name already! You thirsty, mate? Come on, we'll get out of here and find you a drink'.

And there began Gary's total devotion to the dog he called Wolf, who clearly no-one had ever loved and who had long ago lost his fighting spirit.

Chapter 3

Maria Murphy, known to her colleagues as 'MM', was fifty-nine years old. As a medical psychotherapist, she was entitled to retire at any time from sixty onwards. Maria Murphy had no intention of going on longer than sixty-five, although she had no idea what she would do in retirement. Her work was her life. She had no husband and no children.

No-one could understand why MM was not married or at least had a partner. She looked years younger than her age, was slim, still shapely, and her smartly styled blonde hair showed no signs of greying yet. Even the most hardened professor of psychiatry would have to acknowledge that Maria was brilliant at her job as well as being an attractive woman: compassionate, empathetic, and very tough when she needed to be. She took on many of the patients who were displaying particularly recalcitrant and challenging behaviour. She was passionate about her work and had never had any desire to be deflected from it by social interaction of any kind with the opposite sex except in a professional capacity.

'Why is it that people forever make assumptions that I *wanted* to be married?' she would sometimes ask.'It's the height of sexism. Men simply can't believe that some of us can function quite well without them!'

If people had not asked the over-used question about marriage, then they might say, 'Have you any children?' Maria would make some flippant reply - 'No time for them,' or 'Too messy!', but inside, the scars from her pain never fully healed, and the deep ache, though dulled by time, was a permanent feature in her life.

Years ago, Maria Murphy had lost a child at birth and had sublimated her grief into dedicated study. She was blessed with a high intelligence and an intellectual zest that never failed her, acquitting herself with distinction in every school examination that she took. Embedded in her psyche, however, ran a deep-seated lack of self-worth, probably caused in part by over-critical parents with their setting of impossibly high standards for their daughter. She felt she never quite belonged anywhere. Her pious Roman Catholic parents, Henry and Emily O'Neill, were cold, severe, and Victorian in outlook and had been aghast when their only child had told them she was pregnant. They abandoned her at the tender age of seventeen to a hostel for 'Fallen Girls' in Ireland, albeit one with a dubious reputation. She was informed without sentiment that her baby daughter had died at birth and that Maria herself had narrowly escaped death. The nuns running the hostel immediately and possibly misguidedly, on seeing there were complications at the birth, had her transported to the local hospital. She lay on the ambulance stretcher plugged up with towels and pads to try and stem the uncontrolled post-partum bleeding. The nuns were shocked but, unfortunately, fairly familiar with these haemorrhages. They swiftly wiped the blood from their garments, washed their hands of the matter Pontius Pilate style, and deleted both mother and child's existence from their records. They had their reputation and credibility to consider, did they not? They did not want the Bishop to lose faith in them and close the convent down as a result, did they now?

On hearing the baby had died, Maria's parents decided their daughter could come home once her tummy became flat again after the birth—probably in two or three months' time. They did not want anyone guessing about her pregnancy, especially as she had been banished for seven months and questions had already been asked as to her whereabouts. They had recommended to Maria a temporary stay in the local convent after the birth. Maria was appalled and deeply wounded by her parents' attitudes and, from then on, steadfastly refused to go home ever, permanently damaged by their rejection of her in her hour of need. There were no words of compassion or understanding from either of them about her baby—their unacknowledged grandchild. The child was born in sin, and God had metered out His punishment to their daughter accordingly.

They were wealthy people and seemingly without conscience, but not quite. Knowing that their daughter, as a gifted individual, was highly intelligent and had been set for academic excellence, they offered to pay for her training or higher education for as long as she needed but were secretly relieved that their daughter, tainted by immorality and corruption, had refused to live under the same roof as them again. Money had been her parents' answer to practically everything in life. They gave away vast sums on occasions, usually to people or situations where they could influence some kind of outcome for their own purposes. 'The Conscience of the Rich' Maria thought witheringly, having just read the recently published book by C.P.Snow of the same name; however, despite her principles, she defiantly accepted the money for her long training, tuition, and accommodation.

Maria moved to England, far away from them, and applied successfully to Cambridge to study Medicine and then Psychiatry. Her subject choice was due in part to an unacknowledged drive to understand her parents and the workings of their minds and try to find some glimmer of an excuse for their attitudes. Maria could never fully accept that their rejection of her was motivated solely by feelings of shame and disgrace over their daughter's pregnancy. Was their love for her so superficial? Just what *were* the workings of their minds, and how had they become so hardened?

She took their money, a vast lump sum, but her heart was permanently set against them from that time forward. She felt no guilt in exploiting them, regarding it as the very least they could do for her. In her heart, a bitterness had taken root: a rogue strand in the fabric of her generally balanced psyche had been sewn there largely by her parents. In addition, Maria had absolutely no desire to forgive them for the hurt they had inflicted on her.

Maria's wartime man friend disappeared without a trace as soon as he learned of her pregnancy. Her affair with him had been driven by her longing to experience warmth and unconditional love. While he appeared to give her both of these whenever he was with her, even telling her that his marriage was a sham and he was going to leave his wife, he nevertheless managed to disappear without trace when she needed him most. During his last visits, their lovemaking had taken a rather different turn. Each time he visited her, he seemed more violent and demanding, asking her to do things she felt unhappy about, even cracking two ribs on one occasion. She assumed it was the result of his having experienced the horrors of war and that he was working them out in some bizarre way. She tolerated it because she loved him and wanted to keep him, and besides, she needed him. She was pregnant.

'Same old story,' she reflected years later when hearing of the havoc wrought on other abandoned wartime lovers. Maria took into her adulthood a hardened mistrust of men and a withering attitude towards Christianity in general and the Roman Catholic Church in particular. Her parents, of course, never shared with her the fact that both of them had disliked the sex act after the very first fumbling and painful physical encounter on their honeymoon and never ever broached the subject in their marriage again, let alone indulged in further lovemaking efforts. Maria was conceived on their one and only attempt. To learn much later that their daughter was having an ongoing affair with a married man, and what was more, clearly approached it initially with abandonment and passion, was more than they could bear. Her pregnancy simply rubbed salt in the wound—a tangible sign of what their daughter had been up to and, in their secret hearts, what they were missing.

'Sin' was the word they whispered frequently to each other. 'Shame' was the potent emotion they felt.

Chapter 4

In the fullness of time, Maria qualified from the University of Cambridge with flying colours as a Psychiatrist, having first read medicine and then on for further training to become a Medical Psychiatric Social Worker, the eight years of training all funded by her parents. She fleeced them mercilessly and without conscience for money. Having witnessed the appalling conditions within the hostel for women all those years ago, she was determined to do anything she could to alleviate some of the mental suffering brought about by social deprivation, isolation, and rejection. For Maria, trying to fathom the complexities of the twisted threads of the mind felt like an essential first step in her training.

Her last ten years had been spent attached to a large South London Psychiatric hospital doing 'on call' emergency medical psychiatric work. She loved the buzz of being called by the Casualty department of the hospital to come and deal with a patient who might have arrived in an uncontrollable suicidal state or mental breakdown and was maybe running amok in the outpatient department or sitting immovably in a catatonic trance. She had used different types of restraint on very troubled patients, including, on one occasion, the largely obsolete straitjacket when there was no other immediate answer to stem violent physical behaviour.

On this particular evening, she really hoped it would be quiet and without trauma. She was on call all night and would be in the designated room in the hospital for a few hours' sleep before cooking herself two scrambled eggs on the two-ring gas stove provided before starting her day's work in the Outpatient clinic. Most nights were without incident. On a more demanding night, she might be called to a ward when a patient was particularly distressed, or else someone would be brought in by ambulance in a poor mental state. On rare occasions, she drove to a patient if he or she were deemed by the paramedics to be too ill psychologically to transport.

Maria slept very lightly in a set of clothes that she could combine sleeping in with visiting patients: usually, a navy tracksuit bottom and pastel tee shirt over which she always put on her smart/casual mid-blue jacket. The fact was that if Maria dressed herself in sackcloth, she would still look attractive. Many commented that she appeared to be only a little over forty. It was not unusual for her patients (or rather, 'clients' as the medics had been directed to call them) to fall in love with her. Maria encouraged them to talk about it with her, thereby taking the first step to defuse the situation. She was totally without vanity and self-deprecating about her appearance generally, even though she spent more time and money than she should on her hair. The fact was that Maria Murphy could have done with some psychotherapy herself when it came to her lack of self-worth.

She had drifted off to sleep by about one a.m. when her phone rang. It was the Casualty department of the local hospital.

'Professor Murphy. We have a problem. The paramedics were called out to a young man who was presenting as extremely disturbed. He is now sitting on the floor here, wailing and saying all sorts of incoherent things. We've tried to calm him. The Consultant on call has given him ten milligrams of Diazepam intravenously, but he's still ranting and thrashing around. Please could you come? It's rather urgent'.

'Of course, Nurse – em?

'Staff Nurse Maureen Wilson'

'Of course, Staff Nurse Wilson. Put him in a side room if possible and reassure him as much as you can. Poor chap's obviously traumatised by something. I'll be there within fifteen'.

Maria quickly put the kettle on, straightened her clothes, put a brush through her easy-to-manage hair, grabbed her car keys from a dish by her bed, gulped a few mouthfuls of the strong instant coffee she had hurriedly made, went to the car park and drove to the hospital, keeping just within the speed limit. She had been fined twice already in the last two months, so she watched the speedometer carefully this time.

She parked in her priority bay, put her identification badge on the dashboard, and went up to the Casualty department. The doors swung open for her.

'Oh, Professor Murphy, are we glad to see you!' said a nurse holding the door. 'Never seen anything like this one'.

Maria was ushered into one of the small side rooms and came face to face with a young man, keening in grief. Maria had heard the sound once or twice before. She had never forgotten the howling of the twelve-year-old girl in the bed next to her all those years ago in Ireland when her newborn baby had been pulled unceremoniously out of her arms forever for adoption. The young girl had wailed inconsolably like an animal for many hours. It was the most intense, guttural sound that Maria had ever heard and seemed to come from the very depths of the mother's soul. Maria's own extreme loss of blood had rendered her so weak that all she could do herself was sob silently into her pillow, but her heart and insides were indeed keening mournfully at the loss of her own baby. She had four pints of blood replaced and was turned out of the hospital in three days to fend for herself.

XXXXX

Maria addressed the distraught young man who was now crouched, foetal position on the floor, and rocking from side to side.

'Now, let's see what's happening here, shall we?' Maria said gently as she drew a chair up alongside him and began talking softly.

'What's the matter, fella?' she crooned with a soft Irish lilt.

She moved to take his hand. The young man quietened for a few seconds and then snatched his hand away.

'Let's see if we can help'.

The young man clenched his fist and thrust his arm out sideways at her aggressively, intending to hit her, and narrowly missed her chest.

'Get out! Get away, sod you, woman' he yelled, suddenly finding his speaking voice.

This was definitely not going to be over in five minutes. Suddenly, the young man was up on his feet and storming around the room again. He swept a small pile of medical equipment off a trolley, picking up a chrome nasal speculum.

'Oh dear; mistake', said Nurse Wilson aloud to herself.

In her desperation to contain the flailing patient, she had finally coaxed him into a side room used for emergency ear, nose, and throat examinations, amongst other things. The young man started swiping the air with the speculum and moved up to Maria Murphy menacingly, brandishing the pointed end near her throat.

'Leave me alone, I said '*Leave me alone!'*

For only the second time in all her years as an on-call Medical Psychiatrist, Maria thought about a straitjacket. In a gentle whisper barely audible to anyone but her patient, she said,

'Has someone you loved died, sir?'

He crumpled immediately and sank to the floor, collapsing like a badly stacked pack of cards.

'Yes', he whispered back, dropping the speculum to the floor, causing it to rattle and vibrate several times before it was still. He started sobbing uncontrollably.

'Yes, I said '*Yes',* and through gritted teeth, and punctuated by sobs, he hissed,

' Now will you *fuck off?'*

Chapter 5

Gary Johnson stayed under the care of Maria Murphy for twenty-four hours. She gradually pieced together fragments of Gary Johnson's story. He and Wolf the dog had lived in the shadows for three years. He had found it was harder than before to stay invisible with the dog. Occasionally, people stopped to talk to Wolf and ask Gary questions about him, terrifying him when this happened. He knew the Law and he were always a stone's throw away from encountering each other, which made his invisibility imperative. On occasions, when desperate for food, he would sit at the edge of an obscure tunnel or shop doorway, his old wool hat pulled over his eyes, head bowed, his dog by his side, bowl in front of him, waiting silently for someone to throw them a few coins.

The money he accrued, which was generally a pittance, was spent mainly on dog food for Wolf. As Wolf gradually put on weight, so Gary lost it. Gary was wafer thin now and very hungry most of the time. He raided bins outside restaurants for any food that was thrown away, and much to his advantage, some places were sickeningly wasteful.

Gary had gone to a primary school for three years before he was expelled, having been deemed 'unteachable' by the more hard-nosed teachers and 'needing extra special care that we are unable to provide' by the more understanding ones. Gary remembered one line from 'All Things Bright and Beautiful', which the children often droned out in assembly, during which most of his time was spent flicking pointed paper darts surreptitiously at other children. The words often ran through his head now when he was foraging for food:

'The rich men in their castles, the poor men at their gate.'

Many of the hotels seemed to Gary to throw away food indiscriminately. Life on the run was challenging but far preferable, Gary knew, to spending the rest of his days locked up. During his three years on the run, he carried with him a burning desire to see his daughter Lucy. Once, when she was less than two weeks old, he had stolen her from her pram and looked after her for a few hours. These were probably the happiest hours of his life (although the baby's mother died inwardly of anxiety while she was missing). The discovery that Lucy had an identical medical condition to Gary's thrilled him. Her tiny webbed toes were Gary's toes in miniature and reminded him of his mother's webbed fingers. Lucy had the same condition, which proved beyond a shadow of a doubt his paternity.

Gary was a little ashamed of the group rape he had orchestrated with his gang at Borough Road Market in Southwark. He had been the first to help himself to their virgin victim's goodies as he thrust her onto the ground greedily. Hope O'Neil was a nun, and her black habit and copious undergarments had presented quite a challenge to the vicious and fired-up gang of five. But have their ugly way they all did. When Hope found she was pregnant as a result of the rape, she had no idea which of the five was Lucy's father, of course. Gary, however, enlightened her, pointing out the genetic condition (called 'Syndactyly' she was informed) and declaring that the baby was his.

On Lucy's first birthday, his curiosity won the day to see his daughter again. Gary took a huge risk and hid in the bushes outside Hope's ground-floor flat, hoping for a glimpse of her. He commanded Wolf to be silent, and Wolf, ready to cringe at the first sound of Gary's orders, sank to his belly and remained absolutely still. Gary knew that the police had issued posters saying that he was a wanted man. What he did not know was that the police had visited both Hope and the local vicarage family, who had baled Gary out on many occasions. They were all questioned extensively, but no-one had seen Gary since the night of his disappearance, and probably if they had, they would have had difficulty turning Gary in. No-one had seen him, that is, except Robbie Taylor, an ex-convict turned good who now worked as a youth leader attached to the church. He said nothing.

Gary's long wait outside Hope's flat was eventually rewarded. At around three o'clock on a warm afternoon, Hope wheeled a pushchair down the path, through the gate, and onto the pavement. Gary stared. Lucy, just one year old, was sitting in the pushchair, throwing a soft white toy rabbit out of it and giggling as Hope bent down to pick it up. The whole procedure was repeated, the baby was delighted by her newfound power, and the giggles grew more and more joyful. Gary stared at the baby. She had a soft cap of goldish hair, slightly curly at the ends, and the prettiest little face that Gary thought he had ever seen. Even from a distance of about fifteen yards, he could see Lucy strongly resembled her petite and dainty mother.

Gary's heart ached. He had an overwhelming desire to go up and talk to Hope and the baby. His feelings for Lucy and for his dog Wolf nearly equalled each other in intensity. Gary had never felt love until his encounter, first with his newborn daughter and then with his dog, the one living thing in the world that actually seemed to need *him.*

Gary and Wolf slunk back into the tunnel, and the pair lived the life of the homeless for two more years, skirting various parts of London but always eventually returning for a while to Gary's self-selected home base, which was in the tunnels around Southwark. Wolf turned out to be a soul mate for Gary. He always walked free and was obedient to every tone of Gary's voice. For a dog that had been so rejected in his early years, he was affectionate, obsequious, faithful, and grateful to Gary. Gary never used his belt again as a lead after the first encounter with him in the tunnel. It was a matter of pride to him that the dog obeyed his every command. Besides, Gary had lost so much weight that his one and only pair of jeans sank well below his hips unless he wore the belt in the tightest hole to hitch them up.

Gary and Wolf were inching back towards the tunnel after one of their scavenging expeditions, dodging between bushes when necessary and out on the pavement when he knew they were not the police's particular patrol area. He was incredibly street-wise over these kinds of timings and routes, just as he had accrued detailed knowledge of the tides of the Thames when he lived in the tunnel near Southwark.

Quite suddenly, an urbanised red fox, bold as brass, ran in front of them. Wolf, normally passive and law-abiding, lost his head completely and raced after it as if possessed, through the bushes and out onto the road in hot pursuit of the insolent fox. Gary raced after Wolf, calling him to heel, but Wolf was gone. The next thing Gary heard was a terrifying screech of brakes, a loud and chilling howl, and then silence. Gary reached the road. A woman had got out of her car and was bending down over the lifeless dog. The fox had completely escaped, but Wolf had not been so lucky.

Gary was frozen to the spot for a few seconds, then raced up to the car.

'I'm so sorry', said the woman, pale-faced with shock. 'He just ran out. There was nothing I could do. He's still got a heartbeat, but he's not responding'.

Gary stared at Wolf, feeling as though his own heart was severed in two. He knelt down.

'What d'ya go and do that for, boy? A fox ain't worth it'. He stroked Wolf's head. 'Come on, boy, you're all-right. On your feet. Wolf – *UP!'* he commanded desperately. The dog remained immobile. Gary tried to move him, but it was impossible. Wolf was as still as a rock, and a trickle of blood was slowly seeping out of his mouth.

'I'll drive you to the Vet', said the woman. 'I know where the RSPCA is. It's not far. Let's lift him into the car'. She glanced at her watch.

Gary and the woman awkwardly began to lift Wolf, who by this time seemed to rouse slightly. He looked at Gary and licked his hand softly, leaving a smear of blood over it. A man of business-like appearance ran up.

'Let me give you a hand. You sit in the back', he said to Gary, 'and I'll straddle the dog across your lap. Support his head'.

He helped them lift Wolf into the car, not seeming at all concerned that the dog was leaving a trail of blood on his dapper grey suit.

'Thanks so much', said the lady driver, who was clearly very shaken by the whole episode.

'I lost my dog a few weeks ago. Nothing hurts as much as losing your faithful friend', he said, meaning to be kind but causing a further cold clutch of fear to take hold of Gary's heart. Gary talked to Wolf all the way to the Vet.

'Come on now, Wolfie, you're gonna be O.K. You and me, we belong togevver, innit?'

He carried Wolf up the steps of the Vet. The driver of the car profusely apologised that she had to leave, saying she had small children to collect from school. Seeing the state of the dog, the Receptionist immediately knocked on the Vet's door.

'Emergency here, Carl. Dog run over. Needs urgent attention'.

The Vet was out within two minutes, full of apologies to a perfumed woman carrying her minute Pomeranium dog, who was wearing a glitzy pink coat with the word 'Angel' emblazoned on it in purple. The dog was holding stiffly a bandaged paw. Angel looked the epitome of a pampered little princess.

‘There, there. Mummy’s little darling’, the woman whispered to Angel in a baby voice, without so much as a glance at the bleeding dog lying inertly in Gary’s arms.

‘Let’s have a look at him’, the Vet said kindly to Gary. He glanced at the young man on the point of collapse. ‘Stay with Maggie here’, he said, waving a hand towards his receptionist, ‘I’ll be out as soon as I have any news for you’.

‘Please save him’, said Gary in a whisper, and then collapsed onto a chair, white as a ghost, with his head in his hands.

After what seemed like a lifetime to Gary, the Vet reappeared, looking grim.

‘I’m so sorry. Your dog had internal bleeding, and I suspect a ruptured spleen. He had taken such a hit from the car. I have to tell you that he died while I was examining him. There was no hope. I’m very sorry’.

Silence.

The Vet turned on his heels and went quickly back into his surgery. He hated breaking this sort of news, and the youth looked as though he was going to pass out. The Receptionist put her arm round Gary.

‘So sorry. It’s very hard. They are such pals, these dogs, aren’t they?’

Eventually, Gary whispered,

‘I want to see him’.

Suddenly fired up, he angrily broke away from the Receptionist, barging straight into the Vet’s surgery. There on the table, spread out, was Wolf, eyes wide open, his mouth covered in blood. The Vet and his assistant were about to clean him up and shut his eyes before asking Gary if he would like to come into the surgical room. Gary froze. Quite suddenly, his grief opened in a torrent of the wildest abuse towards the Vet.

‘You’ve killed him, you’ve gone and killed him!’ he screamed. ‘I’ll get you for this’. He picked up the syringe that was lying in a metal dish on the table beside the dog.

‘Look! You’ve killed him with this. You’ve done him in!’ he yelled, waving it menacingly at the Vet.

‘That was adrenaline’, the Vet spoke sternly. ‘It was a last attempt to revive him. Put it down’, he commanded.

Suddenly, as quickly as the storm had broken in Gary, it subsided, leaving him sobbing uncontrollably.

‘We need some help here, Maggie’, said the shaken Vet. ‘Please phone 999 for backup’.

Gary was trembling uncontrollably when the paramedics arrived. As soon as he saw them, he lashed out again.

'I don't want none of your lot. Get away!' He started kicking the two men and immediately wrestled one to the ground. The other paramedic managed to get Gary in an arm lock hold, wrenching his shoulders and arms backwards. The other paramedic was up on his feet by this time, nose bleeding but otherwise unharmed, and ran ahead to open the ambulance doors. Gary was pushed in, whereupon he started howling piteously all the way to the hospital.

After several attempts to pacify him at the hospital, including an injection of Diazepam, the Consultant on call suggested that Nurse Wilson should call the Medical Psychotherapist on call – Professor Maria Murphy.

Maria Murphy saw immediately that this was a young man in deep distress.

'What's the matter, feller?' she crooned again, her soft Irish lilt revealing itself for the first time.

After she had repeated the phrase, Gary finally began to quieten a little at the sound of the soothing words,

'Let me help you'.

Somewhere in the back of his mind, though he was hardly aware of it, the tone and warmth of Professor Maria Murphy's voice reminded him of the people at the vicarage who had taken him in unconditionally when he so badly needed help: Connie, the sweet and tender mother of the children; Sadie, her sister, who had lost her own son tragically; and Hope, the mother of his child, who had opened her heart to him despite everything. There was a gentleness in Dr.Maria's voice that had finally acted as a soft touch of healing balm to his grief.

Chapter 6

'Tell me about what tragedy has caused you so much pain, Gary', Maria said.

'My dog', he finally whispered.

'What's happened to your dog?'

'Gary, we're here to help. What's become of your dog?'.

'Killed', murmured Gary.

Maria Murphy gently took his hand again, and this time, Gary did not pull it back.

'Got run over, didn't he? Some fucking fox'.

'Your dog chased it?'

'Yep'. Gary hung his head.

'I'm afraid dogs lose all reason over foxes', she said quietly.

Silence.

Gary suddenly started ranting again.

'The bloody woman killed him. Didn't stop in time. The sodding fox got away scot-free and...' his voice became more hysterical 'and – and my Wolfie got clobbered. And what's more...' Gary started storming round the room again, 'The fucking vet finished him off, didn't he?'

Gary suddenly rolled to the corner of the room, hugging himself and rocking. Maria Murphy knew that she had to try to defuse some of the anger that was continually bubbling up in Gary's cauldron of grief and was a potential danger both to himself and others. The consultant who saw him initially when he arrived had given him a suitable amount of Diazepam, which was clearly not having the required effect of calming him down. She was well aware that, occasionally, the drug could work adversely.

'Tell me about Wolf if you can, Gary', said Maria softly. 'He must have loved you very much'.

'He was the best. He was mine. Me and 'im we belonged together. Like that, we was'. He entwined two fingers. 'I rescued him'. Gary was replacing his ranting with quiet sobbing. 'He was the best', he repeated.

'I'm sure you gave him a lovely life, Gary. He was probably happier with you than anyone else in the world, you know'.

'Oh, I do know', replied Gary. 'I rescued 'im', he repeated.

'Then he was a lucky dog. You did him proud. Gave him a great life'.

Silence. Gary was suddenly quiet and gazing at the floor. Eventually, Maria said,

'Gary, can we call someone for you?'

'Ain't got no-one'.

'Nobody?'

'I said it, didn't I?'

Maria was silent. Eventually, she said,

'Where do you live, Gary?'

'No-where in particular'.

'Where did you spend last night?'

'Wolf and me like tunnels'.

So here was another of life's casualties who had slipped between the fingers of what was meant to be a caring society.

'Would you like us to fix you up with something for a few days? Perhaps a Church Army Hostel? There's one near Southwark'.

Gary felt as though a bolt of electricity had shot through him. The Church Army was exactly where he had lived until.....until the deed was done with his mother. Panic overtook him, momentarily obliterating all thoughts of Wolf. He rose to his feet, approached Maria, and thrust his chin out aggressively.

'NO. No, I bloody wouldn't', he shouted.

Maria reeled backwards. Finally,

'Gary, I can't let you go like this. You're in no fit state for the moment. I'll ask Staff Nurse here to find you a bed in the hospital, and we can call Social Services tomorrow to see what they suggest'.

'O.K. O.K. I'll give you an address'.

'Who will this be then, Gary?'

'The Vicarage lot. They take anyone in. They took the mother of my kid in when she was pregnant and.....'

'You have a child?'

'I said it, didn't I?'

'How lovely!' Maria said and meant it. 'What's the little one's name then, Gary?'.

'Lucy Grace Erin O'Neill,' he said, proud for a moment. 'Dunno about the Lucy or Grace bit. Too fancy for me. Erin's after Hope's mum. She died. Never even knew 'er mum she didn't. Mind you, some muvvers aren't always what they're cracked up to be'.

Maria's insides felt as though they were going to drop out. Her face drained rapidly of all colour, and her legs were in danger of giving way. For a moment, she hardly knew what she was doing. She was shaking inside.

Finally, she found her voice and spoke in crisp, staccato sentences.

'Er, Staff Nurse. Take Gary to the little kitchen you have here. Fix him a sandwich. Now. Please'.

Staff Nurse Wilson stared at Maria and was about to question the wisdom of her request, but Maria barked,

'NOW, Staff Nurse Wilson. I said, 'NOW!'

Staff Nurse Wilson was loathe to contradict Maria. She certainly had never seen her like this before, but she knew it was not safe to have Gary with her alone in the kitchen in his extremely volatile state. She thought of the sharp knife they used to cut the bread.

'Dr. Murphy, I'm sorry, I - I really don't.......'

Maria shook herself, and her professionalism kicked in.

' Yes, yes, of course, you're right.' she said. 'I should have thought. Now, Gary, can you give me the details of the vicarage, please?

She reached for a notepad and pen from her bag. Gary started to speak.

'I dunno the number, but I know the address. It's St. Lu...' he stopped suddenly.

What was he doing? By giving details of the vicarage, he was laying himself open to the possibility of the police finding him.

'This is between you and me at the moment, Gary', she said, sensing his apprehension.

'You not involving the Fuzz – the Bill – are you?'

'Why should I, Gary? You haven't done anything wrong, have you?'

She stared at him intently and did not avert her gaze.

'*Have* you, Gary?'

Gary suddenly felt like a writhing worm struggling on the end of a hook. Anything wrong? No. He had only drowned his own mother, and that was just for starters.

'Nuffink wrong', he said, sliding his eyes furtively up to Maria.

Maria knew in that moment that she was looking at best at a liar and, at worst, a hardened criminal. However, she had not been called to make a judgement on Gary but to support him.

'Carry on, Gary. Name?'

She notated the details, outwardly calm, although her hand trembled. A furnace of confusion had been ignited inside her, which she would need to subdue in order simply to continue to function.

'Gary, I'd like to book you a follow-up appointment to check how you are doing. Is that all-right with you?'

'S'pose so', replied Gary, having no intention of following anything up whatsoever except a dark tunnel, his private grief, and his anonymous life.

Chapter 7

From her home in Southwark, Sister Hope O'Neill pushed her daughter Lucy's pushchair along the embankment in the direction of the Rotherhithe tunnel. It was a long walk, but the day was bright and sparkling, and little Lucy loved being out. Hope heard the loud and penetrating squeal of brakes in the distance and hoped to goodness the sound did not indicate a serious accident. She decided to turn back. It wasn't her business, and there would be other people around to help, wouldn't there, she told herself. The real reason, however, which she barely acknowledged to herself, was that she had actually become quite squeamish and fragile since the birth of her baby.

Motherhood was wonderful but had taken its toll in terms of her levels of anxiety. The memories of the rape revisited her more times than she cared to acknowledge. At the time, despite the kindness of the vicarage family, she had escaped back to the solitude and peace of the convent in Ireland to recover, where she would have stayed had she not gradually become aware of her pregnancy. The Mother Superior then made it quite clear that, as she had the reputation of the convent to consider, of course, she would arrange for Hope to give birth to her baby in a local mother and baby home, and the whole matter would carefully be forgotten.

Sadie Connors, Hope's newly discovered half-sister, had scooped her up and brought her back to England to have the baby. Hope had originally come to London in search of her father, whom she had never known. She did, however, discover a half-brother and three sisters, Sadie being the eldest of them. Hope's mother had died in childbirth, so the nuns had informed her, and they—the nuns—subsequently became her surrogate family. Although sometimes impatient with the constraints of convent life, Hope knew it was her safe haven in terms of security. She had researched long and in-depth to see what she could discover about her family and learnt that her father had lived in Southwark. He was clearly one of the many men who indulged in at least one extramarital relationship during the war when away from home.

Sister Hope was granted a sabbatical by the convent for her travels and had arrived in London full of happy anticipation. Her happiness increased when she met the Vicarage family at Southwark, who welcomed her with open arms.

In London, without warning, she was brutally raped at Borough Road Market at dusk by a gang of five youths which included Gary Johnson. Her little daughter, the legacy of the rape, had been born nine months later, and half-sister Sadie was intent on buying the three of them a small house or ground-floor flat in the Southwark area so that they could share their lives. There, Sadie discovered, to her shock, that her love for Hope was more than purely sisterly, and she desperately hoped that in time, Hope and she might have a full, loving relationship as a couple. Hope loved Sadie, but not in 'that' way, as she gently expressed to Sadie one evening during an intimate and honest talk.

Six months later, reacting to how she felt about the rejection, Sadie found another partner, and the pair decided to move back to her mobile home in Scotland. Sadie was sorrowful to part with Hope, having already lost her precious disabled son in a fatal road accident, but was driven by another dynamic force in her life—a partner who shared her sexual persuasion and reciprocated her love in full measure. Hope was quietly grief-stricken. She and Sadie were soul mates, or so Hope thought, but looking at the transformation that had occurred in Sadie as a result of this new and all-consuming love, she could not resent it. Sadie had been through many traumas, including losing her beloved son, Jack, in a tragic road accident. She deserved some happiness, Hope decided, even though 'deserving' was a word she rarely used to describe any element in the Christian life. Her faith told her that good things were a matter of God's graciousness rather than a 'right', hence giving her daughter Lucy the middle name of Grace—'goodness and graciousness'. Lucy Grace Erin was the baby's full name. Erin, as the Nuns had informed her dispassionately, was her dead mother's name—the mother she had never known but always mourned.

Chapter 8

Hope loved visiting the Lockwoods, known as 'The Vicarage Family', who only lived a fifteen-minute walk away from her ground-floor flat. Since Sadie left, Hope had been a more frequent visitor there. The family was warm and expansive, and in no way was Hope regarded as a visitor or an intrusion. Besides, Connie, the children's mother, was her other half-sister, they discovered, sharing the same disgraced father. Hope frequently looked after the younger children at the vicarage.

Two days previously, Connie had given birth to two healthy and beautiful little twin boys, giving her a total of four sons and one daughter. Their young daughter Rosy had been desperate for a sister, so little Lucy Grace Erin's visits went some way in providing this for her.

Hope, hugely excited, visited Connie in the hospital.

'You'll never guess what Lucy wants to call the babies, Hope. Pharoah and Elvis!' Connie laughed.

'*What!*' retorted Hope.

'We took her to see Jason Donovan in *Joseph and his Amazing Technicoloured Dreamcoat'* as her

Christmas present at the London Palladium. It was brilliant, actually, and Rosy was besotted with the King Pharoah scene. 'Pharoah' does an amazing take-off of Elvis'.

They both laughed.

'So what *are* you going to call them?' said Hope

'*Not* Pharoah and Elvis!!'

'Jason?' Hope laughed.

'Oli and I have agreed on Joseph and Benjamin – from the story, and Rosy seems reasonably satisfied with that'.

'Can I pick one up?' said Hope, gazing at the enticing newborns in their cradles.

'Yes, yes, of course', replied Connie, smiling proudly.

Hope very gently picked up one of the tiny boys.

'Hello, little fellow. Which one are you then, I wonder? Connie, which one is he?' she asked, gently holding the baby towards Connie.

'Don't ask *me!'* said Connie, laughing. 'I'm only his *mother!* Could be Joseph, or could be Benjamin!'

'They really are identical, aren't they?' said Hope. 'Actually, I think this one is Pharoah. He has a double chin!'

They laughed so much that a nurse came in, rosy-faced, puffing, and of extremely ample proportions.

'Now, mother, I think you're getting over-excited. Time to leave her to sleep, please', she said, wagging her plump finger at Hope, who was leaving anyway.

'I think we've just met Potiphar's wife!' whispered Connie when the nurse had gone out of earshot.

'Hardly!' replied Hope, in fits of giggles.

Chapter 9

Sister Hope returned to the vicarage after her visit to see the babies at the hospital. She and little Lucy were staying there temporarily to assist with Oliver and Connie's other three children until Connie brought the twins home.

'What are they like?' Rosy asked excitedly before Hope was even inside the door. 'Come on, Auntie Hope, *what are they like?!'*

'They are beautiful little babies', said Hope, smiling broadly. 'You wait till you see them!'.

'What colour hair?' pursued Rosy excitedly. She adored babies and always demanded full descriptions of any newborn.

'Quite a lot of dark, like your Dad's', said Hope, smiling at Oliver. 'But much more handsome!

'Hey, steady on! I can't be outdone by my sons!'.

'And they are *identical.* We're never going to tell the difference', she said, laughing.

Rosy, ecstatic, danced a jig around the hall with Lucy, who screamed with laughter.

'We've got two babies, we've got two babies!' she chanted again and again.

‘Cup of tea?’ said Oliver to Hope, ‘Or something stronger?’ he smiled.

‘I think it’s going to be you who needs something stronger!’ laughed Hope.

‘And keep off the communion wine, Dad’, said James, Oliver’s eldest son, coming into the kitchen. ‘I’ve seen you putting an extra drop or three into the chalise for when you finish it off at the end of communion!’

‘Now, James, that’s a trade secret!’ Oliver laughed. Normally, he would have given James a warning shot not to go too far, but the family was in high spirits. The twins had been born safely, and Connie was well. What more could they ask?

The phone rang. No-body rushed to answer it. It rang many times a day in the vicarage. Most calls were parish-related for Oliver; a few were for family members. Oliver took his duties as vicar of a busy London parish very seriously. He rarely resented the phone, whether it interrupted a meal, cut through sermon preparation, or even interrupted his day off. He regarded himself as a servant of the people chosen by God and regarded it as ‘a duty and a joy’. But today was different. He was meant to be having two weeks off to look after his family while his wife was in hospital and then to welcome her home. It was part of his allocated annual leave.

‘Don’t they *know* it’s my break?’, he said exasperated. ‘I’ve put it in the church news sheet for three weeks running. If this is Mrs. Tweedy on the edge of one of her nervous breakdowns, I’m putting the phone down’. But of course, he wouldn’t. Mrs. Tweedy was an attention seeker who was known to be besotted with Oliver Lockwood. Mind you, it was fairly easy to feel besotted with him, as Connie had pointed out. He was kind and gentle but strong and steady, good-looking in a way, and could take a firm line with situations if needed. Connie didn’t mind about Mrs. Tweedy. She was no threat. If she had been a sultry blonde or a blazing redhead, it might have been different, as she frequently said with a laugh to Oliver, but half meaning it nevertheless.

‘Hello. Vicarage here’, Oliver said, trying to disguise his frustration. Suddenly, he put his hand to his head.

‘*What!*’ he said. Everyone in the room looked up. Even little Lucy stopped cavorting with Rosy. Oliver sounded stunned.

‘No. We haven’t seen him for three years. He seemed to disappear without a trace. You say you’ve got him there?’

Oliver dragged a chair up to the phone whilst holding the receiver to his ear.

‘Well, yes, I suppose so’, he said slightly reluctantly after listening for a minute and sitting down, looking stunned. Taking a grip on himself, he added,

‘Please do bring him along, and we’ll do what we can’.

As soon as he put the receiver down, James and Rosy said in unison,

‘What’s up, Dad?’

‘I’ll tell you later’, said Oliver

‘Oh, Dad, you always do that. When it comes to boring us with Mrs.Tweedy and her obsession, we have to listen. But anything *really* interesting and you don’t fill us in’, replied James, who was more than ready to leave home for University.

‘Maybe you’re right. But it remains within these walls. Rosy, do you understand that? No sharing of secrets’.

‘O.K., Dad. Got it’, said Rosy coquettishly, twisting her brown ponytail round her fingers and going to sit on Oliver’s knee.

‘Gary Johnson has turned up’.

At that moment, Peter, the Lockwood’s son who had been diagnosed with autism as a young child, walked into the room.

‘I suppose he’s going to stay again, is he? Well, he’s not having my room, Dad’.

‘Peter, would you go up and call Robbie down for me, please? Tell him it’s a bit of an emergency’.

Peter loved Robbie Taylor. Robbie had a way with youngsters and seemed to understand Peter without patronising him. Peter was the cleverest child in the family but needed sensitive handling. Peter knocked on the living room door of Robbie’s top-floor flat in the vicarage.

‘Robbie. Dad wants you. Got some news’.

Robbie came to the door.

‘Oh. Right. Good or bad, Pete?

‘Depends on your viewpoint’, said Peter cryptically, keeping Robbie guessing and enjoying his moment of power.

‘Hmm. Now that’s a mysterious answer, Peter Lockwood’.

Peter smiled, which was an event of scarcity value in itself. Peter found social communication difficult, but with Robbie, he was always ready to talk. Robbie had a relaxed manner with Peter, and secretly Peter hero-worshipped him. They jumped the stairs two in tandem on their way down.

'Hi, Robbie. Sorry to disturb you. I've got some news'. Oliver paused. 'Gary Johnson has turned up. I've had a phone call from a Professor Maria Murphy. She's a Medical Psychiatric Social Worker apparently', he said, reading from the scribbled note he had made on the back of an envelope.

'Good luck to her', said James. 'What's she doing? Sorting Gary's head out, Dad?'

'That wouldn't be possible', said Peter.

'Hey, come on, Peter. We probably all need our heads sorted out!' Oliver smiled at Peter, but Peter knew his tone, and it was serious.

'What did the Psychiatrist want us to do, Oliver?' asked Robbie.

'Take him in', replied Oliver. 'He gave this address as his home address – or rather, us as his next of kin'.

'He can have my bed', said Rosy. 'I will sleep in my tent in the garden'. Shall we, Lucy, shall we?' she added excitedly.

'I don't think so, Rosy', said Hope quickly. 'It's getting chilly at night now, and you need to be indoors'.

'He'll be here in about an hour', said Oliver, so we'd better make some contingency plans. They're packing him off in a taxi with a chaperone'.

'What sort of state is he in?' asked Hope.

'The doctor didn't say', said Oliver, 'but she said he had been 'traumatised by a death', he added grimly.

Robbie said nothing. He knew more about Gary than anyone else. He had witnessed events on that sinister foggy night three years ago, had seen Gary leading his drunken mother to the end of the pier, and had subsequently found the battered, high-heeled emerald green shoe of his mother's washed up on the beach at Bankside in Southwark. A body had been found some days later, which no-one came forward to identify.

Robbie had never told anyone about these observations on that murky night. In a sense, it was a case of honour among thieves. Robbie had spent two spells in prison for grievous bodily harm, amongst other things, and he was not going to betray Gary, even if Gary had committed an unspeakable crime. Besides, Robbie had spent a lot of time trying to draw alongside Gary, even taking a chance and talking to him about God, and he had been frustrated not to be able to find Gary during the last three years despite searching rigorously. Robbie would probably have remained a criminal with little chance of a decent life had not the Reverend Oliver Lockwood scooped him up at the prison gates on his release. Oliver and his wife Connie had shown Robbie unconditional love, and eventually, Robbie began to respond and soften, eventually maturing into a young man who could take responsibility and who had magic all of his own when it came to the youth of Southwark. He had met Gary and tried to draw alongside him, with a limited but definite modicum of success.

Robbie pushed his dark hair out of his eyes, a repetitive habit of his, and let the air out through his teeth.

'So he's back, is he? Any information on what he's been up to during the last three years, then?'

'Not yet', replied Oliver, already weary of the prospect ahead.

'Something criminal or wicked, I bet', said James with a toss of his head. 'He's as thick as two short planks, and he only has two ways of thinking—with his fists, and you know where else!' Oliver glowered at him. Something or someone had got to work on his eldest son's arrogance. He felt he'd failed somehow. Connie said it was 'just a stage' he was in, but James seemed to have been at 'that stage' for rather a long time now.

Robbie decided he had time to put a quick call through to Kitty, Connie's niece. Robbie had always turned to Kitty when he had anything to mull over. Although she was sixteen years his junior – she was nineteen, he was thirty-five, she had a wise and loving head on her shoulder. Robbie barely knew it himself, but after all these years of simply being playmates and friends, he was beginning to fall in love with Kitty Connors.

Chapter 10

The doorbell rang. There, on the porch, stood the shrunken figure of a young man, wafer thin, with his head hanging so low that Oliver could see the blond roots showing through the dyed brown of his hair. Had Oliver not been told that Gary Johnson was on his way, he would have thought he was looking at a complete down-and-out stranger standing in the rain. Gary Johnson was wearing an oversized black bomber jacket that the hospital had found him in their lost property store and an almost new pair of white trainers, also provided by the hospital, as the shoes he owned had been worn right through, and the soles were hanging off.

'All-right, Guv?' said the taxi driver to Oliver. 'I'll leave him in your tender mercies. Best of luck, mate. I haven't got a peep out of him. Taxi's all paid for, courtesy of the National Health. No wonder the country's in a mess. It's a bloody....'

Cutting him short of further expletives, Oliver said a brief thank you and made it quite clear that the taxi driver should go immediately.

'Gary', he gently, 'Come in, my friend, and I'll make you a cup of tea'.

On hearing the familiar gentle, kindly voice, Gary crumpled in a heap in Oliver's arms. He sobbed. James, Peter, and Rosy all peered round the door and into the hall and then retreated quickly. Oliver led Gary into the kitchen, and for several minutes, Gary continued to sob. Eventually, through muffled crying, he said,

'Me dog's died. Only friend I had in the world. Run over he was. Vet finished him off'.

'That's terrible, Gary. I'm so, so sorry. I'm glad you've come here'.

Just then, the door opened, and a diminutive little girl with strawberry blonde curly hair, wearing dungarees and a pale blue jumper, and pretty as a picture, tottered into the kitchen. Gary stopped crying and stared.

'Is that my kid? Is that Lucy, my kid?'

Before Oliver had time to shape an answer, Hope scuttled in, head down, embarrassed.

'Lucy! Come here! Come to Mummy, there's a good girl'.

She scooped up the child swiftly and exit the kitchen, avoiding Gary's stare.

'Wot they doing here?' said Gary.

'Hope's been looking after our children while Connie's in hospital. She's just had twins. Two boys'.

'Blimey mate!', said Gary. He gulped his tea down.

Oliver agreed. 'Blimey Mate!' seemed the expletive most appropriate to how he was feeling at the moment.

'Thanks, Rev. Sorry I used your address. Didn't know what else to do'.

'Don't worry about anything now. Robbie says you can sleep up in his flat until you're ready to think about the future'.

'Ain't got no future, Rev'.

'Yes, you have. You just can't see it now. Losing your dog must have been terrible'. He paused. 'Gary, you're amongst friends here. You know that, don't you?' Oliver's stomach lurched as it always did when his compassion quickened.

Gary nodded almost imperceptibly, but Oliver saw it.

'Robbie will be off the phone in a minute. He'll be glad to see you. Anything to eat, Gary?'

'No, ta. I want to see my little'un. Can you fetch 'er, Rev?'

'I won't be a minute', said Oliver non-commitally. That depended on Hope, and by the way she beat a hasty retreat from the room, suggested the answer would be a firm no. Oliver left Gary piling spoonfuls of sugar into a second cup of tea, returning the wet spoon back into the sugar bowl, which Connie always reprimanded the children about. Oliver asked Robbie to come into the kitchen.

'Watcha, mate', said Robbie 'Where you bin, then? I've been looking for you for nearly three years. Regular Houdini you are'.

Gary said nothing.

'Come 'ere Mate. You look done in'. Robbie gave Gary a bear hug before Gary could back away. 'Now you just stay here until you've got a bit stronger. Guess you've been dodging around every tunnel in London, avoiding the Fuzz, haven't you? Yes?'

'My dog died', said Gary. 'I flipped me lid, didn't I, and a shrink was called from somewhere or other. At least I got a new pair of trainers', he said with a hint of a smile. 'They gotta be worth something. Adidas, innit'.

'Nice one! Come on, mate. Come upstairs with me. Where's your bag?'

'*Bag?* I don't 'ave a *bag*, mate! You must be joking. The only thing I've got is me belt, and no-one's havin' that cos that's precious. Used it when I first found Wolfie in the tunnel, didn't I?'

Gary caught his breath as if he was about to cry again. Suddenly, his mood changed. He turned to Oliver. 'I want to see my kid, Rev. Can you fetch my kid? Ask 'Ope'.

'Listen, Gary. I know Hope. She'll need time to think about it'.

'Try, Rev' and added, 'Try, please, mate?'

Oliver left Gary and Robbie in the kitchen, but when he went into the sitting room, he found Hope and her daughter Lucy had gone and the front door open.

It was the second time that Hope had bolted. The first was the night before she was due to be examined after the rape. Hope was a decent, honest, loving, and God-fearing young woman, but some things were just too traumatic for her to face. Her upbringing had been severe. Gary turning up would take Hope time to process and work out what was best. Meanwhile, she needed time and space. Robbie returned to the kitchen, knowing that Gary would refuse to take no for an answer.

Chapter 11

Maria Murphy kicked off her shoes, poured herself a large whiskey, grabbed a packet of salted peanuts from the larder, threw herself into her squishy olive green armchair, and turned on the television as she did every evening on her return home from work. Normally, she would reflect on the day a little, flick through the newspaper, switch channels to find the news headlines, and settle comfortably for at least half an hour. This was her favourite time of day.

Tonight, outwardly, her routine was no different from every other day, but internally, her whole world had been shaken. She gulped her double whisky in one go, poured herself another large measure, and, leaving the empty glass on the coffee table, went to her bedroom. There, she rummaged in one of her divan bed bottom drawers and drew out a bulging box file held together precariously by a thick, half-perished elastic band. She returned to her living room, poured herself a third whisky, and opened the over-full box file, spreading out on the table papers, certificates, receipts, old photographs, newspaper cuttings, and letters that had been stored in the box at random records of her life before she had been unceremoniously turned out of her parental home at the age of seventeen.

She picked up the only photo she had kept of her mother and father, Henry and Emily O'Neill. There they were, in faded black and white, standing formally arm in arm and unsmiling towards the camera. Her mother was short and petite with fair hair in a loose hairnet, and her father, well over six feet tall and grey-haired, towered over his wife both in height and his sense of self-importance. In her father's arms was a small tabby cat, the only sign that there may possibly have been a beating heart somewhere buried inside the outward severity of his demeanour. Maria had kept the photograph only because of her devotion to Milly, the cat at the time. Looking at her parents' faces made her stomach church. In an instant, she heard her father's voice booming down the years.

'You've brought shame on us, child. You have sinned, and we are no longer prepared to keep you here.' he had said, delivering the lines formally as though he had rehearsed them. His face reddened as it always did when he was upset. Maria often wondered if he would have a heart attack during one of these episodes.

Her mother thrust her chin up towards Maria.

'I hope you enjoyed it, you brazen hussy. I've spoken to Father O'Sullivan, and he is sorting you out a place at St. Brigid's Home for Fallen Women. As you know, that is two villages away from here, so you will be anonymous there. The Father will come and collect you on Saturday. Your home is run by the blessed Nuns but funded partly by our long-suffering Government, so you will be well looked after'. Her mother paused and looked at her daughter's belly disparagingly. 'You must be gone before your sins show. You've brought shame on us, to be sure'.

She continued, this time using a strange, robotic voice as if rehearsing a speech. Years later, Maria began to understand that her mother may have used this mode of delivery in order to disguise her breaking heart, but at the time, she interpreted it as simply cold cruelty.

The summer before, Maria had acquitted herself with distinction in all subjects in her school examinations and had been accepted by Trinity College Dublin to take up their offer of a place on their prestigious degree course in Medicine. These achievements counted as nothing in her parents' eyes now, despite their intense pride in her at the time. All they could think about was the disgrace Maria had brought upon them.

'You're nothing but a *whore* and a *prostitute*', spat out her father with venom and hatred, 'We're *ashamed* of you'. (She was surprised they didn't add, Bronte style, 'Lock her in the red room!').

Maria quickly found her fighting spirit.

'I loathe your puritanical...' her anger almost prevented her from finishing the sentence - 'Your puritanical – *wicked* - ***hypocrisy!'*** she shouted. 'Call yourselves Christians? All those years of making me pray to a God I have never believed in - punishing me if I opened my eyes when I was meant to be praying - you're totally under the thumb of that Father O'Sullivan'.

In a fury, she picked up a garish-painted china crucifix from the sideboard and threw it hard at her father. It missed him and crashed to the ground, chipping the paint off in several places and partially knocking its head off. Quickly, her mother went to the open window and shut it, saying,

'Keep the noise down, will you? The neighbours will hear. Don't you dare blaspheme about one of God's representatives on earth'.

Her father picked up the crucifix and held it close to his chest.

'You've defiled the blessed Son of God and His mother, Mary, and you will be punished. How *dare* you damage the sacred face of Jesus!'

'That's nothing but an ugly graven image if you did but know it', Maria retaliated. 'You're trying to locate your God in a gross effigy! Is that all He's worth?' she screamed.

'Leave now, this minute!' said her mother, at last breaking free from the robotic voice. 'This is no longer your home. You are not our daughter from this day on. You're a sinner, and God will punish you accordingly.' Her mother turned away from her, folded her arms emphatically, and stood staring into space at the large garden outside.

From that day forward and for many years, Maria had no respect for religion of any kind, particularly that represented by the Roman Catholic church, her views having been formed and tainted by the example of her parents and based more on anger and resentment than anything rational. Years later, her stance on atheism was to make a seismic change, but for now, her heart was set against God, the church, and everything that they both represented.

xxxxx

Maria poured herself another whisky, which she knew was foolish. An inevitable headache would follow. She was extremely agitated by her thoughts and memories as she sifted through more papers from her box file. She alighted on an old printed postcard in faded brownish-black. It depicted 'St.Brigid's Home for Fallen Women'. The postcards originally had been stacked up on a table for visitors to buy, as if the institution was something to be proud of rather than the hard and merciless place that it was.

The memories flooded back and made her weep. Most of all, she remembered the verbal abuse from several of the nuns, denigrating the girls with derogatory remarks. There were one or two kindly nuns and orderlies, but whenever they stopped to show their humanity through warm conversation or enquiries about how this or that particular girl was feeling, they were reprimanded harshly and told to move on. The work was arduous, and the hours were long. Maria carried her pregnancy well and was neat rather than bulky, but even she puffed and staggered in the last month from work on hands and knees cleaning floors. The work she hated most was in the laundry picking heavy, soaking sheets with wooden tongs out of the huge copper boilers, then lifting them sopping wet and poking them through the mangles. There was *always* work in the laundry. Heavy, unrelenting work. Maria reflected that it was actually a wonder that more mothers did not miscarry in their third trimester, but these little unwanted babies seemed to cling tenaciously to life in utero.

She remembered one occasion when Father O'Sullivan came to see her in the Home. She expected only a patronising pat on the head at best or the usual conversation about the nature of sin, but when he reached her bed, he put down a heavy brown parcel tied up with string. Father O'Sullivan had been privy to the celebrations that had taken place when Maria had passed her exams and gained a place at Trinity Dublin.

'Here you are, child. You have sinned and are being punished, but that is no reason why your fine intellect should go to seed, is it? I thought you might like these'.

He had bought for her several books on Medicine: *Text Book of Pathology, Gestalt Psychology, The Complete Medical Handbook.* Maria treasured them all and read them avidly. This was the first kindness she had been shown apart from the one or two nuns who broke the rules and talked softly to her. Her opinion of Father O'Sullivan rose considerably. She never forgot this gesture of kindness.

In the mother and baby home was a twelve-year-old orphan girl – Cathy Ryan. Maria shared a dormitory with her, as well as with six other pregnant girls. Cathy Ryan, not even a teenager, had just given birth to a healthy baby boy, the result of an uncle's rape, who she quickly named Callum before he was unceremoniously whisked away after an hour of his birth for adoption, leaving Cathy distraught. She had returned to the dormitory to recover from the birth and spent one day keening piteously over her loss, followed by several days in a catatonic state in a dark, unresponsive stupor. No-one went near her apart from to bring her scanty meals, which she hardly touched. Normally, girls who had given birth were set to work within three days, scrubbing floors or cleaning paintwork. Cathy, however, was left alone. No one could gain a response from her.

'Now stop this nonsense, child! Your baby has gone to a lovely home. You should be glad for him. Other women have been through the same thing and haven't made this fuss. Thank the holy Mary Mother of God that he is going to have a good life', chided one of the sisters. 'By the way, they liked the name 'Callum Patrick', and they're going to keep it, so that's nice, isn't it?'

'They better bloody had', replied Cathy, 'because *those* are his names'.

Maria was relieved to see this flash of spirit, but it didn't last long. Cathy turned her face to the wall once more and remained there for several hours. Maria, now eight months pregnant, stroked Cathy's head and held her hand. Her insights told her that Cathy needed the safety of her catatonic stage where she could nurse her pain and her grief in a cocoon of silence and privacy. Eventually, though, Maria spoke gently to her, 'Cathy. Can you talk to me? Cathy? It's dreadful what's happened to you. Talk to me, please?'

After a minute, Cathy slowly turned, her face white and wizened, and simply said,

'They've taken him'.

‘That’s dreadful, dreadful. Did you have a chance to hold him?’

‘Yes. For a few seconds. He was beautiful’. She turned her face back to the wall.

‘Cathy, when I have given birth, I will take you out of here. I have money. You must come with me, and we’ll start a new life away from the people who have hurt us. Maybe England’.

Cathy turned back again and, this time, looked Maria full in the face.

‘Thank you’, she said, ‘but I must stay near him, wherever he is. I have no-one else’.

‘We’ll track down your son, Cathy, so that you can at least see him. ‘We will find Callum’ said Maria. ‘I promise you’. Cathy stayed facing her. After a minute, Maria said, ‘How was your labour, Cathy?’

‘I was slapped when I screamed. Slapped and shouted at. I didn’t know it was painful. No-one told me’.

Maria was silent. Her baby’s birth was four weeks away, and suddenly, she did not want to hear any more.

Maria went into labour early the very next day and without warning. Her waters broke suddenly while she was scrubbing a floor, and she was whisked into a basic room for the humiliating ritual of pubic shaving and an enema. There was no time to get her to hospital where girls generally were transferred to give birth. Within an hour, the baby was delivered.

'You're a sinner, and God will punish you'.

Maria remembered those words of her mother's during her contractions and again when the nurse quickly removed her baby.

'Your baby is dead, I'm afraid. Born too early. No chance of survival. Sorry, dear'.

Maria turned her head to the wall in silence. After a minute, she muttered through her tears,

'Was it a boy or a girl?'

'A wee girl'.

'I want to see her please', she whispered.

The nurse immediately replied,

'You can't *see* her. She's dead. She's just 'remains' now. Her spirit has gone to live with Jesus'.

'*Please,* I must see her. I want to hold her. Just once?'.

The midwife Nun noticed that Maria had begun to bleed heavily. Several postpartum haemorrhages in their care ended in death before the sufferer could ever get to the local hospital. The midwife Nun looked at Maria – so young, so pretty, and in a way, yes, despite her church's teaching on unmarried women – so *innocent.*

'Wait a minute, dear', she said. She ushered another nurse in to find more pads and towels and came back after a minute carrying a Swan Vesta matchbox.

'Tuck this inside your nightdress,' Then she whispered, 'It's a wee curl from your baby's hair'.

The matchbox containing a tiny, fine blonde-gold curl had remained Maria's most precious possession from that day onwards. As soon as she could, she tied the curl securely with a narrow pink silk ribbon, put it back in the matchbox, and for many years kept it tucked into her bra and close to her heart.

Before she left the hospital, Maria paid one last visit to St. Brigid's to find Cathy Ryan, with a plan to invite her to England so she could oversee responsibility for this abandoned child of twelve years who had not a friend in the world. Cathy, however, had left. No-one apparently knew where she was going or if she had an address. Probably not, Maria decided, seeing that she had no-one at all to care for her. She vowed she would not forget Cathy Ryan and made a promise to herself to trace her when she could.

Maria herself felt that God, whoever or wherever He was, or *if* He was at all, had indeed punished her well and fully, as her mother had predicted. She found not a modicum of sympathy or understanding coming from her parents, either for herself or towards the grandchild they had lost. Their hearts were hardened against her, and her mother maintained her coldness towards her daughter, even though in the depths of her being, her heart may have been beating out another tune altogether.

As soon as she could, Maria journeyed to England, leaving her old life, with no sense of loss for her parents, but grieving for the baby daughter she knew she would have loved. She carried with her a suitcase, a parcel of books done up with string, money from her parents, and a Swan Vesta matchbox. She was borne along by an ocean of sorrows and bearing thoughts that lay deeper than any tears she could shed.

Once in England, Maria visited the deed poll council offices in Cambridge Immediately. She had important business to attend to before she could free herself sufficiently mentally to concentrate on her studies and her future.

Her Cambridge days were the usual mix of intellectual and academic rigour and rich and heady social experiences. Others observing her would have agreed she was socially adept and could converse vibrantly with the most gifted amongst both students and dons, but the more discerning and insightful detected in her a need to keep her emotional wings tightly folded, guarding closely whatever was going on under the surface of her socially competent exterior.

During parts of her training as a Psychiatrist involving the study of behavioural sciences, it was necessary for her to take part in sessions of psychological self-exposure. While she revealed enough of herself to satisfy her colleagues and tutor, the most significant event in her life remained hers and hers alone, and the little matchbox with her daughter's curl in it stayed close to her heart. She had put a wrapping of lint around the box, which she changed frequently as the box had sharp edges that were beginning to mark the tender skin on her breasts.

xxxxx

When the troubled and violent Gary Johnson disclosed he had a daughter and that her name was Lucy Erin O'Neill, Maria was stunned and shocked to the core. She concluded, after rational reflection and a huge discipline of her mind, that this had to be one of life's enormous coincidences. Her baby had died. She had never questioned that, although she had tried to find where her daughter might have been buried. She had heard grizzly rumours about the manner in which dead babies were discarded, including secretive massed graves, but chose not to follow those up in case her heart broke completely in two. Besides, no-one was at all forthcoming on the subject, and she concluded there was a conspiracy of silence between the nuns in holy orders and the misogynistic attitudes of male authorities towards unmarried mothers both in the church and in society at large, most particularly epitomised by her own father.

But as for her baby, having survived and being alive now? That, quite simply, was impossible. Her baby had been declared dead at birth.

She thumbed through the papers from her box file. She had just one sheet of typewritten paper in effect, signing her out of the mother and baby home and into the hospital when she was haemorrhaging. There was no discharge notice from the hospital and certainly no birth or death certificates for her daughter; in effect, reflected Maria, a tiny persona non grata, only fit for a mass grave.

Chapter 12

Meanwhile, The Rev'd Oliver Lockwood had persuaded Gary that, for his own health's sake, he should stay for a few days in the vicarage as he had done previously. Secretly, Oliver was worried about Connie returning home with the tiny twin babies and finding yet another person in the house. Connie and Oliver had agreed from the early years of their relationship that they wanted to keep an open home. In their eyes, God had bestowed on them a huge vicarage, and it was their duty and their joy to open their door and their hearts to the needy and dispossessed of the parish. Out of this had come the blessing of Robbie, who was evidence of a life transformed by love. Could they help Gary in the same way? That was Oliver's hope and prayer, but he was realistic and worldly wise enough to know that Gary was severely damaged with deep psychological scars.

He reflected. Professor Maria Murphy sounded warm and well informed on the phone and said she would need to schedule a follow-up appointment for Gary. Perhaps she would be willing to support Gary for a few weeks to see if she could work on the first steps of unravelling the twisted threads of a childhood that had damaged him so profoundly. He would ask her and, if necessary, find the money to pay for three or four private sessions. He had a parish fund drawn up by generous parishioners to support particularly needy cases, and Gary's fell into that category without a doubt.

Oliver had no idea that actually he would be supporting a murderer, even if that murderer had many reasons to commit the crime. Had Oliver known, he would have reluctantly concluded that Gary should be handed over to the police to serve his sentence, undoubtedly a very long one, even given the extenuating circumstances of his childhood. Added to this, Oliver would have been sure that bringing two newborn babies with a recovering wife and a vulnerable son on the autistic spectrum to live under the same roof as a murderer would not have been such a good idea.

Oliver discussed the matter with Robbie, whose streetwise wisdom could always be trusted. Robbie said he was prepared to see to all Gary's needs if he stayed, to cook for him upstairs, to supervise his days, and, if deemed appropriate, to attend his psychological counselling sessions with Gary. Still, Robbie said nothing about what he had witnessed on Bankside beach on that foggy evening three years ago. He did not see its relevance now; besides, there was honour among thieves. He never forgot that there, but for the grace of God, he could have ended up like Gary.

It was not going to be easy persuading Gary to accept psychological counselling sessions—call them what you will—nor to stay for more than a night or two at the vicarage. They sensed an intense restlessness in him, and time and again, his grief bubbled over about his dog. The one thing that might keep him would be the thought of being in close proximity to his little daughter.

Meanwhile, Hope had slipped quietly out of the house with Lucy and made her way back to her own home in the town. She had thinking to do. Currently, her head was a swirling mass of confusion.

Oliver rang Maria Murphy to arrange a follow-up appointment for Gary and to enquire about future sessions to help him. Maria felt almost as though she had a guilty motive for accepting, with some alacrity, Oliver's request for her to do some work with Gary. She knew she had an ulterior motive, and that was to find out more about Lucy Erin O'Neill and, more importantly, her mother. Also, however, she cared about all her 'clients', and Gary was no exception. An appointment was arranged for two weeks' time, and Maria would come to the Vicarage and simply observe Gary interacting for the first session, then decide on her way of approaching things. First, however, she needed to be filled in about Gary's past and how the Lockwood family fitted into it, and Robbie Taylor in particular. If she could hear something of his background, she could start fitting the pieces of the jigsaw together and have an idea of where to start. She and Oliver agreed that they would spend half an hour the following day chatting and writing a few relevant notes to help her.

Meanwhile, Hope knew she must return to her beloved family in the vicarage to honour her promise to help them when the babies first arrived home. She would go there first thing tomorrow morning, but sleeping in her own bed at the moment, with Lucy quietly tucked up in hers in the adjoining room, was very welcome.

xxxxx

When Maria knocked at the vicarage door the following day, Peter answered. Maria, experienced in dealing with folk with all sorts of mental and neurological differences, detected within a few seconds that Peter fell into that kind of category, albeit mildly. She noticed the avoidance of eye contact, the agitated hands, and the shyness, which was in excess of normal. High-functioning autism, perhaps?

'Hi. You're Peter, aren't you? Good to meet you again'. She held out her hand a little to see if that would be too much for the lad. It was.

'Hi', replied Peter monosyllabically, turning away slightly.

‘Peter, I’m Professor Maria. Can you fetch your dad for me, please? He’s expecting me’.

‘If he was expecting you, he would be here. Dad’s never late’, replied Peter.

‘Where can I find him, Peter?’

‘You can’t *find* him because he isn’t missing. You can only *find* someone if they are lost, and he isn’t lost’.

The logic and linguistics were actually flawless and typical of the bright autistic mind, Maria thought, and also inevitably irritating, especially if you had to live with it all the time! Maria found the syndrome fascinating and had a strong emotional connection with folk who fell into this category, having delved deeply into it during her training years at Cambridge. Experienced as she was, she was not sure of her next move, however. Fortunately, Oliver appeared, drying his hands on a tea towel.

‘I do apologise, Dr. Murphy. I....’

‘Please – it’s Maria’, she interrupted.

‘I was just finishing the kitchen’, said Oliver. ‘My wife is due home from hospital tomorrow, and I don’t want her to find anything amiss. She’s going to have her work cut out. We’ve just had two healthy twin boys’, he smiled proudly.

'That's two amounts of crying', said Peter, 'and I do *not* like that kind of noise'.

'We're going to buy you a headset, aren't we, Peter'.

'Yes', replied Peter, smiling at last and glancing directly at Maria, 'and it's going to be top of the range, Dad says'.

'That's an absolute 'must,'' replied Maria. 'You're certainly going to need top-of-the-range to drown out the noise of your little brothers!'.

Peter gave Maria a discerning look. This lady seemed to 'get it'.

'Rosy wanted a girl', said Peter, 'They would have been quieter, but I'm glad it's two boys'.

'What makes you think girls would be quieter, Peter? Asked Maria.

'Rosy will love them when she sees them', said Oliver, intercepting what could be an interminably long-winded and philosophical answer from Peter. 'Now give us a few minutes, please, Peter. Go and look at that catalogue and mark the ones you think will be most suitable for you, and then perhaps you could come back and show Maria and see if she approves?'

'Aye aye, Captain von Trapp', said Pete, performing a mock salute. 'Bye, Professor Maria. I do trust the hills are alive with music for you'. He ran upstairs, singing in a mock, high operatic voice.

'The hills are alive with the sound of music, tra,la,la,la'.

Maria and Oliver laughed. Peter could be great fun if he felt relaxed.

'You've scored a hit there', said Oliver, relieved. Peter could be very tricky to visitors. 'Come in – Maria', said Oliver, opening the door wide. 'I hope my son made you feel welcome when he greeted you. He can be a bit of an unknown quantity', he smiled wryly.

'He's perfectly lovely', replied Maria. She smiled fully and warmly, and Oliver was suddenly reminded of someone, but he could not place exactly who it was. Oliver made Maria a mug of coffee, and they sat facing each other in the sitting room. Maria thought again what a nice-looking man Oliver was, in a slightly offbeat and casual kind of way. She liked his worn brown corduroy jacket slung casually over his shoulders. She liked his warm manner and direct gaze. She just liked *him.* Connie Lockwood was a lucky woman, she concluded.

'Can you fill me in with what you feel at liberty to share regarding Gary Johnson - um – ? '

'Oliver, please'.

'Oliver', Maria said, thinking how his charm seemed genuine. She was familiar with the austere Roman Catholic priests she had met up until this time (with a few exceptions) who mainly inspired fear and, in her case, loathing. This man somehow seemed totally human but also had what she had to confess could be described as a kind of spiritual aura about him.

'Where shall I begin?' he mused, twisting his biro several times and then making hundreds of rapid dots on his notepad. 'It's a long and rather sad saga'.

'Perhaps tell me about Gary's parents?' said Maria.

'Oh well, they were *shocking*', Oliver said, 'so don't say I haven't warned you!' he smiled. 'You may not have heard the likes of it before'.

'Try me', Maria smiled back.

'Humanly speaking, Gary has never had a chance in life. His parents were in and out of prison for all of their lives, and Gary was simply farmed out to anyone who would have him while they were inside, or else he was left to scavenge on the streets – literally'.

'That's more than enough to cause a child deep distress for a start', Maria interjected.

'Oh, you haven't heard anything yet!' replied Oliver.

Maria looked at the priest in front of her, who was struggling with the content of what he was about to deliver. The dots on the paper were coming thick and fast.

'I've heard most things in my work, Oliver. I see people in all sorts of states and conditions from all kinds of horrendous backgrounds. Almost without exception, the early years of abuse these children suffer have a lasting impact on their lives'.

Oliver did not reply to this. He was remembering his wife Connie's early sexual abuse at the hands of her father and how damaged Connie had been when he first met her. He also remembered the stories from Connie of how their father bullied his three other children and that the oldest boy, James, had tragically taken his own life. Theirs was a seriously dysfunctional family, wrapped in a veil of respectability against the outside world. Their father had proved to be a rogue thread within it, and his black influence caused damage, heartache, and pain in all of his four children, not to mention his wife.

After a minute, during which Maria had the insight to remain silent, seeing this man was in pain, he continued.

'Gary's parents were had up for crimes of bestiality. They used their son in depraved acts in order to take pornographic photographs of him with animals and sell them on the black market'.

Maria was silent. Finally, she said,

'How involved was Gary, and how old was he?'

Oliver went on to explain Gary's involvement from the age of six upwards. He went into some detail about the exploits Gary was involved in and acts he was forced to perform by his immensely cruel and depraved parents. Oliver tried to downplay these for the sake of Maria's sensitivities, but even the watered-down version was horrific. Finally, he said,

'As a result of years of this kind of perverted expectation of their son, Gary himself regarded the female sex simply as vehicles to use mercilessly for his gratification. To put it crudely', Oliver added, 'he stopped abusing animals and started on women, treating them in much the same way—as objects. Rape was his standard calling card'.

'That doesn't surprise me one bit,' remarked Maria, matter-of-factly. 'He was simply swopping one violent act for another'. Oliver looked over at her. Outwardly, she appeared unmoved by the grimness of the story, but he had a feeling that her external demeanour belied her deep sense of tragedy.

He was right, as quite suddenly, Maria's tears fell.

'I can't bear to think how damaged so many of our children are', she said passionately, her feelings spilling out from behind her professional exterior. She wiped her eyes. 'I see many, many people in my surgery who are suffering grievously as adults, and in most cases, nothing has been their fault at all, although they always blame themselves. 'The sins of the fathers are visited on their children, etc'.

'Yes. yes', replied Oliver, jumping up out of his seat and speaking passionately too, 'but remember this: 'The son shall not bear the iniquity of the father, neither shall the father bear the iniquity of the son'. Without that, Maria, there would be no hope for any of us. We would just be part of a downward spiral of blame and guilt. The whole point is that God can redeem us'. He swept his arms wide open. 'That is what the resurrection is all about. Standing instead of us and taking the blame'.

Oliver sat down suddenly and put his head in his hands.

'I'm sorry, Maria. I get carried away. Where were we?'

Maria wanted to continue the discussion. She had never met anyone who seemed so lit up by his faith and, she felt, could explain it so clearly and so fervently and in a way that was acceptable to her, but there was ground to be covered about Gary, and Oliver was on a tight timescale.

Oliver continued:

'This is the part of the story where Hope O'Neill comes in. Shall I continue?'

Maria's insides jumped and lurched. She nodded, 'Yes please'.

'Sister Hope O'Neill came from Ireland in search of her father four years ago. She was a Nun. She went from a children's home over there into Holy Orders. It seemed the only option as she had no money. But it suited Hope. She is a devoutly Christian lady and lives out her faith in a wonderful way. She's never known either her father or her mother. Her mother died in childbirth, and her father was an adulterer. He had four children back in England, and when his girlfriend in Ireland told him she was pregnant, he abandoned her and never saw her again'.

Oliver paused and started joining up the dots on the pad again with his biro.

'Can you guess who her half brothers and sisters turned out to be, Maria?'

'I think I can. How extraordinary. How sad,' murmured Maria. 'What a dirty rat! It's a familiar story, I'm afraid', she said, not without irony. She could hardly believe what she was hearing. Oliver paused. Hope was entirely open about what had happened to her in Southwark Market four years ago. It was no secret to those who were close to her. This Professor Maria invited confidence, unsurprisingly, considering her work, and she seemed to have an abundance of understanding and compassion. Taking a chance, Oliver decided to fill her in. He would tell Hope afterwards. After all, this was the part that concerned Gary Johnson and was relevant to her background knowledge of him. He would explain that to Hope, and he knew she would understand.

'Hope had just been to lunch with us. We all liked her enormously. She was gentle, and she was fun, not at all pious, just holy. You will know the difference, Maria'.

Half an hour ago, Maria might have had to say that no, she wasn't sure what the difference was. Now, looking at Oliver, she was able to simply answer 'Yes'.

'Hope set off after lunch in high spirits. I think it was probably the first Sunday Roast she had eaten for a very long time. She lived very frugally'.

Oliver paused again. Here was another difficult part of the story. He pushed his hair out of his eyes, looked down, stabbed the paper with the pen several times, and continued.

'Sister Hope was viciously raped in Borough Road Market, down the hill from here, not by one but by five brutes – louts – sorry – *animals,'* he said through gritted teeth. 'Needless to say, she was torn, bleeding, and totally traumatised. She was due to go to the police station the following morning to have all sorts of swabs and tests and examinations, but she disappeared back to her Convent in Ireland. It was too much for her to cope with'.

'Poor girl', murmured Maria. 'What a dreadful, dreadful thing'.

'Yes', replied Oliver, 'and one of the men, the instigator of the gang rape, was Gary Johnson.

Maria gasped but said nothing. They sat in silence for a while. Oliver then continued.

'Connie has an older sister, Sadie, who lives in Scotland, but at the time of the rape she lived with us. Very sadly, her disabled son was killed outside here'.

Again, Maria gasped. Was there no end to this chapter of terrible tragedy and accidents?

'Sadie was lovely with Hope, and the two half-sisters struck up a special relationship. Sadie bought them a shared house down the road with the insurance money she received from the wheelchair company. The wheelchair was seriously faulty, and it was that malfunction that had caused the accident'.

'Are Hope and Sadie living there now?' asked Maria.

‘Hope has gone back up to Scotland’. Oliver paused, and the biro began stabbing again. Another awkward moment for him.

‘Um, I don’t know what your feelings are about the gay issue, Maria, but you might as well get the full picture’. He paused. Maria said nothing.

‘Sadie fell in love with another woman, and they live together as a couple’, he said.

Maria shrugged her shoulders.

‘So? It shouldn’t be an issue, should it? I hope they’re very happy’.

Oliver looked at her. That was the response in a way that he had hoped for. Yes, it was 1992, but many minds were still set against homosexuality. The homosexuality issue had become a burning one within his own family – his wife’s sister – and he had done some very serious thinking about the issue. He was a priest, and the line of his church was that the ideal scenario was that of one man, one woman, and one union for life in marriage. Oliver had seen the very special love of Sadie, his sister-in-law to her partner, and was forced by the sheer quality and depth of their love to re-evaluate both his own and the church’s view on this issue.

‘So – they are very happy living in Scotland. Sadie gave Hope the home to herself and Lucy for as long as they need it’.

Oliver paused again, suddenly feeling bewildered that he had shared the information about his sister-in-law. His life involved many keeping of confidences.

‘I’m sorry, Maria. I have told you too much. Forgive me’.

Maria simply went on to the subject, which was burning a hole in her heart.

‘Where does the little girl fit in? Lucy Erin isn’t it?’ Maria asked disingenuously, knowing full well that it was this name that had caused her search in the first place.

‘Yes. Named after Hope’s mother. The baby was the result of the rape, and because of the condition Syndactyly that both Gary and the baby have, it was clear Gary was the father. He stole her when she was a newborn and discovered her webbed feet, which were just like his. It’s an inherited condition’.

Maria had heard a lot of things during her work as a Medical Psychiatric Social Worker, but she had never heard a saga quite like this.

‘So Gary has feelings for this baby?’

'He seems to, but with Gary, his feelings can – um-
'

'-Turn on a sixpence', filled in Maria.

'Precisely', replied Oliver.

'Well, there's plenty of material to be getting on with', said Maria with a wry smile, closing her notepad. 'My problem is knowing where to begin!'

'A person of your experience will find a way in, I've no doubt', said Oliver, and meant it.

A way in was found much more quickly and dramatically than either of them could possibly have imagined.

Chapter 13

Hope was excited that her half-sister, Connie, was bringing the babies home to the vicarage the following day. She knew it would be hard work for all of them, but Connie was a very organised person, and as long as the babies fed well, Hope thought she herself would only be needed for about a week or ten days to cook and look after the other children, Rosy in particular. Her own little girl, Lucy Erin, had loved the company at the vicarage, and it would be no hardship for her to go back there for a little while longer.

Connie, Oliver, and Hope had decided that the Lockwood family – Mum, Dad, James, Peter, Rosy, Joseph, and Benjamin – would spend the first night on their own and indulge their joy of being together. That was the theory, anyway. What they had not reckoned on was that Rosy would cycle into her parents' bedroom at four a.m., ringing the shrill bell as she came; that Peter would rage down the stairs with a face like thunder complaining about the noise; and that James, who knew everything at the age of seventeen, would come in loudly advising his parents in a voice booming like the prime minister's at Question Time to '*Put the babies as far away as you can,* preferably in the kitchen with the door shut, and simply *leave them to cry, for goodness' sake!'*.

The tiny babies weighed five and a half pounds and nearly six pounds, respectively, and although they were a really good weight for twins, they nevertheless needed three hourly feedings for a while. Connie had already decided that breastfeeding both babies might be too much but was planning to alternate with breast and bottle. She had been a trained nursery nurse, so babies and young children were her particular field of expertise. All the training in the world, however, could not have covered every eventuality of the first night of the babies' homecoming. In the end, Oliver and Connie sat up in bed at five o'clock a.m. with a cup of tea and rocked with laughter, or was it hysterical exhaustion?

The following day, Gary Johnson had plans to execute. He had been living upstairs in the vicarage for three days, overseen by Robbie. But enough was enough. He knew that the Professor Maria woman would be coming for him soon and would start ferreting around in places in his life that were none of her business, so it was definitely time to disappear. He was always half expecting the police to come roaring up to the doorway, but so far, no-one had spilt the beans about his past – the multiple rapes, including that of Sister Hope, violent stabbings in the streets, and latterly the disposal of his mother. Time to move on and back into the shadows before the game was up.

First, he must see his daughter; no, much more than that, he must *claim* his daughter. After all, his beloved

Wolfie had died, so all he had left in the world was Lucy Erin, yes it was. He knew Hope's address in Southwark as Oliver had re-addressed a couple of letters that had come for her at the vicarage, which Peter had forgotten to drop into Hope's home on his way to school.

Gary moved stealthily towards her house, identified it, then slunk away and moved in and out of the crowds in Borough Road Market, his old stamping ground. He remembered stealing his belt from there some years back. This had now become his most precious item as it had doubled as Wolf's lead, and it still had a faint whiff of him on its leather. Gary smelt it frequently.

Oliver had given Gary thirty pounds to set him up a bit, with which he bought from the market some rope and a large red scarf. From the grocery counter, he purchased a few biscuits and sweets and an inexpensive pink polyester blanket. Mission accomplished. Clutching the goods in two plastic carrier bags, he walked up to Hope's house. It was dusk now. The drawing in of the evening figured as part of his plan – seven thirty in the evening, to be precise.

He knocked at Hope's front door. Hope was already in her cotton nightdress, wrapped round with a cream candlewick dressing gown. As soon as she put Lucy to bed each evening, she was used to dressing comfortably, getting ready for bed, and curling up in front of the television or with a book for a couple of hours. This was her routine. She opened the front door a little, naturally cautious, as she and the toddler were there on their own, and Hope always felt a little vulnerable. The Convent had been such a safe place, surrounded by thick walls, so living in a busy city centre was quite a contrast for her.

When she saw Gary on the doorstep, her instinct was to slam the door quickly, but Gary already had his foot in it, wedging it open.

''Allo Hope. It's only me. Can I come in for a few minutes? I've come to see me daughter'.

'She's not here, Gary. She's staying at the vicarage,' Hope lied.

'You sure? Her pushchair's here'.

'Yes, I brought it back with me. I'm going to stay up there tomorrow morning when Connie and the babies come home'.

Already too much information, thought Hope, especially about Lucy Erin. As long as it deterred Gary temporarily, that was all that mattered. Her protective instinct rose in her like invisible hackles rising and spiking along her spine. Gary was already hatching his alternative plan. He eyed Hope up and down, his animal lust kicking in. Why not? He had done it before, and this time, he was on his own, so he could take more time. Enjoy it. Play with her. Taunt her. And what's more, she didn't have all that Nun's garb to negotiate before he reached the prize.

Hope saw the look in his eyes and froze inside. This man was evil. She hated the word, but sometimes there seemed no other. She instinctively folded her arms over her breasts, which inadvertently left the bottom of her nightdress and dressing gown open for Gary's viewing.

'No, Gary. *Please.* Don't do it. It would be wicked. You're better than that now', she said desperately, 'You're a much nicer man now.'

But it was too late. Gary bounced her onto her sofa, pushed her flat, and lifted up her garments. Hope started screaming for help. Gary reached for his carrier bag, pulled out the scarf, and gagged Hope tightly, mouth and nose, the bright red scarf like a thick stripe of blood on a wound. She could not breathe and began to thresh her legs and arms around. He reached for the rope and bound her arms tightly. Ah. That was it! Just her legs free. That was quite exciting. A kind of bondage!

'It's OK, *Sister* Hope. Soon be over. You know what, you might even enjoy it this time. You ain't a virgin now, are ya? I saw to that, didn't I - well, me and the lads'.

He lifted her nightdress up beyond her breasts and surveyed her.

'Not a bad kit for a nun', he said as he prepared himself. 'You can kick as much as you like, darlin'. I'm made of tough stuff. Lean back and enjoy it, why don't ya? Have ya had it since I helped myself before – me and the lads, that is?' he said, giving her a painful bite on her neck.

'Don't worry. I won't hang about,' he said, almost visibly slobbering at the mouth in anticipation, like a loose-jowled bulldog salivating for food.

Hope died inside, and furthermore, she was struggling to breathe. Just succumb, she told herself. Don't fight it. Gary, full of pent-up animal lust, began to do the deed - viciously, angrily, violently - as if punishing Hope in some way. He was hurting her mercilessly. Suddenly, before Gary could complete his vile act, a little voice called out:

'Mama. Mama. I need a drink'.

The little girl stood on the stairs, bewildered by what she saw. Quick as a flash, Gary withdrew from Hope's body as roughly as he had entered, pulled his jeans up, and moved quickly to Lucy, who was standing on the stairs, blonde curls tousled, holding her white toy rabbit. Hope tried to call out to Lucy but could make only the smallest muffled sound. The scarf was tied round her mouth in several layers.

‘’Allo Lucy. I’m your daddy. You spoiled me fun, but never mind, you’re coming with me. Like to come with your daddy?’ He turned to Hope and, with a face like thunder, said, ‘You lied, Sister ‘Ope. Now that’s not very good considering you’re a *Nun!*’ He spat out the word ‘*Nun*’ as though it was poison in his mouth. ‘That was a *very* silly thing to do, wasn’t it?’

Lucy backed away, frightened and whimpering now, ‘You hurt Ma-ma’. Gary picked her up decisively.

‘She loves it, Lucy Locket. Come on. We’re gonna have some fun’.

Gary took the belt off his jeans, which had remained unfastened, with his flies undone. He was going to use the belt as a dog’s lead on Lucy. Lucy looked at Hope.

‘Why you hurting Mama? Naughty man to hurt Mama. Ma-ma, I can see your bottom’, she said, distressed and beginning to cry. ‘I can see your bottom, Ma-ma. Pull nightie down, pull nightie down, Ma-ma’.

‘Ma-ma’s all-right, yes she is’, said Gary. He went up to Hope and bent right down into her face.

‘You’re all-right in’t ya? Quite comfortable down there, innit? Sorry, I deprived you of my goods there. You missed a treat. But I’ve got me daughter instead. Thanks, Hope’ he leered. ‘But rest assured, I’ll be back for me finishing off, oh yes, I will. A man's got to 'ave his finish, hasn't he?'

With that, he dumped Lucy hard into the pushchair, leaving the belt on the table as he negotiated the pushchair straps but failed to lock her in. Lucy was struggling and kicking her legs.

'No. Nasty man hurting me'.

'Wow. You're a feisty little thing, ain't you? Just like your Muvver' he leered. 'Bye, Hope. I shouldn't shout if I was you. You'll run out of breath. Don't worry. I'll look after me daughter, oh yes I will'.

With that, he opened the door and was gone, the child now sobbing in bewilderment. He reached into one of the bags and gave her a sticky, sweet lolly, then ran like the wind with the pushchair until he reached the tunnel at Southbank, leaving Hope terrified, distraught, and fast running out of breath. She tried to wriggle her body downwards towards the telephone, but it was up on a ledge out of the way of Lucy's little fingers, which were adept at dialling random numbers. She wriggled further to the door, but her feet could not turn the door knob. The red scarf was completely covering her nose and mouth, and she knew that if she struggled further, she would run out of breath.

'Lord, help me', she whispered inside her muzzle before she passed out into oblivion ten minutes later.

Chapter 14

The following morning found Connie slightly bewildered. She had definitely arranged with Hope that Hope would be up at the vicarage by eight o'clock that morning to help with breakfast and get Rosy off to school. Rosy had been crooning over the babies and was not dressed, and it was now eight-thirty-five a.m. It was not like Hope to let anyone down or get the time wrong.

'Rosy, you really must concentrate, sweetheart. You can see the babies for as long as you like after school, but you will be late for Sarah's mum. You'll both miss the register if you don't get a move on. Now where's your other shoe?'

Connie eased herself out of bed. She still had stitches that were sore from her episiotomy during childbirth, and she felt lethally tired. Where was Oliver? He was always so good at breakfast time except for Thursdays, when he took an early morning communion service. Oliver was, in fact, phoning Hope. He didn't want to harass her, but this first morning was important. He rang twice and received no answer, so he concluded that Hope must be walking up the hill pushing the pushchair this very minute towards them. He called out of the door to Peter, who was just going down the path.

'Pete, if you don't pass Hope on the way up, could you just ring her bell and see that she hasn't overslept, please?' Pete grunted without moving his lips, which in any other language meant yes, he would.

Oliver returned to the bedroom, where Connie was on her hands and knees, looking under the bed for Rosy's other shoe. One of the babies was crying furiously.

'Hey, Con, what are you doing out of bed? Thought you were going to stay there until the kids had gone to school'.

'Well, you weren't here, and Hope's not here,' said Connie, sounding scratchy for the first time. 'Rosy's being a slowcoach'.

Oliver put his arm round her.

'I've been trying to get Hope on the phone, Con. I'm sure she's on her way. She wasn't answering, so she must be. Rosy', he spoke sternly, 'Now, this isn't the way to carry on. How many times have we said you must put your shoes at the end of the bed before you get into it at night time? You need to help Mummy. Get a move on'. Rosy scurried around and, within seconds, had found the offending shoe.

Suddenly, Oliver exclaimed, 'Has anyone seen James this morning? Don't tell me he isn't even up! He wasn't down at breakfast time. That boy is a pain in the neck. He's got mock exams today. Rosy, run upstairs quickly, will you, and see if he's awake, please? We're going to have to get into more of a routine than this'.

The second baby had begun crying. Momentarily Connie covered her head with her pillow, overwhelmed, before she picked up both the babies one after the other and lay them on the bed next to her. They were quiet for a few moments. The doorbell rang. Rosy bent over and kissed Connie and then both her little brothers, which started them crying again.

'We really do need Hope, don't we?' Oliver said. 'Wonder where she's got to. It's just not like her to let us down like this'. He picked one of the babies up and put him over his shoulder. 'Is there a bottle made up in the fridge, Con? I'll give him a top-up. He seems hungry'.

Just then, James appeared, hair tousled.

'Oh no! Why hasn't anyone woken me?'

'And why haven't you set your alarm, Jamie? It's your responsibility'.

'I know, I know', he said, grabbing a piece of cold toast from the pop-up toaster.

'How were they in the night, Mum?' he asked Connie.

'They're always hungry', Connie said. 'I seem to have been feeding them all night. Little guzzlers!'

'It runs in the family', said James, munching toast and spreading crumbs everywhere. 'When do they start having other stuff besides milk?'

'Oh, not till three months earliest', replied Connie.

'Oh, blimey. Will you be feeding them all that time, then?'

'Me and the bottle', said Connie with a wan smile.

'I've got five minutes, Mum. Give me that one' he said, pointing to the baby on the bed, 'I'll fetch another bottle'.

'No, no, Jamie, you must get yourself off. Thank you, though. Good luck with your mocks'.

'They're lovely, but I can't wait for these boys to grow up a bit. They don't do much at the moment, do they? Just cry and feed, it seems to me', said James.

He bent down to kiss her.

'You're brilliant, Mum'.

James could be such a lovely person, Connie reflected, when he forgot to be seventeen going on thirty-seven and a world authority on absolutely everything. Connie knew there was great potential there. It was just a case of living through the 'know-all' phase and treasuring the golden moments in between.

Chapter 15

Peter was approaching Hope's house. He rang the bell once as his dad had asked him to check on Hope. Then he stood and rang several times. Receiving no answer, he peered through her letter box. There on the floor, to his horror, he saw Hope, gagged with the red scarf, arms tied with rope, and clearly, at the very least, unconscious. Peter, horrified, knew he had to act quickly. There was no time to run back to his father, so he began heaving the door with his shoulder. He had always been exceptionally strong, even as a small child, but he couldn't budge it. He kept on heaving, making his shoulder sore in the process. Strangely, no-one came to help or seemed to react. Maybe, thought Peter, it's not so unusual to see a boy trying to bash down a door in Southwark. Weird.

A few seconds later, James came running down the street, late for his sixth-form registration. Catching up with Peter, he was flabbergasted to see him vandalising Hope's door.

'What on *earth* are you doing, Pete? You having a brainstorm or something? Peter caught his breath, held his shoulder, and replied,

'Jamie, look in there! Quick! Hope's in trouble. We've got to get in'.

Jamie peered through. He immediately began to panic.

‘Pete, Pete, what are we going to do? She could be dead’, he whimpered, completely losing his cool. ‘And where’s Lucy?’

‘This is what we’re going to do, James’, said Peter authoritatively. ‘We are going to bash the door down between us and then use Hope’s phone to call an ambulance. While I’m waiting for the ambulance, you are going to run back home and get Dad’.

Jamie was glad to be given instructions. He could not cope at all with this crisis. Most of his life, he had taken the lead in situations with his younger, somewhat strange brother, but not this time.

‘Right, right, yes’, he said and immediately started putting his shoulder to the door.

‘No, James. We need to exert the pressure equally for the best result. Now, after three, we will both heave’.

Jamie stared at his brother. This transformation was extraordinary.

‘One – two- three’. They both heaved. The door creaked but stayed on its hinges.

‘Again, James. Don’t stop. I’ll keep counting’.

'One –two – three'. Several times, the boys heaved until, finally, the door groaned in submission and caved in. Peter bent down to Hope and felt for a pulse in her neck.

'What you doing, Pete?'

'I'm feeling for a pulse', replied Pete. They taught us this in First Aid. Sshh! I must concentrate'. After a few seconds, he whispered,

'She's alive. James, ring for an ambulance, then run quickly and get dad'.

Jamie hesitated. He had mock exams at school. Momentarily torn, he then dismissed the thought. Not important. He gave instructions to the voice at the end of the 999 number but was so shaken that the woman on the other end had to ask him to speak up and speak clearly and slowly. James handed the phone to Peter, his hand trembling.

'Hallo. I am Peter Lockwood, the brother of James Lockwood, who was the last voice that you heard. I am calling about Sister Hope O'Neill. She has collapsed on the floor and has a weak pulse. She needs an ambulance urgently. You can drive it right up to the front door, which is now destroyed. She has clearly been attacked as she is gagged with a red scarf, and her arms are bound with rope'. He gave the name and address and added, 'Please hurry. She is very bad. We need the police too'.

Jamie started running back up the road to tell Oliver the bad news. Robbie was just coming out of the vicarage front door and bumped into the frantic lad.

'Robbie, Robbie, something dreadful's happened. You must come down to Hope's. She's collapsed'.

Robbie didn't wait to ask questions or for explanations. Jamie was in a highly distraught state.

'O.K., O.K. Jamie, I'm on my way. Do you want to go inside or come back with me? Who's with Hope?'.

'We've called the ambulance', panted Jamie as he ran back with Robbie. Peter's down there.'

'Oh no! Is he coping?'

'He's brilliant,' murmured Jamie. 'Just brilliant.'

When they reached the house, an ambulance and police car were waiting outside the house, their blue lights flashing, and a small crowd of onlookers had gathered. Peter was inside the house with the paramedics and police. The red scarf had been released from around Hope's mouth, and her hands were untied. She began to stir.

'Lucy', she whispered. 'Where's Lucy?'

The policemen looked at Peter.

'Who's Lucy, lad? Her nipper?'

'Yes. She's three years old, blonde hair, blue eyes, sweet nature, can talk well for a three-year-old', said Peter authoritatively. 'Can I give you anything more of a description?'

'You are doing just great', said the paramedic. 'Well done, lad.'

'I *am* a lad', said Peter, 'but actually I have a *'name'*. Could you call me by that, please?'

The policeman looked a bit taken aback.

'My name is Peter. By the way, only those who are family call me 'Pete', so please don't call me that.'

Hearing his brother talking in familiar pedantic terms somehow brought comfort to Jamie, who had arrived back on the scene. It reassured him. He wasn't sure about this competent, authoritative brother who had emerged. He felt more secure with the return of the status quo. The paramedics worked on Hope, giving her oxygen and adrenaline and putting a portable drip up. Still, she kept repeating in a voice barely audible,

'Lucy, Lucy. Where's Lucy? Find Lucy'.

Robbie bent down, narrowly avoiding knocking the hanging drip.

'Hope, who did this to you? Tell us, and we will find Lucy'.

Hope began mouthing a name. Her lips were bone dry, and she could barely speak.

'Was it Gary?' asked Robbie.

Hope nodded briefly before sinking once more into oblivion.

Robbie's fury boiled up inside.

'Right. That's it. No more chances. Jamie, Pete, we've got to search for him. Come with me'.

'Not so fast, sir', said the policeman, putting a restraining arm on Robbie. 'We need a full statement from this young man. Now – um – Pete –'

'I told you – it's Peter; not Pete ever. *Peter'*.

'Now, *Peter,* we're going to ask you a few questions. Can you manage some answers for us?'

'It depends on what you ask me', replied Peter. 'If they are erudite questions, the answer will be no. If they are relevant, yes'.

The policeman looked across at the other Paramedic and raised his eyebrows. The brief glance expressed it all: 'We've got the right one here!'.

The Paramedics put Hope on a stretcher and carefully carried her out to the waiting ambulance. They had to manoeuvre around the crowd of people.

'Mind your backs', said one. 'We need complete access please'.

Robbie ran out after the stretcher. 'Can one of us come with her? Doesn't seem right that she should be all on her own'.

'Who is her next of kin? Is the child's father around?' asked one of the police.

Perish the thought.

'Well, Connie Lockwood is her sister....' started Robbie,

'Actually, that is not strictly accurate', interjected Peter. 'My mother, Connie Lockwood, is Hope O'Neill's *half*-sister. You see-' Peter took a deep breath and was about to launch into the entire history of the Lockwood household.

'O.K., Pete. That's enough now', Robbie said, putting a restraining hand on Peter's shoulder. 'The police need to get on'.

'Whoever's done this has got a lot to answer for. Look's like he's raped her too. What did you say his name was?' asked the Paramedic.

Robbie had no hesitation this time in handing over Gary Johnson's name to the police. Robbie had, by his silence, been protecting Gary for three years. He had been down at the quayside on that foggy night when

Gary had led his drunken mother towards the water, lifted her into the rowing boat, and rowed silently off. Robbie had lurked a few paces behind on the quay, unbeknown to Gary.

He had seen Pearl, Gary's drunken mother, being hauled into the boat. He had picked up the emerald green shoe that had fallen off into the shallow water and then lapped it onto the beach. When, a little while later, the police found Pearl's body downstream, they displayed notices and a picture of the remaining soggy green shoe all around South London, asking if anyone had any information about drowning or a woman that was missing. Robbie had seen the posters but chose to say nothing.

Gary's final action of the molestation of Hope, of attempting to rape her and of stealing her precious little girl, had provoked Robbie finally into telling the whole grizzly story.

'I know him', he said, 'and I'd like to make a full statement about him down at the station', he said, 'but mate, the first thing is to find her little girl. God knows what mood Gary is in. The kid ain't....'

'*Isn't'* Robbie, '*isn't',* interjected Peter.

'*Isn't* safe. And what's more, Gary usually carries a knife and is not afraid to use it. Anything could happen if he was that violent with Hope'.

Chapter 16

Oliver was concerned. There was no sign of Hope, and he had just seen his eldest son, James, running back down the road with Robbie. What on earth was James doing? He had important mock exams. Oliver didn't report what he had seen to Connie. She'd had a bad enough night and started the morning as it was. It was amazing how the presence of two tiny babies could have disrupted life so much already. Oliver finished feeding the tinier baby, Joseph, put him over his shoulder to wind him, and then said to Connie,

'I'm just going down the hill, Con. Maybe Hope is struggling with the pushchair or something. It could be a wheel has come off. It was a bit rickety. Won't be more than a few minutes. Are you ok, darling?'

'I'm fine, thanks Oli. I'll get up soon, but I'll wait till you're back, then have a quick shower'.

He kissed his wife briefly, closed the front door, unpadlocked his bicycle, and cycled down the hill. Phew! It was nice to get out in the air, even for a few minutes; however, as soon as Hope's house came within sight, Oliver froze. The ambulance was just drawing off with its blue light flashing, and the police car was still there. Robbie, Jamie, and Peter were all standing outside the house talking to the police officer, who was taking notes. Oliver was generally a calm sort of person, but his stomach flipped, and his imagination raced at the sight of the blue lights. He swung his legs off the bike, leant it against Hope's wall, and immediately went up to the group.

'What's going on? What's happened?'

'And you are, sir?'

'I'm Oliver Lockwood, priest of this parish'.

One of the police officers smirked.

'Well, if you'll forgive me saying so, you don't look much like a priest to me, no dog collar and a nappy draped over your shoulder, sir'.

Oliver was too anxious to comment on his observations.

'What's going on? These are my sons, and Hope is my sister-in-law. Where is she?'

The police, aided by Robbie, Jamie, and Peter, told the story of their morning and what had happened to Hope.

'The worst thing is that Lucy is missing', said Robbie. 'He's gone and taken her, hasn't he?'

'Oh my God!' exclaimed Oliver, and meant it. What to do now?

‘I’m going to look for Lucy’, said Peter, ‘Come on, James and Robbie, you too’.

‘Not so fast, son,’, said the officer, ignoring the withering glance of Peter, ‘We need you down at the station to verify everything you’ve told us’.

Peter was about to object to the word ‘son’, but Oliver interjected, ‘Yes, of course, just tell us what to do and we will do it’.

‘I’ve given you a statement’, said Robbie, ‘and I think I may know where Gary might be. He will have sped along to Rotherhithe tunnel probably. It used to be one of his favourite hiding places’.

The Officer radio-d to a patrol car.

‘Rotherhithe tunnel, mate. Quick as you can’.

Oliver remembered Professor Maria Murphy and how she had managed to draw alongside Gary. She lived a stone’s throw from the tunnel. He phoned Connie and, without explaining why, asked her to reach for Professor Maria’s number, saying that Gary was in ‘a spot of bother’. Connie reached for Oliver’s address book. Oliver could hear both the babies crying in the background. Poor Connie. Not such a good start for her. He would get back just as soon as he could.

Oliver borrowed the officer’s mobile phone and rang Maria.

'Maria, I can't go into the ins and outs of it now, but Gary Johnson is in serious trouble and appears to have stolen Hope's daughter Lucy. He has raped and gagged Hope'.

He heard Maria gasp on the other end of the line. '

'She's desperately ill. Left like it on the floor overnight we think. Gary may be heading for Rotherhithe tunnel. Is there any chance at all you could get down there to help the police? He will need to be talked into handing her back if he's holding her as ransom for anything. I immediately thought of you. I know it's an imposition'.

Maria hesitated. Her diary was crammed full of appointments.

'I know it's a really big ask, but we are terribly concerned for the safety of Lucy'.

'I'll get down there as quickly as I can', she replied, 'but I'll have to make a few phone calls first. Stay calm, Oliver. We'll talk him round'.

'Please, God', she said to the God who she didn't believe in. She'd hedge her bets in this situation just in case.

xxxxx

Maria arrived at the entrance of the tunnel. She was quicker than the police cars even though they had used their blue lights and sirens throughout the journey. Morning rush hour in the south of London almost always meant gridlocked traffic right along the length of the Embankment. Maria had run as fast as she could to the tunnel, which was less than five minutes away from where she worked. She hated its gloom and the way poisonous car fumes became trapped and turned the atmosphere inside toxic. Surely, he hadn't brought the little girl down here? Maria picked her way along the narrow pavement towards the centre. A few cars passed her, but generally, traffic was restricted in the tunnel. There was no sign of Gary. Maybe this had not been his preferred hiding place after all? The air became thick with fumes towards the centre. Maria gritted her teeth, covered her mouth with her patterned purple scarf, which she had slung on for this express purpose, walked further in, and then stopped.

There on the pavement was a parked pushchair, and Gary and Hope's daughter Lucy huddled up together and fast asleep under the new purpose-bought pink fluffy blanket. Maria stared at them. There was something strangely moving and even beautiful about the way the unshaven, unkempt, disturbed young man lay entwined with the innocent, beautiful little child. Maria hesitated, not sure for a moment what her next move should be. In the distance, echoing down the murky tunnel, she heard the sound of the police sirens. Maria must wake the two before the police approached. She didn't want Gary startled and reacting violently or the little girl frightened even more. She knelt down and very gently stroked Lucy's mop of gold curls.

'Come on, little one, let's go and find Mummy, shall we?' The child stirred. Maria was incredulous to find the little girl then immediately smiled a radiant smile and held up her arms in acceptance to her. She realised in those few seconds that this was what it should have been like with her own daughter had she survived. Would her own little one have looked like this? She held the child close and thought she would explode with the myriads of unexpressed and half-formed thoughts and feelings that flooded through her.

Gary began to stir. Suddenly, he was bolt upright.

'What you doin'? Give her back, give her *back,*' he hissed. 'She's *mine'*. He began tugging Lucy from Maria's arms. The child started screaming.

'Gary. You must let her go, please. You have done a very wrong thing. You know that. Hope is in the hospital. She was nearly dead at the scene. For all I know, she might be by now. Let Lucy go and see her mother quickly, Gary, *please*'.

'I never killed her, I didn't. I just tied her up to keep her quiet so as I could take the little-un'.

'Shut up!' he shouted loudly at Lucy, who was crying loudly. 'I'm your daddy, and I'm havin' yer, make no mistake about that!'

At that moment, the police car arrived, swerved to a halt, kept its blue lights flashing, and discharged two officers. They clamped handcuffs on Gary immediately, one of them saying:

'Gary Johnson, I am arresting you on suspicion of rape, grievous bodily harm and kidnap of a child....'

'I never raped her', Gary yelled as he struggled. 'Never got the fucking chance. The kid saw to that, didn't she? Interrupted us she did', he said, ruining his case in one fell swoop.

The officer continued:

'You do not have to say anything, but it may harm your defence....'

'-and the bit about kidnap ain't right', Gary snarled. 'You can't kidnap what's yours, can ya? She's my daugh'er in't she?' Gary started kicking the officer.

'...If you do not mention when questioned something you later rely on in court....'

'And I ain't going to court either. Tell 'em, doc. She's me daugh'er in't she?'

'...Anything you do say may be given in evidence'.

'Yeh, well, you can tell 'em this. I ain't had a chance in life, have I, Doc?'

Maria was about to respond in some way when Robbie came running up the tunnel.

'And you can accuse him of murder, too', he said in between laboured breathing. 'And you'll have to do me too, 'cos I've sat on the information for three years and said nothing. I wanted to give him a chance', he said, 'but not now'.

Gary stopped kicking. They all stared at Robbie. There was silence apart from the drone of traffic in the distance echoing through the tunnel. Robbie spoke almost in a whisper.

'Gary's right when he said he didn't have a chance in life, but I know he murdered his mother. I saw him take her down the jetty at Bankside beach last November. He got her drunk, dragged her into the rowing boat, and then took her downstream. I didn't see him tip her over because it was a pea-souper, but I found her shoe and then saw the posters'. He turned to Gary with a look of sorrow and regret, 'Sorry, mate, 'I've stood by you, but I've got no choice now you've raped Hope again and stolen Lucy.'

Gary crumpled in a heap, almost bringing the police officer who was restraining him down with him.

‘How d’ya know that?’ he murmured. ‘It was so bloody foggy’.

‘I followed you, Gary. I thought you were up to no good, and I was right, wasn’t I?’

Gary slowly nodded.

‘Was that a ‘yes’?’ asked the second police officer sharply.

Gary did not respond, but looked finished.

‘Gary, we’ll find a way through this’, said Maria softly, handing the little girl to Robbie and kneeling down beside him. ‘There *are* extenuating circumstances, and I may be able to speak up for you if you tell me more of your history’.

‘All I want is to be able to see me daughter. Lost me dog, haven’t I?’ whimpered Gary.

‘Well, I doubt you’ll ever be able to do that, son’, said the second police officer harshly. ‘You should have thought of that when you raped that woman and dragged the little girl away. Look at her’.

Gary looked up. Lucy was sobbing softly and shrunk back as she saw his gaze.

‘No. No. Nasty man hurt Ma-ma’, she said. ‘I want Ma-ma’.

'Doctor Murphy', said the restraining officer, 'Please take the little girl and the pushchair and bring her to the station while we deal with this one', he said, now struggling again with Gary, who had found his second wind. 'And you, mate', he said to Robbie, 'must come with us. Officer, handcuff him.'

'There's no need to do that. I'll come'.

'Ah, but you see, deliberately withholding information from the police during a criminal investigation may result in charge of felony and is a punishable offence. Put the handcuffs on him, officer, as I said'.

The handcuffs were clamped on Robbie for the third time in his life. He said nothing but looked at the ground. He had been waiting for this for three years. The second officer, the more senior of the two, had decided that it was not a good idea to let Lucy out of their sight.

'Doctor, I think the officer and I must take the child back to the station. It's not right to let her go with you. We have a duty of care to protect her, as you probably know, being medical and all that.'

Medical Social Psychiatrist Professor Maria Murphy rose to her full height (albeit only five feet two inches) and tapped into her rarely used ability to silence people in an instant with her intimidating air of authority.

'Officer, have you heard of the O.H.C.H.R?'

Both officers looked blank.

'It stands for The Office of the High Commissioner for Human Rights. I'm surprised in your line of work, you haven't heard of it' she said witheringly. 'What about the United Nations Convention on the Rights of the Child, 1989? Heard of that?' She looked at them.

'No. I thought not. I suggest you go to night school to inform yourselves', she said with an oversweet smile. 'Let me quote something to you from it:

'The best interest of the child shall be the primary consideration in all circumstances'. The *primary* consideration, gentlemen. I am a Medical Psychotherapist, Professor Maria Murphy, and I am therefore taking the child back to my surgery to check her over. I will then return her to the Reverend Oliver and Mrs. Connie Lockwood, who often act in loco parentis to her; or if her mother is well enough, straight to the hospital, where they can be reunited - whichever is deemed to be in her best interest. Which option do you prefer, Constable – um.....?'

'Er - Walters, and its *Sergeant* Walters'.

It did not fit easily with Maria's philosophy of ethics to treat the policemen as in some way inferior beings as she had just done, but she was determined that Lucy would not go back with two unfamiliar men to a clinical and cold police station. Lucy was already so traumatised that Maria knew it would have a lasting impact on her for many years to come in some form or other.

The little girl was screaming at the top of her voice, a loud, penetrating, shrill, terrified scream which reverberated round the tunnel.

'Yes, perhaps you'd better get her out of here. Blimey, what a racket! Nothing wrong with her lungs, anyway!'

'I will take her and check her over, and then I will wheel her back to the Vicarage. Both the vicarage and the people in it are familiar to her. You could call it her second home.

Without further discussion, Maria put Lucy in her pushchair, strapped her in, fumbled with the complicated harness for a few seconds, and then walked purposefully away from the two police officers and Gary, the latter protesting loudly and alternating between shouting and sobbing.

'Give 'er back; she's mine. I ain't done no harm to her. I love 'er, I do. I love 'er. You better tell Hope I'm sorry, and I just wanted my kid. She's mine, in't she?'

Chapter 17

It was turning out to be one of those days when Oliver returned speedily to the vicarage. He found Connie ashen, pale, and clutching her abdomen. Both the babies were finally asleep in their respective cradles, but Connie was in trouble.

‘Olly, I’m afraid I’ve got to go to hospital. I’m bleeding really heavily. Can you call an ambulance? I’m in difficulties, I know, but whatever happens, I’m taking Ben and Joseph with me’, she added. As she spoke, she was clutching her stomach with one hand and pulling a couple of pairs of knickers and a large packet of sanitary towels from a drawer with the other.

‘Oh, Con. Oh, darling. Any idea what could be wrong? This is bad’. He looked with growing fear at the accumulating pool of blood that was beginning to seep into the patterned carpet. ‘We must get you seen to quickly. Poor lamb. They’ll sort you out, Con’.

‘Sorry about the carpet, Oli. I’m stuffed up with towels, but the bleeding has gone wild’.

Oliver phoned 999 immediately, and the ambulance arrived within ten minutes.

‘It’s probably some rogue remains of placenta need clearing out’, said Connie, adopting a matter-of-fact tone, but her ashen face told Oliver that it might be a whole lot more than that.

'I expect it will be a D&C. They're routine with this kind of thing'.

She smiled at Oliver, trying to hide her growing alarm.

'Thank goodness Rosy is at school', replied Oliver, whose insides were now churning with anxiety.

'At least we've got a few hours. Come on, Con. Let's get you by the front door so that you can whip into the ambulance quickly. I'll bring the twins'.

When the paramedics arrived, however, they insisted on Connie lying down on a stretcher with her feet slightly raised. They strung up a saline drip once Connie was in the ambulance. Oliver put both the babies quickly into one carrycot. The rolled together sweetly face to face but remained asleep. He covered them lightly with a cream pram blanket, carried them up the steps of the ambulance, and kept watch over his precious cargo.

In the ambulance, Hope whispered weakly, 'Where was Hope, then, Oli? We could do with her now. It's so totally unlike her'.

'She's not around', whispered Oliver back evasively. 'I'll phone Bruce and Clara and see if they can come and help. It won't hurt Clara. She's in between shows, and Bruce said she's wandering around feeling very frustrated and aimless'.

Connie said nothing. Her ambitious and rather hard-nosed sister-in-law was not now her favourite person, although years ago, they had been very close.

However, nowadays, Clara had become rather a cross to bear in the family, and Connie had to muster all her Christian love to cope with her. Connie adored her brother Bruce, Clara's husband. Bruce had gentle, long-suffering, and noble, yes noble, nature Connie always felt. Noble because he had stuck with Clara through thick and thin, including her short-lived but spectacular flings with men at the theatre. He had also been Connie's soul mate when they were children. Clara and Bruce's kind-hearted and beautiful daughter Kitty, their one and only, would have been a better bet to come and lend a hand, but she was away filming for *Vogue* magazine.

There was another thing. Connie knew about the sexual encounter Oliver and Clara had long before Connie and he were an item. This one-off event appeared to result in Clara becoming pregnant, but the baby – Kitty – turned out to be her husband Bruce's 'miracle' baby, conceived despite Bruce's apparent impotence. Connie had long since come to terms with this aberration of Oliver's, but the thought of Clara coming to stay in the vicarage was nevertheless rather a challenge for her. What Oliver had never shared with

Connie was that there had been another time when he was extremely stressed and had very nearly succumbed to the wiles and charms of temptress Clara. There had been no need to tell her that. He remained deeply ashamed.

Connie lay back, feeling more and more weak, and gave up trying to sort things out. With the last vestige of energy, she murmured, 'Olly, is Hope all-right?'

Oliver said nothing. With all the strength she could muster, Connie propped herself up on one arm and scrutinised his face.

'Should I be worried?

'It's OK. She's in good hands. I'll fill you in later'.

'And Lucy? Who's got Lucy then?' she whispered.

'Like I said, I'll fill you in later'.

Hope was not at all reassured by his answers but gave up the unequal struggle to communicate. She knew she was in dire trouble as the bleeding was increasing by the minute. The babies were being jiggled around by the ambulance as it sped through the city centre, its blue light flashing, but they remained unperturbed and fast asleep, having cried and fed alternately for much of the night and worn Connie out.

Connie was quickly admitted and examined. In the waiting room with his two new little sons, Oliver sensed urgency and danger. He ran his hand through his dark hair several times. This was already a dreadful day, but everything else paled in comparison to the plight of his wife, who was his world. Still, the babies slept.

‘Thank you, God, for that, at least’, prayed Oliver, although he wasn’t so pleased with God today, even though he acknowledged that He did have other things on his plate, for example, a little matter of a war raging in Bosnia. Oliver would have eagerly and comprehensively put such faulty theological thinking straight if a member of his parish had voiced anything of that nature. God was universal and everywhere and a constant God of love who entered into our suffering, wasn’t He, didn’t He? He felt absent in Southwark just at the moment, thought Oliver ruefully.

Oliver was anxious and desolate. He spent an extremely stressful hour waiting for news of Connie. He tried to pray for her, but his thoughts raced wildly, moving into the zone of ‘What if’s’ and it was only with an iron hand on his imagination that he kept his mind under control. Eventually, a surgeon appeared.

‘Reverend Lockwood? Please come this way. Nurse McIndry, could you keep an eye on the babies for ten minutes?’ Nurse McIndry gazed in the carrycot and looked delighted.

Oliver's heart was pounding. There was a sombre note in the surgeon's voice.

'Is she all-right?'

'I'm very sorry, but we've had to perform an emergency hysterectomy. A delayed postpartum haemorrhage is sometimes difficult to control, and it was the safest option for your wife. I'm sorry'.

'Is she going to be all-right?' Oliver repeated, stunned.

'She'll be fine. We're putting some blood back in her, and she'll be up and around in no time. Have you other children, Sir, or were you hoping for more?'

'I have three other children', replied Oliver, not really taking in the conversation.

The surgeon glanced at the twins.

'Five in all? Oh well, you won't mind a bit of free contraception then!' he replied, 'We've done you a favour!'

'Can I see her?' replied Oliver, ignoring the crassly timed comment.

'In a while when she's round from the anaesthetic. We'll keep her in Intensive Care for a few hours, and then, providing she's on the road to recovery, we'll call you. Leave your infants here, and we'll reunite them with their mother as soon as possible'. He looked at

Oliver's strained face. 'You get off home now, Rev'd, and take a few deep breaths on your way!'

'Thank you', said Oliver. His head was still reeling regarding the implications of the operation, but really, all he cared about was the safety of his wife. He phoned Clara, Connie's sister-in-law.

'Hi. This is Clara. Leave a message'.

To the point, thought Oliver.

'Hi Clara. Oli here. We've got - er - a bit of a family emergency here. Connie is in hospital, and to be honest, I – I need a hand taking and collecting Rosy from school, and a few other bits and pieces. I wondered if you might be able to help for a day or two, Clara - just whatever you can manage? I'd be really grateful. Many thanks. Sorry to have to ask. 'Bye'.

In Reception, he remembered to enquire about Hope. He explained that his sick wife was Hope's sister. The secretary, who was trying to do the job to the best of her ability, looked doubtful.

'I'm sorry, sir, but we're not allowed to give out information about other patients. Only to the next of kin'.

'But Connie, my wife, is next of kin, and I am Connie's husband'. He grew a little taller than his six-foot height. 'I am also vicar of Southwark parish, so I hope you can take my word for it'.

The secretary, embarrassed, telephoned the Intensive Care ward to ask if there was anyone by the name of Hope O'Neill in there. Eventually, after more telephoning, she gave Oliver information.

'A Sister Hope was brought in three hours ago with breathing difficulties, multiple bruising and symptoms of shock. She has received treatment and is now sleeping'.

Oliver was torn. He desperately wanted to see Hope but knew Rosy would be home from school very soon, and she had to be his top priority. He thanked the secretary and asked if she would mind ringing for a taxi.

'Yes, your Reverend. Of course. It will be a pleasure', she replied obsequiously, her tone completely changed from before, which often happened when people were impressed by the vicar title. Oliver hated its influence, but on this occasion, he was grateful that it had worked in his favour. The taxi arrived within three minutes. It was amazing sometimes what a dog collar could do.

Chapter 18

Meanwhile, Professor Maria Murphy had taken Lucy Grace Erin O'Neil home with her from the wretched business in Rotherhithe tunnel with Gary Johnson. She cleaned her up and made her some scrambled egg with soldier fingers of toast, singing old Irish folk songs to her all the while. The little girl clearly was familiar with some of them and joined in, so Maria knew her mother must have also sung to her frequently. The miracle was that Lucy seemed entirely happy with Maria. It was almost as if the little girl felt a kinship with her. Lucy had had such a traumatic time with Gary that Maria presumed that anything and anyone would have been better than that. She did not assume that it was actually a comfortable relationship for Lucy.

Maria's self-esteem did not stretch that far. However, it was amazing, she thought, how her latent maternal instinct seemed to kick in regarding Lucy. This little one was so easy to love and pretty as a picture with her gold-blonde curls, blue-green eyes, and winsome smile. Very Irish, Maria concluded – not so much the hair colouring, but definitely those eyes! She talked and sang softly to Lucy throughout the two hours before strapping her back in her pushchair and setting off for the vicarage in Southwark. Maria realised she had just had amongst the happiest few hours of her life with Lucy. 'I wonder if it could have been like this', she mused.

Once at the vicarage, of course, there was no answer. Only the dog barked vociferously. Maria looked through the letter box. The handsome family golden retriever dog jumped up.

'It's all-right, boy. They'll be back soon. Good dog. Now lie down and be a goood boy. Goood boy' she said soothingly through the letter box when the dog obeyed.

Lucy laughed.

'Goood boy, goood boy, goood boy!' she mimicked, laughing. 'Teddy!'

'Is that his name? Teddy?'

'Teddy, Teddy, Teddy', Lucy sang.

'In your bed!' Maria commanded Teddy through the letter box. Hearing his name and the command, the dog immediately recognised both, turned round, tail between legs, and walked away from the door and into the kitchen. 'Goood boy, goood boy', said Maria through the letterbox once more, at which Teddy came bounding back and started barking excitedly again.

Maria was in a dilemma. She didn't want to go to the police station with Lucy. Should she take her back to her home or simply wait on the doorstep of the vicarage? At that moment, Oliver provided the answer as he came steaming up in a taxi, paid the driver quickly, and ran up the steps.

'Maria, I'm so sorry about all this. We've had an emergency. Lucy! Sweetheart! You're safe!' Oliver held out his arms to Lucy, who jumped into them as he swept her up in a huge bear embrace.

'My goodness, little one, you've had an adventure, haven't you?'

'Nasty man hurt Ma-ma'.

'Yes, but Ma-ma's going to be fine, Lucy. Maria, thank you so very much. Come in for a cup of tea if you have time, and I'll explain everything'.

'And so will I!' replied Maria. 'There are enough happenings in this family to fill a novel!'

Maria had readily agreed to stay at the vicarage with Lucy and Rosy while Oliver visited Connie in the hospital. Oliver had not heard back from Clara, so Maria was proving in a hundred different ways to be a godsend. He thought how blessed they were as a family that she, a high-powered, enormously busy, and respected medical psychiatrist, had appeared at the family's point of deepest need.

xxxxx

As Oliver entered the intensive care ward, he was struck by the unnatural quietness of it all, apart from the few bleeps from life-saving monitors. When Oliver reached Connie, she looked very calm and very pale but was able to smile softly at him. She always had the ability to melt his heart and reassure him, whatever the situation. He thought again how much he adored her. The surgeon had told Connie about the hysterectomy. It did not seem to perturb her unduly. All she was worried about was how it would affect her ability to be able to breastfeed the twins. Hormones and all that, she explained in a whisper.

Oliver saw ahead of them at least six weeks' recovery for Connie, and already his mind was in overdrive. How would they cope? He then reminded himself that they had already had numerous meals delivered to them by well-wishing parishioners, and doubtless, this would continue when parish folk heard about the latest drama at the Vicarage. What Oliver and Connie did not know was that most parishioners were only too delighted to repay the kindness of the vicar and his wife, who were universally loved. Somebody had already drawn up an evening meal rota to make sure the new mother did not have to cook during the first ten days at home with the babies.

All Connie wanted to do now was hold her newborns. She was very weak but, with the aid of three pillows, was propped up by the kindly registrar to watch for Nurse McIndry to enter with the babies. In stage whispers, Nurse McIndry gave Connie a bulletin as to how they had slept until ten minutes ago, how she thought they looked like their father but had their mother's nose, and weren't they going to be just the most handsome men when they grew up! She whispered incessantly so that Connie had to strain to hear her. How was the birth? What was it like to push out two babies instead of one? What about *two boys!* Connie shut her eyes in weariness. She just wanted to hold her sons. The Intensive Care nurse gave permission for her to do so for just two minutes on the understanding that if the babies cried, they would have to be whisked out immediately. Oliver thanked Nurse McIndry, saying they were fine now and, using skills well honed during parish life, steered her carefully and naturally towards the door. He picked up one baby gently, putting him into the crook of Connie's right arm, careful not to knock the blood transfusion drip, and then picked up the smaller baby and put him into the left arm crook.

Quite suddenly, Oliver was overwhelmed with feelings of immense gratitude to the hospital, to Connie, to the surgeon, and to God, and tears quietly fell down his cheeks. Connie saw them.

'I love you so, so much, Oliver Lockwood. You are the best husband in the world. I don't need my womb now, do I? It's done its work'.

‘It has, and very well, too’, replied Oliver, looking at his sons. Suddenly, it felt like a new beginning, full of promise.

xxxxx

Rosy ran to the door when she heard Oliver’s key in the latch.

‘Dad! Is Mummy all-right? What’s the matter with her?’

‘Just let me get inside, Rosy, and I’ll tell you all about it. Yes, she’s going to be fine’.

He greeted Maria, thanking her profusely for holding the fort.

‘Listen, Oliver. I’ve phoned my hospital. I have some leave owed to me. I rarely take it, so I have told them this is – um – a family emergency, and I may need a week off. They will postpone my appointments or refer them to someone else’. She hesitated, the old insecurity kicking in. ‘That’s if – if, well, if I could be of any use. I don’t want to force myself....’

Oliver went up to her and briefly put his hands reassuringly on her shoulders. Maria had not let anyone near enough to do this for a very long time. His gesture felt strong and affirming.

‘Maria, this is most kind of you. I’m sure we would love some help. I can’t believe you’re doing this for us!' he said. He paused. 'There is just one thing. I have texted my sister-in-law Clara to see if she might help. She hasn't replied, but it's a bit out of her comfort zone, to be honest'.

Maria smiled to herself. Up until twenty-four hours, the whole thing would have been way out of *her* comfort zone, but there was something about this family—the warmth, the need, the sheer honesty and integrity. Besides, she wanted to see Lucy safely reunited with her mother and was intent on taking her up to the hospital, subject to Oliver's approval, to see Hope as soon as she was able to receive her daughter. Lucy had already taken up residence on Maria's lap, and Maria knew the little girl needed her mother as quickly as possible. She already had her thumb in her mouth, grabbing Maria's soft jumper as a comforter whilst twirling a curl with the other hand. Maria couldn't work out whether Lucy was simply tired or the shock of it all was kicking in. Maybe a bit of both, she concluded.

Oliver drew Rosy aside and gently explained to her as much as he felt appropriate about Connie's operation, emphasising that she was going to be fine and they would see her as soon as possible. Rosy, at first anxious, asked a million questions and then settled herself, satisfied with her father's careful and patient explanations.

Suddenly, there was a loud and long ringing at the door. Somebody pretty persistent, thought Oliver. He opened the front door, and there was Clara Connors – beautiful, seductive, flirtatious Clara with whom he had fallen briefly but hopelessly in love before he had met Connie and with whom he had an hour of all-consuming physical passion.

She swept in, tossing her chestnut mane in a gesture that used to send shivers up and down Oliver's spine. She was just as beautiful now as she was at twenty-one, he thought.

'Hi, Oli. Trouble in camp, then? Well, if you will have all these children,' she smiled, 'What do you expect?'

Oliver laughed. Clara never changed.

'I thought I'd come as quickly as I could', she said, moving with familiarity into the kitchen, where she stopped short. Rosy ran up to her, and Lucy stirred on Maria's lap.

'Oh. Hi. Looks like you have help already!' said Clara, an edge to her voice. Clara liked to be centre stage in everything she did, whether in a performance role or outside of it.

'Clara, this is Professor Maria Murphy. She scooped Lucy up when she had been stolen from Hope by Gary Johnson. It's a long story. Coffee?'

Clara went quickly up to Lucy and tweaked her hair.

'Well, Hi Lucy. Wow! You've had an adventure, haven't you?'

Lucy shrank closer to Maria and buried her head further into the black cashmere jumper she had used as a comforter, now damp in one patch. As a medical psychiatrist, Maria was astute at assessing body language, albeit initially on a superficial level. Lucy's spoke volumes, and so did Clara's. She was certainly attractive, vibrant, and apparently enviably confident. Maria, too, felt like shrinking back as the old feelings of inadequacy swept over her. She was cross and impatient with herself for it. Here she was, with a five-year degree in Medicine, plus a five-year professional training in Psychiatry, a member of the prestigious Royal Institute of Psychiatry, feeling insecure and intimidated! Maria knew she had overcome so much in her life, achieved so much, done so much, but all the self-talk therapy in the world did not seem to inform her psyche at this moment when it came to feelings of self-worth, especially when she most needed to feel confident in the face of this overwhelming woman.

'Oh, all-right, be like that, Lucy Grace Erin', Clara said witheringly as she turned away, swishing her hair. Oliver caught the old familiar whiff of apples that had sent him into a frenzy of desire all those years ago.

'She's been extremely traumatised', explained Maria.

Rosy moved towards Lucy and stroked her leg. Lucy took her thumb out of her mouth, saying, 'Nice Rosy'. Clara saw the difference in the welcome. She softened.

'Yes, of course, she's clearly had a traumatic time. Poor Lucy,' Clara said, clucking up to her in a baby voice. Still, there was no response from Lucy.

'Sorry, little one. O.K. In your own time....'

Clara went up to Oliver.

'You going to tell me about it then, Rev?' she said, moving too near, ruffling his hair and calling him by the name she had used in their intimacy.

Oliver backed off a fraction. He was *not* going to encourage Clara's wiles. He had just left his wife in hospital, who he knew without a doubt was beautiful inside and out. Connie always seemed to have a spiritual aura surrounding her, which many people felt, and Oliver had noticed the first time he met her when she was a nanny. Connie had been handling her rosary then, but Oliver had not needed this outward sign to intuit that Connie was a deeply spiritual person.

He looked at Clara. She was wearing black denim jeans and a tight-fitting bright red top, which enhanced the shape of her breasts and nipples, doubtlessly chosen to remind Oliver what he was missing. Oliver noticed. Her hair was just as chestnut in colour, just as beautiful, and her face showed almost no sign of ageing. She was as coquettish as ever. Oliver knew it had been an aberration all those years ago when he had broken his self-imposed vow of celibacy and then again three years ago when he almost succumbed again in a moment of bleakness. He had paid for both dearly. Never again, he vowed. Anyway, apart from anything else, he had much too much respect for Bruce, who, as Connie's brother, bore the same marks of humility as she did. They had both inherited their mother's kind natures, fortunately, and had endured the slings and arrows of their father's cruelty, although both still bore the scars, some physical, most psychological, from their childhood.

Maria noticed Clara's body language and saw her immediate invasion of Oliver's body space. Here was a dangerous woman whose life probably revolved around attracting men and gaining admiration from them for her beauty and overt sexuality. What would she have at the end of it all, though, when her seductive powers no longer provoked the responses she relied upon to feed her ego? What Maria did not know was that in the early years of her marriage to Bruce Connors, Clara had remained sexually frustrated as Bruce struggled time and time again to make love to her. Instead, he always collapsed inside her when they were nearing the peak, and thus, both remained unfulfilled and, in the end, very lonely in the marriage. Had Maria known this, of course, she would have realised that there were some historically extenuating circumstances for Clara's behaviour. Actually, Maria long ago learned that there were, without fail, *reasons* behind behaviours. No-one, she believed, became problematic without a historical reason, which was why she was prepared to work with Gary Johnson to delve into the damage wrought on him by his terrible childhood. When she understood it, she could put up a defence for him and work out suitable treatment and therapy accordingly if asked for her advice.

'Come on, then, Oli. Tell me what's been going on. I'm burning with curiosity', Clara said.

'It's a long story', replied Oliver.

'I've got time', replied Clara. She turned. 'Miss – um?

'Murphy', replied Maria, 'Doctor Maria Murphy'.

'Dr. Murphy, I've come to hold the fort', replied Clara. 'I'm here to do a rescue job. Oliver looks as though he needs it. There's no need for you to stay. Its family business really, isn't it?' she added, going up to Oliver and smoothing his hair.

Maria winced inwardly at both the phrase 'rescue job' and the way Clara was so outwardly flirtatious and seductive with Oliver and was, in effect, summarily dismissing her.

'Maria has offered to stay, which is very kind of her. She's phoned into work to let them know'.

Clara gave Maria another of her withering looks and then set off on a verbal roll:

'Good job, you're not in the theatre. 'I can just see what would happen if I phoned the director to say, 'Sorry, but I'm not in today. I'm holding the fort for a family'. They'd replace me immediately with my understudy. Although I suppose they will put a second-in-command in your place, will they? That's dangerous because it could be like an understudy who turns out to be better than the real thing! Quite threatening, really', she laughed mirthlessly.

Oliver and Maria stared at her. This was Clara at her most thrusting and haughty. Clara sensed their reactions and once more attempted to soften her tone.

'It's very good of you to offer, Dr. – um – what was it again?'

'Murphy', replied Maria icily, holding Lucy more closely.

'It's very good of you, Dr. Murphy, it really is. But I guess this is where the family pulls together, so please do feel free to leave. I'll take Lucy', she said, moving towards her. Then she paused. 'That's if you want to, of course', she added over sweetly.

'Maria, what would you like to do?' asked Oliver quietly. 'Would you prefer to go now?'

'What is better for you, Oliver? Stay or leave?'

'Stay', replied Oliver immediately.

Clara responded quickly.

'Well, I can see I am surplus to requirements here, but Oliver, I've dragged all the way over here to find you are fully catered for. You should have let me know', she said witheringly, picking up her bag and flouncing towards the front door.

'Clara, don't go like this', he said, following her into the hall, leaving the kitchen door open. 'It's lovely of you to have come. It's just how it worked out'.

'Yes, well', she said, flashing her eyes at Oliver, 'I have a memory that there were other ways of coming with you', she replied boldly, brashly, inappropriately, with which she pulled Oliver to her and kissed him fully on the lips. He pulled away, mentally furious with himself for the familiar surge that he always felt when in close proximity to Clara.

'No, Clara, no. This is out of order', he said shakily. 'Please go now'.

Clara walked down the rectory steps. As she reached the bottom, she turned, blew a kiss to Oliver and said,

'I'll leave you to the tender mercies of *Doctor* Murphy, then. Have fun. Sorry I've interrupted you, *Rev*,' and with a swish of her chestnut mane, she was gone.

Oliver returned to the kitchen. Neither he nor Maria spoke.

'Auntie Clara was in a bad mood', said Rosy, helping herself to a biscuit, 'I don't like her when she's like that. Dad, can I go and watch *The Worst Witch?*' she said, hardly taking a breath between the two thoughts.

'Go on then, Rosy. Take just one more biscuit as you go. Maybe we can see Mummy in the hospital tomorrow'.

'Are Ben and Joseph staying with her? Is Mummy looking after them?'

'Yes and no', replied Oliver. Mummy will hold them and feed them a bit, but she's rather weak, so a nurse will help her'.

'Who will change their nappies then?'

'One of the nurses for now', replied Oliver.

'Yuk, Daddy! You'd better warn them that they do the yellowest, most squidgy, smelly poos on the planet!'

They all laughed.

'Are you going to stay, Professor Maria?'

'Yes, if your dad would like it'.

'*I* would like it!' she said.

Putting her hands on her hips theatrically and making a face, she added,

'Much better than Auntie Clara when she's in *that* sort of mood!'

Oliver and Maria both laughed, but inside himself, Oliver felt confused. He never wanted to hurt Clara; after all, he had loved her briefly once, but really, she had been very out of order just now.

Chapter 19

The doorbell of the vicarage rang a few minutes later, not so insistently this time. It was Bruce, Clara's husband, Connie's brother.

'Bruce! Good to see you. Come in, come in. Tea? Coffee?'

'I came to see how Clara's getting on and especially how my sister is', replied Bruce, 'but I've just met Clara getting into her car. She was crying and looking angry. What's been going on, Oliver? Anything I should know about?'

'Oh yes, plenty', thought Oliver.

'First, let me introduce you to Professor Maria Murphy, Bruce'.

Introductions done, coffee in hand, Bruce asked again,

'Did something happen to upset Clara, Oliver? Mind you, it doesn't take much. She's hopeless when she's not performing. 'Resting' is the worst possible thing for her. She becomes like a bear with a sore head'.

‘I could see that’, said Oliver, half smiling. ‘I’m afraid I asked her to come over unnecessarily. I didn’t know that Professor Maria would be here to help’.

‘Well, Oliver, you’d better get your prayer mat out on my behalf. Clara is all over the place at the moment. There’ll be fallout, knowing her. You know what she’s like’.

Oliver did indeed. Bruce looked at Maria. Lucy was nestled into her chest and now fast asleep.

‘I can tell you have the knack with young children’, he said to Maria, smiling.

‘Well, actually, I only have contact with a few in my work’, she replied. I don’t have any of my own, but this little one’, she stroked Lucy’s soft curls very gently, ‘This little one has stolen my heart’.

‘Yes. She’s like her mother and her auntie’, replied Bruce. ‘Sweet-natured, all of them’.

‘Maria rescued Lucy from Rotherhithe tunnel’, explained Oliver. ‘Gary Johnson was up to his old tricks again – and worse. I’m sorry to tell you this, Bruce, but he almost raped Hope – again - gagged her, tied her up, and left her struggling for breath’. Bruce gasped, horrified. ‘He took Lucy and hid her in the tunnel with him - right in the centre where the fumes are dreadful, poor mite’.

For a minute, Bruce was speechless.

'How's Hope? What a dreadful, terrible monster he is. Prison for life, I'd say, and throw away the key'.

'I agree he's pretty dire, but remember he saved your daughter, Bruce. He's got another side, thank God.

'Yes, he saved my daughter, Oli, but don't forget he tried it on with her too, and she was only fifteen'.

Yes, Gary Johnson was a serial rapist, Oliver conceded. There was a lot to unravel there, Professor Maria Murphy concluded as she listened to the conversation. She looked at Bruce. He was tall and muscular, with square shoulders and a mop of brown hair that was just beginning to show flecks of silver. Handsome, she thought, and personable with it. She liked him already. There was something very honest about him.

Bruce pulled out two small parcels from a brown corduroy rucksack slung onto his back, which he had used when cycling. The presents were beautifully wrapped in bright blue paper.

'These are for the wee bairns', he said, smiling. 'Two more sons, Oliver! What an achievement!' he exclaimed but looked down shyly when Oliver opened the parcel to reveal two exquisite miniature carvings.

'Bruce, these are beautiful! They really are! Look, Maria, these are Bruce's handiwork. He is a master carpenter, and doesn't it just show?'

He handed one of the two finely crafted wooden boats to Maria. She examined it closely. It really was exquisite. The one had red trimmings on it, and on the hull was hand-painted the name 'Joseph'. The other, trimmed in blue, had 'Benjamin' on it. The woodwork was beautiful.

'When did you do these, Bruce?' Oliver asked.

'As soon as Connie heard, your twins were boys. Marvellous these ultrasounds, aren't they?' replied Bruce. 'Bought me some time before their birth. I wanted to mark it somehow, of course. Identical twin boys in the family don't happen every day. Clever old Connie always looks as though a puff of wind will blow her away. How is she, Oli?'

'She'll be all-right', replied Oliver, 'but I think it might be quite a long haul – as long as that puff of wind doesn't blow her away first!' he smiled. He knew what Bruce meant.

Lucy stirred. She opened her eyes and looked across at Bruce sleepily. Bruce went up to her and tickled her gently in the stomach.

'Hello, Little Lucy Locket! I've got something for you'.

Lucy immediately sprang into life and, clambered off Maria's lap and ran towards him.

'What you got, Uncle 'Rusey?'

Bruce dipped into what was fast becoming a bag of delights and brought out a tiny parcel wrapped in rainbow-coloured paper and tied with a white ribbon.

'Here you are, Lucy. We mustn't forget you in all the excitement of the babies, must we?'

Lucy unceremoniously tore the beautiful paper off the parcel to reveal a miniature carving of a pony.

'Like it, like it!' Lucy exclaimed and immediately ran to Maria.

'Look, Mummy M'ria! My horsey, my horsey!'

Mummy Maria! Maria was stunned by the name Lucy had spontaneously called her. Tears welled up unbidden in her eyes. Bruce saw them.

'It's beautiful, Lucy, beautiful', Oliver said. What are you going to call him?'

Lucy thought for a second.

'She's Erin. Like granny. Ma-ma says - she's a – an angel now,' she explained haltingly to Maria.

'That's a good name, Lucy. Hello Erin,' Bruce said to the wooden pony softly, immediately on Lucy's wavelength. He looked at Maria, whose tears were now falling down her cheeks.

'Lucy's mum Hope is our half-sister', he explained gently. 'We share the same father. He was a complete rat bag, unfaithful to my mother, and probably many times, we think'.

Bruce paused, unsure how much to complete the picture. After a few seconds, he continued,

'Hope's mum died in childbirth. Her name was Erin, Hope was told'. He paused. 'Hope talks to Lucy a lot about her'.

'He Rat bag! Rat bag! Rat bag!' Lucy repeated laughing, enjoying the word. Maria's tears kept coming, and she dabbed them constantly with a tissue, pretending to sneeze in the process, desperate that no-one should see. But they all did. Bruce continued.

'Hence this little pony's name', he said, smiling at Lucy. 'Hope was the result of my father's adulterous relationship with Erin. We're none of us proud of our father, and that's the understatement of the year'.

'But tell Hope the last bit, Bruce. You managed to forgive him, didn't you?' said Oliver.

'In the end, I did in a way, thanks to you, but I haven't forgotten the damage he did. We all had our fair share of that', Bruce replied.

‘So who looked after Hope as a child’, asked Maria, quietly.

‘She was brought up in a children’s orphanage in Ireland’, he paused and thought. ‘‘St. Brigid’s Hospital for Illegitimate Girls’ of all the dreadful names, and then she went into a convent. She came over here trying to track her father – our father –Connie’s, mine, Sadie’s, my brother James’s- he died – and it turned out – Hope’s too. That’s the sum total of what we all know. He turned out to be a pretty awful man, our father. I hated him for a long time’.

‘What was his name then, Bruce – just out of interest?’ Maria asked, mustering up an air of nonchalance as best she could.

‘Albert Connors’.

Maria’s heart seemed to skip several beats. Becoming lightheaded, she put her hand to her forehead. Bruce misread the gesture.

‘I’m sorry,’ he said quickly. I’ve bored you with too much information, but it’s a fascinating story for us, and we’ve only known we had a half-sister for four years’.

Definitely *not* too much information, thought Maria. She had just received the verification she was seeking and had only had to ask a single question.

‘That’s very interesting,’ she said, trying to sound nonchalant. ‘A complicated story, to be sure it is’.

Oliver unobtrusively studied Maria. Why so many quietly shed tears? What had provoked such an emotional reaction? Should he ask her, or was that too intrusive? Perhaps later, he decided, if it felt right. Something had struck a deep chord in her.

Bruce was staring at her directly.

‘I’m sorry. I seem to have touched a nerve. Please forgive me, Maria. It was totally unintentional’.

‘No, no, Bruce. It’s a very interesting story.’

She suddenly wanted to share her story with these two rather special men, but she simply said,

‘I had a child, but she died at birth, and one never quite comes to term with that. I don’t speak about it usually’.

Maria, in fact, had never in forty years shared that fact with anyone ever. Oliver understood now why she was so moved by Lucy’s utter trust in her. ‘Mummy M’ria’, Lucy had called her. He decided there was a story to be unravelled here, but it was not for him to unleash more pain in the otherwise pragmatic Professor Maria Murphy.

Neither man said anything, but Maria sensed their strong empathy.

‘Will it be all-right for me to visit Connie?’ asked Bruce after a silence had elapsed.

‘Lovely’, replied Oliver, ‘but perhaps stick to a few minutes’.

‘Is Hope in St.Thomas’s, too?’ Bruce asked.

‘She is, but I haven’t managed to get up to see her yet. She’s still in intensive care. Next time I go up....’

Maria interjected.

‘I’m thinking it might be good to take Lucy to see her. I think you said Hope was asking for her even when she was barely conscious.

I know she’ll be desperate to see that she’s all-right. What do you think, Oliver?’

‘See Ma-ma, see Ma-ma, see Ma-ma’, chanted Lucy. ‘*Now*, please, Mummy M’ria’.

There it was again. So it wasn’t just a slip of the tongue or a fluke the first time!

‘I’ll phone the hospital and see if a short visit would be suitable’, Maria said.

Suddenly, Lucy’s face clouded over. She took Maria’s cheeks in both her hands and put her face very close to Maria’s.

‘Not horrid man, not horrid man!’ she said intensely, the panic in her voice rising.

'Not the horrid man, Lucy. The horrid man has gone away forever'.

Maria held her close again and found the little girl was trembling. As Maria knew from experience, the effect of the trauma on Lucy would be profound and probably long-lasting.

Maria phoned St. Thomas's hospital and was told that yes, it would be a very good idea for her young daughter to see her mother as Hope had been asking constantly for her.

Maria warned Lucy that Hope would have bruises and maybe plasters but that she was getting better. The taxi dropped them right outside the imposing building. Maria found her heart pounding as she negotiated the maze of corridors and lifts to find Hope's ward. She knew the pounding had less to do with the exertion than with the anxiety, excitement, apprehension – call it what you will – of seeing Hope in the light of the new knowledge freely offered by Bruce about her parentage.

Hope was in a ward of four beds, having been moved after twenty-four hours of intensive care. It seemed that she had been suffering from the deep shock and trauma of the incident as much as from being bound and gagged. She had a wide bandage round her head where Gary had banged her down, as well as bruises and grazes on her legs and knees from trying to drag herself along the floor to reach the door handle. Her intimate parts were also torn from the attempted rape. Apart from these wounds, she was fairly unscathed physically. She'd had a 'lucky escape', as the doctor had pronounced in a somewhat cavalier manner.

Chapter 20

Professor Maria Murphy immediately assumed an air of authority as she entered the ward. It was an unconscious attitude that covered her like a mantle whenever she was in any kind of medical establishment. The effect on others was that nurses went scuttling, and doctors became withering behind her back in an attitude of 'Here's one who thinks she knows it all'. It was nothing of the kind. It was actually the result of years of coping in an environment that was still male-dominated as far as medical hierarchy was concerned. She likened female consultants to female pilots. Female pilots had a reputation for working even more tenaciously, striving even harder, and growing considerably thicker skins than their male counterparts in order to reach similar levels in their careers.

A chirpy young nurse was at the reception desk.

'Can I help you?'

'Yes, please. I've come to see Hope O'Neill. I presume that's O.K?

'Yes, of course. The bed by the window. She'll be glad to see her little one. I presume that's little Lucy? The police have been asking lots of questions. Hope has been asking for her daughter constantly. Got stolen, didn't she? That's what the local news said, anyway'.

Maria Murphy ignored the last comment, finding it too intrusive for comfort. She decided to let Lucy walk into the ward rather than keeping her strapped into her pushchair. Lucy ran ahead of Maria until she found Hope. Hope was lying back on her pillow with her eyes shut.

'Ma-ma, Ma-ma!' Lucy cried, before Maria had a chance to restrain her from clambering onto the bed and smothering Hope with kisses. Hope winced as she opened her eyes but then broke into a broad smile and held Lucy's face between her hands.

'Lucy, my little darling!. Oh, am I *glad* to see you?!'

Maria spoke gently.

'Hope, we thought you'd like that. She's desperate to see you too'.

'Nice Ma-ma, nice Ma-ma. Bad man gone'. Lucy stroked Hope's hand gently.

'Yes, Lucy. Bad man's gone. That's good, isn't it? We must pray for him, mustn't we?'

These Christians! Here was Hope, recovering from rape, bondage, and the theft of her daughter; here was she, damaged and bruised, yet reminding her daughter to pray for Gary! It crossed Maria's mind that by talking to God about Gary, Hope might be doing something not dissimilar to Maria. By probing into Gary's psyche, trying to work out the damage that had been done to him and why he had acted the way he did, trying to understand with a positive attitude, even forgive his actions, all these sprang from a heartfelt desire to support. The motivation for them both, as Maria saw it, was to try to explain rather than judge, support rather than discard, and help to heal rather than meter out punishment. Only the focus was very different.

Hope would probably have agreed with that explanation, but for her, there was another more profound dimension—that of handing over Gary into God's hands. Justice was certainly due for Gary and his vile actions, yes absolutely, but mercy was also required in abundance. In Oliver's eyes, Gary had always been more sinned against than sinning, as King Lear had put it.

Lucy snuggled into Hope. Hope twirled one of Lucy's gold-blonde curls around her finger.

'Hope, how are you feeling?' asked Maria.

'A bit weak and wobbly but nothing that a few days won't put right, thank you'.

'Very, very frightening for you', said Maria.

‘Yes’, said Hope simply, and Maria knew she must not ask anything further.

‘Why you got ban –idge, Ma-ma?’ Lucy asked, stroking Hope’s hair gently.

‘I’ve got a bump on my head, like when you fell off your tricycle. Do you remember, Lucy? But it’s getting better. Don’t worry, your Ma-ma is getting better. I’ll be home soon’.

’Mummy M’ria look after me now?’ said Lucy, smiling shyly at Maria.

‘You’d like that, wouldn’t you, Lucy Grace Erin?’ said Hope, kissing her daughter’s forehead.

Lucy nodded.

‘Till you home, Ma-ma’.

‘Until I’m home’, affirmed Hope.

Hope looked earnestly at Maria.

‘I can’t thank you enough, Professor Maria, for everything you’ve done. The police who came yesterday said you had removed Lucy from the scene to protect her’.

‘She’s a wonderful child’, replied Maria, smiling.

Lucy slid herself down from the bed.

‘Horsey, Mummy M’ria. Horsey. Pretty please?’

Maria opened her shoulder bag. Lucy dipped into it and triumphantly drew out Bruce's carving.

'Look Ma-ma!'

'Oh, isn't he *beautiful!'* exclaimed Hope, examining it. 'That's Uncle Bruce's handiwork, to be sure. What's his name, Lucy?'

'Silly Ma-ma! Not a 'he' He's a *she!* She's called Erin'.

Hope laughed. 'You never forget your grandma, do you, Lucy? It's a lovely name for a lovely horse'.

She turned to Maria and explained.

'Erin was my mother's name. She died giving birth to me'. Hope paused, suddenly thoughtful. 'I have nothing at all to remind me of her. No photo, no memento, nothing. I just know her name was Erin and my father abandoned her. Now *that* has been hard to forgive', said Hope, and lay back on the pillow, suddenly exhausted.

'She will have loved you very much', said Maria almost in a whisper.

There was silence. The room seemed charged with a stillness, as if everything around Maria was holding its breath. 'I came from Ireland to find my father', said Hope, staring at the ceiling.

‘And I came to Southwark to find my daughter’, said Maria in a whisper.

Hope sat upright.

‘You have a *daughter?’*

‘I was told she had died at birth just as you were told your mother died in childbirth’.

Silence.

‘Hope, when I left Ireland after my baby died, I came to Cambridge and immediately changed my name. I wanted to leave everything behind, including my parents, who were unforgiving and merciless. I changed it to Maria Murphy’.

Maria paused and stared intently at Hope.

‘Hope, my name was Erin O’Neill’.

Lucy had fallen asleep on Hope. Hope stared with incredulity at Maria, then rested her head back on the pillow. Tears slowly filled her eyes as Maria stroked her hair.

‘Hope, I think you are my daughter’.

Chapter 21

'Now, there's a picture!' said the chirpy nurse, bustling in. 'Three generations, and like peas in a pod! I don't need to ask if *you're* related. Mother, daughter, granddaughter – all blonde and beautiful! Aren't family genes a wonderful thing? I came to ask if anyone would like a cup of tea?'

Hope shut her eyes, feigning sleep. Maria mouthed, 'No, thank you. Ssh!'

'You mustn't stay for much longer, dear. She's had a very bad time, you know', the nurse said in a stage whisper.

'Fifteen minutes more', replied Maria, and her tone said, 'and don't you dare contradict me'.

'Fifteen minutes it is', she said, scuttling out.

Hope sat bolt upright.

'You must tell me everything you know. I will never sleep again till you do'.

'Rest your head on the pillow, Hope. I'll tell you what I know, but it's not actually very much'.

Maria's voice was soothing and gentle. All that could be heard in the ward was the regular bleeping of the monitor fixed to Hope, and a sound delicate as butterflies' wings of Lucy breathing.

'My parents were stifling and strict and very religious, but not in the way that Oliver, Connie, and you are. Their faith was rigid and joyless. I suppose I was desperate for a bit of freedom, and I kicked over the traces. When I was seventeen, I met this rather dashing sergeant major called Albert Connors. At first, he made me feel special and wanted. I fell in love with him. I think it was as much *need* as anything else. He told me towards the end that he had a wife and baby son in England. For me, the damage was done. When I told him I was pregnant, he became cruel and vicious and very, very angry'.

'My father,' said Hope quietly.

'Yes, Hope. Your father, and Connie's and her brothers and sister's. I don't need to tell you how ashamed I was when I realised he was married. But I doubt it would have made any difference. Extreme need led to extreme selfishness on my part. It's no excuse, but that's how it was'.

'His poor wife', Hope said softly. 'I heard from Sadie that he was cruel to all his children and his wife, and he abused Connie sexually when she was only six'.

Maria gasped.

'A paedophile as well!'.

‘That’s a terrible word’, said Hope, in a slightly reproachful tone, taken aback.

‘But that’s what he was, Hope, if he abused her. There’s no way of dressing it up’.

Hope reached for a tissue from her bedside cabinet to wipe her tears, careful not to rouse Lucy, then she laid her head back on the pillow.

‘I think I should go, Hope. You’re tired. I’ll come tomorrow and tell you the rest’.

Hope sat bolt upright.

‘No, no, Maria. You can’t possibly leave it there. Please. Carry on’.

‘Well, my parents disowned me and booked me in at St.Brigid’s Hostel for Fallen Girls’. A dreadful place’, Maria shuddered at the memory. ‘I went into labour more than a month early and was transferred very quickly to the local hospital, also mainly run by nuns. My baby, a girl, was born and whisked away. The nun told me she had died. Apparently, I had what they called a postpartum haemorrhage and nearly died. The nuns at St. Brigid’s simply eradicated my name from their books. Every time a mother was lost, the Home was under threat of closure. It simply couldn’t afford another death, so I was eliminated, and so were many babies. Eliminated -just like that’, she said, clicking her fingers.

'And the baby?'

'I know now that it was you, Hope'.

Hope lay back again, stunned.

'You see, because you were small and seemingly lifeless moments after your birth, the charitable interpretation is to say that a mistake was made. You were put in what they delicately called the 'Disposal Room', where babies were left when they had died or were about to die. Illegitimate babies were not regarded highly unless they were being sold for adoption. It seemed that no-one bothered to see if you could be resuscitated. God alone knows what happened to the ones that died. There are stories of all sorts about where they were buried. Many were untraceable in unmarked graves. I think it will all come to light one day'. She paused. 'History will be updated, Hope, to reveal the truth'.

'Please carry on', whispered Hope.

'I asked directly after the birth if I could hold my baby, even though I was told she had died. The nun was shocked, but she did give me a tiny blonde curl of my baby's hair', Maria said softly. 'I still have it just as she gave it to me—in a matchbox. I tied a tiny pink ribbon around the curl'. Maria drew out the lint covered box from inside her blouse. She opened it and showed Hope. It was Hope's turn to gasp as she gently picked up the tiny golden curl.

At the same time, Maria fingered Lucy's curls very gently, and her tears began to fall.

'I have mourned for you all these years, Hope. Not a day passes when I haven't thought about you and longed for you'.

'How did you find me?' whispered Hope through tears.

'I was called to see if I could sort Gary Johnson out. He told me that his little daughter was called Lucy Grace Erin O'Neill. It had to be too much of a coincidence – and, in addition, your name being Hope....'

'Yes', murmured Hope. 'Yes, it would be - too much of a coincidence.

A soft silence fell. At last, Maria said,

'And now, look at this little one! It feels like a miracle'.

Hope looked straight into Maria's eyes.

'It *is* a miracle, Maria. This is God's handiwork. He weaves patterns in our lives. It's part of Love's tapestry. I know it,' she said.

'Yes', replied Maria, moved. 'Yes, I believe it is. I came to England with nothing except my intellect, and now I have found a daughter and a granddaughter and am beginning to see that there might be a God.'

‘And I have been given my mother,’ replied Hope, gently weeping.

Maria laid her head next to Hope’s on the pillow, and the two women finally clung to each other, the wetness of their tears mingling and falling on the sleeping child, anointing her in the sanctity of the moment.

Chapter 22

It was a Saturday, so the vicarage children were home and preparing to welcome Connie and the babies. Robbie ran up the vicarage steps carrying a huge bunch of colourful helium balloons.

'Nothing like these for a homecoming!' he said, separating the strings and lining the hall with the vibrant balloons one at a time.

'There! Great, aren't they, Rosy? Think your mum will be pleased?'

'Yes, she'll love them,' answered Rosy, 'and Auntie Hope too, and es*pec*ially Lucy! I'm *so-o-* happy they're coming out of the hospital on the same day. How long will Auntie Hope be staying, Dad?' she asked as Oliver came out of his study with garlands of bunting over his arm.

'Did you make those, Dad?' asked Jamie as he leapt down the bottom four steps of the stairs.

'I did', replied Oliver. A nice relaxing task'.

'Cool. Who's looking after the parish while you're off, Dad?' he asked.

'Well, I'll see to a few things, and the churchwardens will do the rest', Oliver replied.

'Oh no, you *won't,* Dad – not even a *few* things', said Jamie, suddenly angry. You just *can't* let go, can you, especially when it comes to family? You're not God, you know. The parish will survive without you. Are you power-crazy or something?'

Oliver sighed. He knew Jamie was right, but the lad had an uncanny knack of making everything sound like a criticism or a cynicism. He could only pray that Jamie would grow out of it. Cynicism was definitely not an admirable trait in his eldest son's desire to prove he was nearly an adult. As if sensing he had gone too far, however, and had hurt his father in the process, Jamie took one end of the bunting,

'Where do you want it, Dad? I'll do the other end. Down the hall or in the sitting room? It's great. Mum will love it'.

'Thanks, Jamie'. Together, they strung the bunting the full length of the hall.

'And I've done these pictures', said Rosy, showing them her portraits of Connie, Ben, Joseph, Hope, and Lucy and blu-tacking them onto the wall.

'Great, Rosy. They'll all love them.'

'I don't see how Ben and Joseph will love them. They can't even focus their eyes yet', commented Jamie.

Jamie just *had* to spoil it for Rosy, Oliver thought. He said nothing, however. He felt he was always reproaching his eldest son. He reached for his car keys.

'Right, I'm off to get Mum and the babies. Now remember, she's had an operation and needs to rest, so we must do everything to help, musn't we?'

The bell went just as Oliver was about to go out. He opened the front door wide, and a parishioner handed in a vast lasagne with two wrapped loaves of garlic bread perched on top of the cling film, plus a huge bowl of green salad.

'I thought these might come in handy', said the young woman with a warm smile, 'and we've drawn up a rota, Oliver, so that you don't have to cook main meals for a fortnight. That'll give Hope a bit of a chance, won't it? And if it's all-right with you, the Senior Fellowship has made a list of people who will come and collect and deliver your ironing'.

'I just don't know what to say, Sue. It's ---'

Sue, a smiling and kindly gift bearer, put up her hand to stop him.

'Don't say *anything,* Oliver. It's our pleasure, and you – well - you're both very special', she said, welling up. 'We're terribly sorry to hear about Connie. Is she going to be ok?'

'She's getting better', Oliver reassured her. 'Say a huge thank you to everyone. You've no idea what this means to us'. Sue waved as she left the vicarage steps,

'Just shout if you need anything, won't you? We're always here'.

Then she was gone, this unassuming, kind, and extremely practical angel of mercy.

'Blimey, Dad. You must have done something right!' said James. Oliver looked at his son. 'And your Mum', he said simply. His dad looked tired. Jamie suddenly realised what an awful strain this whole saga had been for him. He went up to Oliver and punched him gently in his middle.

'Love you, Dad'.

'Love you, son', Oliver said, giving him a bear hug. Jamie did not resist, but hugged his father tighter.

xxxxx

An hour later, Connie was walking gingerly up the vicarage steps and gasped as she came into the house.

'Oh my goodness! Who did all this? It's all lovely! Beautiful! What a welcome!' she exclaimed.

'A corporate effort', said Jamie, smiling, 'and master-minded by your one and only devoted husband'.

Oliver was coming up the steps with both babies in one carrycot. They were crying loudly.

'Oh, here we go', he thought, bracing himself in readiness for the onslaught of his new family of five children. He turned to Connie.

'Welcome Home, Con. It's wonderful you're back'.

Connie kissed Oliver tenderly and made her way into the kitchen, ignoring the babies crying, and pulled Rosy towards her.

'Rosy, us girls must swim together in the midst of this sea of boys, mustn't we? I love your pictures! We must put the ones of Ben and Joseph over their cots in their bedroom so that when they are older, they can see what they looked like'.

'Auntie Hope is coming very soon, Mummy, so everything will be back to normal, won't it?'

'Please, God', said Oliver under his breath, and meaning it. 'Con, I made up a couple of bottles for when you arrived home. Shall Jamie and I feed the babies?'

'Oliver, you're my superhero! Thank you so, Jamie. I've been telling Ben and Joseph they have two terrific older brothers! By the way, where's Peter?'

No-one had noticed that Peter had not been seen for rather a long time.

'I'm sure he'll be playing table tennis or something over at the club', said Robbie. 'I'll run over and tell him you're home'.

'Thanks, Robbie', said Oliver.

Robbie had been through the laborious court hearing and released on bail for three months, pending further enquiries about his withholding of information over the drowning by Gary of his mother. Gary, still outwardly defiant, was locked up in a prison cell awaiting trial. After Robbie was released he pondered on the facts. Was there no-one who would put in a good word for Gary, as Oliver had for him, or were there, in fact, no good things about him at all? The single advantage of prison for Gary was that he got fed regularly, which was more than he had done for the past few years, and the rehabilitation and counselling programmes might help him, although Robbie had his doubts.

Robbie sprinted over to the club, but Peter was not there; neither was he on the football pitch, nor on the school grounds, nor at an after school activity. Robbie was uneasy. Peter could be teased mercilessly and had made very few friends at school. He was often the butt of nasty bullying. Robbie decided he wouldn't go back to the vicarage until he had tracked Peter down. They seemed to have their hands full enough as it was.

Chapter 23

Kitty Connors, age twenty-three, Bruce and Clara's only child, still lived at home. She had similar chestnut-coloured hair to her mother, although a shade lighter. She was a stunning-looking young woman, slim and naturally elegant, and seemed to wear her beauty lightly and without vanity. Kitty worked in the city for the British branch of *Vogue* and was busy saving as hard as she could to buy a flat. London prices were beginning to rise steeply, and she knew it would be a long haul for her. She loved her parents but could hardly bear to live any longer in an atmosphere where her mother called all the shots and her father spent his life humouring his wife. Clara's coolness also extended to her daughter. Bruce had shared once with Kitty in a moment of closeness that he thought Clara might be a little threatened by Kitty's popularity and a wide circle of female friends. Clara herself had few quality relationships with women. Men, however, were a different matter. She knew exactly how to seduce them with a sentence or a look. They provided a natural playground for her to exercise her sexual skills, and this made women keep her at arm's length and regard her as a threatening predator of their men.

Clara had fallen in love with Oliver almost at first sight when she was a student, and he was a theatre chaplain. Neither had ever forgotten their one-off passionate sexual encounter. Clara's husband, Bruce, was impotent at the time, so Clara assumed that the baby she had conceived unintentionally was Oliver's. It was a fair assumption. A pact was later made between Oliver and Bruce that, as long as Oliver stayed completely out of Kitty's life, Bruce would bring her up as his own. Bruce loved Kitty generously from the moment she was born, and, true to the arrangement, Oliver kept out of the family's way. He grieved silently for his daughter.

Kitty developed Leukaemia at the age of three, and matching bone marrow was urgently sought to save her life. Oliver offered to have a test to save Kitty, even though it meant exposure to his fatherhood, so Bruce submitted himself to the test for the sake of appearances. The secret had been sacred between the three of them for almost three years, and all concerned wanted to keep it that way. It was discovered, however, much against the odds, that Bruce was Kitty's bloodline father. In his case, impotence had not precluded the chance of fertility, especially given the fact that Bruce had many attempts at a fulfilment that were aborted just before the point of climax, much to his chagrin. Although statistically rare, Bruce was proven through the bone marrow test to be Kitty's natural father. His own bone marrow, therefore, subsequently saved his daughter, much to his unspeakable joy.

In her heart, Clara held secret feelings of disappointment. So besotted with Oliver was she that she had always secretly wanted Kitty to be his, despite the inevitable fallout. From the moment of receiving the knowledge regarding the bone marrow test results she had never shared this feeling with anyone, and least of all with Bruce. The effect of Clara's secret, however, was that once Kitty had recovered and become fit again, Clara began to resent her. The more attractive and charismatic Kitty became (aspects inherited from Clara herself), and the more she displayed Bruce's nature, which was one generally of gentleness and patience, the more Clara tended to make life difficult for Kitty, not obviously, but with a repertoire of subtle and oblique put-downs and a general lack of endorsement of everything her daughter did, and especially her academic achievements at school.

Clara began to drink heavily to dampen her rogue feelings. She and Bruce shared a bottle of red wine every night, Bruce having one glass and Clara the rest. She also frequently had a couple of whiskies as an aperitif. Bruce was watchful over her drinking but knew it was more than his life was worth to comment on it more than once or twice. Clara's tongue could be very sharp.

Professor Maria Murphy would have had a field day attempting to peel off the layers of Clara's psyche and the resulting behaviour, but she would have found there as many layers to deal with as there are on a tightly compacted onion. Once one layer had been peeled off, another two or three would reveal themselves, all equally as challenging to deal with as the last, with many tears shed in the process.

One of Kitty's favourite occupations on a Saturday was to browse round Borough Road Mark in Southwark, which was a short underground train journey away from the Connors' home in Richmond-upon-Thames. She usually went during the afternoon and lingered until many goods were cut down in price. The market was closed on a Sunday, so all perishable items were reduced to ridiculously cheap prices.

Arriving at the market, she went straight to the fabric counter. It always had a wonderful display of every colour and type of material possible. Kitty loved transforming her choice of material into swirling skirts or flowing dresses. She was an excellent needlewoman. Clara always maintained this talent came from Bruce, the violin maker, repairer and craftsman of wood.

'It certainly doesn't come from *me',* Clara told Connie once. 'I can't even thread the needle in the first place, and I find it all so *boring'.*

Connie, her sister-in-law, was an excellent seamstress, and she knew Clara's oblique remarks to her constituted put-downs but chose simply to reply,

'But you've got so many other huge talents, haven't you, Clara?'

She constantly hoped that by affirming Clara, Clara would eventually become softer and milder, especially towards her brother Bruce. But she did not.

Peter Connors had decided he would buy his mum some flowers as a homecoming welcome. This was uncharacteristic of him, but if truth be told, he had missed his mum a lot and been worried about her. Being autistic, he had not been able to express these feelings satisfactorily in words. When he heard that Connie was due home that very afternoon, he raided his carefully organised tin of pocket money, taking out ten shiny pound coins, which he always carefully collected from the bank in exchange for a ten pound note. The bank knew Peter. As he was always very polite and as he was the popular vicar's son, nobody minded but smiled indulgently as they exchanged the coins for a note.

He arrived at Borough Road Market, found a flower stall, and there the challenge began. So many flowers! So many bunches! So many different prices! Peter found decision-making difficult; that was why it seemed such a miracle that he was able to take such decisive action when Hope was trapped behind her front door by Gary and why James had been so incredulous. Peter seemed to take on an entirely new persona during that episode.

But the flowers were another matter altogether. There were so many ifs and buts. For someone who was not thought to be blessed with the skill of lateral thinking, he did surprisingly well at it. If he bought the pink carnations, then everyone would think he had wanted the babies to be girls. If he bought the red roses for his mother, everyone would think he had an Oedipus Complex. White flowers against their sitting room's white walls would get lost, and yellow was too much like the colour of the babies' mustard poos. He knew Rosy would notice that and laugh at them. What to choose? He had no idea.

His cousin Kitty saw Peter at the stall and watched him for a few seconds. She was extremely fond of him and immediately wanted to help, but no, he must choose these flowers himself, she decided. She knew it would challenge him. Just then, Peter turned and saw her. She noticed he was very red in the face, and his eyes were brimming with tears of frustration.

'Oh, Kit, please could you come and help me? I don't know what to choose'. He looked beseechingly at her. Immediately, Kitty was by his side.

‘I think mixed colours would be nice and bright, Pete’, she said. ‘How about these?’

She had picked out a large bunch of tall colourful gladioli, marked 50% off for a quick sale.

‘Thanks, Kit. Will mum like these?’

‘She’ll love them’, Kitty replied. ‘Don’t hesitate, Peter, or they’ll sell them to someone else’.

Peter handed his money over, counting it out pedantically on the counter. ‘There we are’ he said, ‘£3.50 pence. Not a penny more, not a penny less’.

‘They’re a bargain, Pete. Auntie Con will love them’.

Mission accomplished. Peter was about to turn and set off home when he saw the infamous gang to which Gary had belonged, each of whom had served two years in jail for the group rape of Sister Hope three years ago. Gary had been the instigator of the rape, and this fact was taken into consideration and reflected in the comparatively lenient sentence of the other gang members. Many had thought that misjudged.

‘What’ya up to, Pete boy? Fancy seeing *you*, boyho! And the famous Miss Kitty, Gary’s bit on the side!’.

Kitty should have denied this vehemently but felt paralysed to the spot. She had seen the bullying tactics of the gang three years ago and knew they would beat her to the ground and who knows what else if she tried to get to her feet.

'Oh, look at this! Flowers for your Mummy, Peter? Or for your girlfriend? Or your *boy*friend!'

One of the gang wrenched the flowers out of Peter's hand, and each member picked a stem out of the bunch, hurled it on the ground, and stamped on it, leaving the coloured flower petals scattered and bruised like trampled and long redundant pieces of giant confetti after a wedding.

Peter hurled himself at one of the gang.

'Don't you *dare* do that. Kitty chose them'.

'Kitty, Kitty, Kitty', mocked one of the gang in a high pitched voice as he dealt Peter a hefty blow on his face. Another member kicked him hard in the crotch, making Peter yelp loudly. His nose started to bleed heavily, and he bent double in agony from the assault on his genitals.

'We'll teach you, you little snitch'.

'Take that, you fucking grass', said another, winding him with a blow to his abdomen.

xxxxx

Meanwhile, Robbie, increasingly anxious, had been looking for Peter. His disappearance from the family was uncharacteristic. Robbie had searched all the most likely places, and his final thought was that Peter might be in Borough Road Market, where teenagers tended to congregate. Peter was not a mainstream teenager, Robbie knew, so it seemed unlikely he would be there, but Robbie was intent on leaving no stone unturned. Connie would be seriously fretting by now, and the family did not need any more worries.

As he approached, he saw Peter being buffeted by blows from several fists and Kitty cowering on the ground looking up in fearful despair. Robbie was a quick reactor and not always a wise one. He approached Mickey, the self-appointed leader of the gang now Gary had gone, and with all his force, hauled Mickey off Peter and dealt a hefty blow to his chin. Quick as a flash, with face bleeding, Mickey whipped out a switchblade, pressing the blade out of the handle in one movement as he held it up to Robbie's chin.

'I know you. You're big trouble you are. You grassed on Gary, didn't ya?' he said, touching Robbie's neck menacingly with the point of the switchblade.

'Put that down', Robbie commanded, his voice strangulating with fear. 'The police are going to lock you up for life else'.

'Let them', Mickey said viciously through gritted teeth. 'Since when did I care about them a lot? They're just a load of rubbish'. He pushed the point of the switchblade deeper into Robbie's neck and drew blood from it. Quick as a flash, Peter was on his feet and leapt on Mickey. Mickey swished round and was about to stab Peter when Kitty was up. Finding her courage, she threw herself between Peter and Mickey in a huge effort to defend her cousin and Robbie, whom she had adored since babyhood. Mickey stabbed her hard in her stomach. Kitty reeled, held her wound, which had begun to pump blood through her clothes, then staggered and finally sank to the ground.

'Run!' yelled Mickey to the group. 'Run before the fuckin' Filth comes!'

They all scattered, cowards, every one of them. Robbie yelled to Peter,

'Cover her with your jacket, Pete, and call the police'.

Robbie ran as fast as he could after the gang. Even catching one of them would be a triumph, all that was probably necessary to do the whole lot. But they were scared, adrenalin-fuelled and swift and outran Robbie, even though he himself was fit and fast. In the end Robbie gave in, knowing to catch up with them was a forlorn hope. He ran back to the scene. A crowd had gathered, and on Peter's instruction one of them had phoned the police. From the waist down, Kitty's clothes were now soaked in blood, dark, sinister, and ominous as it seeped its way relentlessly through her underwear and dark jeans. Her face was porcelain white, framed by the burnished brown of her hair, which was splayed out, curiously creating at that moment an image of a tragic pre-Raphaelite Beauty. Peter was kneeling beside her.

'Right, Robbie. Do as I say', Peter instructed when Robbie arrived back, breathless. 'Run back to the vicarage and tell Mum and Dad'. Ask them to phone Kitty's dad and then you come back. Don't let Mum come. Tell her I'm O.K. Bring a blanket with you.'

Here was Peter, taking charge just as he had during the crisis with Hope. Kitty was fast running out of life.

'Kitty. Kitty, babe. We're getting help. Stay with us', said Robbie, kissing her forehead.

'Hang on, Kit. You *must* hang on. Robbie's getting help', said Peter with quiet authority.

An ambulance arrived, quickly followed by a policeman on a motorbike, the first responder. Two other police cars arrived within a few minutes. The paramedics were on the ground, examining Kitty and working on her. One of them looked briefly up to Peter.

'She your girlfriend? We'll do our level best, but I'm afraid you must be prepared that she might not make it, son'.

'She is *not* my girlfriend, I am *not* your son, she *must* make it, and that is *not* a good thing to say in front of her. She may be wounded, but she is *not* deaf', Peter said witheringly.

The paramedic, somewhat taken aback, proceeded to perform chest compressions and mouth-to-mouth resuscitation. The crowd was silent. Such a beautiful girl - the vicar's niece - such a major tragedy right on their doorstep.

After what seemed an eternity, the paramedic shouted,

'Right, we've got an output. Put a line in'.

This done, they lifted Kitty onto a stretcher and very carefully put her into the ambulance. Just at that moment, Oliver came racing down the hill with Robbie.

'Can I go in with her?' he asked one of the paramedics, his foot already on the ambulance ramp.

'Are you next of kin, sir?'

'I'm her uncle. Her father will go straight to the hospital'.

‘Leave us to do our job, if you would, sir. It’s better that way’.

‘Is she going to be OK?’ He asked the eternal question in the face of a deep medical crisis.

The paramedic shrugged and looked serious.

‘You’re the local vicar, aren’t you? Better get your prayer mat out, Father. She’s in a pretty bad way’.

In that second, a myriad of images collided in Oliver’s mind. This was the third time Kitty had been in mortal danger. First, the leukaemia, then her near-drowning during the river cruise boat tragedy, and now this. Had he not been a man of God, he would have thought in a panic that surely her luck was about to run out now, her number up. Third time *un*lucky. Oliver had always had a special bond with Kitty. He spent the first three years of her life presuming she was his flesh and blood, and during that time mourned for the loss of her in his life and grieved deeply over the situation. The feeling that he was inextricably linked to her had never left him.

‘Pete, let’s get you back home, son. It’s been a terrible shock for you’.

‘He’s been magnificent’, said Robbie quietly, ‘So brave, so strong, so in control’.

Oliver put his arm round his son.

'I'm very, very proud of you', he whispered in his ear. Peter smiled up at him, but then his face clouded over.

'I was buying some flowers for mum. Kitty came up and helped me choose. It's Kitty that's brave, Dad, not me. That vicious prick was about to stab me, and Kitty leapt in between us'. He paused. 'Dad, that knife was meant for me'.

'Oh dear God,' said Oliver. 'Thank God you're safe, but poor, poor Kitty –

'They've *both* been brave as lions', said Robbie.

'And you are too, Robbie'.

'He is', replied Peter. 'He had the blade of a knife pointing at his throat'.

'Come on. Home to Mum, Peter, and you too, Robbie.'

'Not so fast, sir', said the police officer. 'We'll need to talk to them, please. They are involved in a crime and are key witnesses'.

'You'll have to follow us to the vicarage, officer. I have to see my mother and reassure her', said Peter, assuming an air of authority once more. Oliver caught Robbie's eye. This was a Peter neither was familiar with, and they were both equally amazed at the transformation.

‘We’ll follow you up, son’, replied the police officer.

Oliver knew the misplaced use of the word ‘son’ would provoke Peter, so he quietly said,

‘Come on, Pete. We have bigger issues to deal with. He means it in a friendly way’.

‘*Really?’* said Peter. ‘Frankly, I call it patronizing’.

Again, Oliver and Robbie exchanged a faint smile, and they all trudged up the hill together, each one shocked to the core by the event.

Chapter 24

When Connie rang Bruce and Clara's phone, there was no answer the first time. 'Leave a message if it's urgent', Clara's voice said crisply on the recording. Connie was flummoxed. How could she leave a message saying that Kitty had been stabbed and was hanging on to life by a whisker? She decided to try again, hoping that perhaps Bruce was in his workshop at the top of the house, with Clara out shopping or rehearsing maybe. The phone rang and rang. At last, just as Connie was about to give up, Bruce's puffed and slightly irritated voice came on the phone.

'Hello. What can I do for you?'

'Bruce. It's Con. Bruce, I'm afraid I have some rather bad news for you'.

Bruce sat down on the stool by the phone, holding his breath. He was conditioned to believe that bad news always involved Kitty. This was the legacy of her leukaemia and near-drowning traumas. Clara said he was neurotic about it all and had a morbid imagination. This time, however, his 'morbid imagination', as she called it, was more than justified. Sadly, it was prophetic.

'Oh, Brucey. It's Kitty. You must get to Charing Cross Hospital quickly. Kitty's - Kitty's been – she's been stabbed'.

Bruce felt he was going to pass out. He clung to the arm of the sofa.

'Bruce. Is Clara there?' she asked, knowing how Bruce would be.

'She's out', replied Bruce faintly, then realising the need for action, he said,

'I'll get up there now, Con. Where did she get stabbed?'

'Borough Road Market'.

'No, no, I mean, where in her body, Con?

'I think it was her stomach. High up'.

Bruce felt himself going again. Perilously near her heart and lungs then.

'Thanks, Connie, thanks. I'll go this minute.'

He put the receiver down and reached for his coat and car keys. He was about to race to the car when Clara came up the path, joyfully waving a contract.

'I got it! I got it, Brucie! The lead in 'Me and My Girl'! It opens in Chichester. Rehearsals start tomorrow. I'll have to......'

She stopped. Bruce had both his hands up to stop her talking and was looking pale and haunted.

'Bruce, whatever's the matter?'

'It's Kitty. She's in hospital. She's been stabbed.'

Bruce was never to forget the words that followed.

'Oh no! What perfect timing! Just as I have landed this....'

'Clara', Bruce shouted. '*Listen!* She may die'.

'*What?* Who told you that?'

'Connie'.

'Well, she's always a bit of a tragedy queen, isn't she?'

Bruce took Clara by the shoulders and shook her.

'Our *daughter,* Clara! Our daughter has been stabbed in the stomach'.

Clara was finally diverted from her obsessive self-interest.

'Where is she? Which hospital?'

'Charing Cross. I'm going now'.

'I'm coming', said Clara. Just let me put this inside. I'll read it later. It *is* exciting, though, isn't it?'

Bruce felt sickened by his wife. Was she really so shallow, or had the news simply failed to sink in? He decided it must be the latter.

'I'm going. Either come now or follow in your car'.

'I'll have a quick cup of coffee first. Haven't had one all day. I'll follow you in five minutes, Brucie'.

In a flash, Bruce was driving far too fast down the bus lanes of central London towards the hospital, his heart full of fear and dread for his daughter, thinking, as others were, that this might be the third time *un*lucky for her.

xxxxx

Back at the Vicarage, Connie was in tears. Her dear brother, her only brother now, was in deep, deepest distress. Every tragedy involving either Sadie, her sister, or Bruce, her brother, reminded her of the fateful day when she had run up the stairs, age six, following her father and Bruce, to find James hanging and her mother and brother's hearts breaking in two. Connie had not been allowed at the funeral, being thought too young to cope with such a harrowing event. In truth, however, she had always felt in some strange way that her exclusion meant she was somehow to blame for the death. Irrational, she knew now, but she had carried that feeling throughout her life, the legacy of wounds inflicted on a young and vulnerable mind.

She sat now in a stupor. Was she exaggerating things, or had the family had more than its fair share of tragedy? Her mother had died of a brain haemorrhage following a clumsy push against a wall by her oaf of a husband, Sadie's precious bright and physically disabled boy had been killed outside their door by a lorry mounting the pavement, and now Bruce's daughter's life was hanging in the balance.

The babies were quiet, and Rosy was watching television in the sitting room. Connie went to the bedroom and pulled out her rosary beads. She hardly used them now. They belonged to a part of her life of yesteryear when she was a devout Roman Catholic instead of a devout Anglican. She needed them now. She knelt by the bed with her rosary beads and prayed fervently and beseechingly for Kitty, Bruce, and Clara. It was all she could do. She believed in the power of prayer, but somehow it didn't feel enough now.

Connie's prayers were brought to a swift conclusion by the arrival of Peter, Oliver, and Robbie. She saw immediately that Peter's face was bloodied, that his shirt was torn, and over his arm, his jacket was soaked in blood. Oliver looked pale and strained, and Robbie was exhausted and dishevelled. She moved as quickly as her post-operative wounds would allow to Peter, took the jacket from him, and flung her arms round her son. Peter did not resist as he sometimes did but put his arms round her and stayed there. Finally, he said,

'I tried to get you flowers, Mum. Kitty helped me, but they came to a bad end'.

She kissed him, then turned to Oliver, held his face in her hands, and said,

'Darling, you poor darling', and gathered him into her.

'Not me, Connie. Kitty', said Oliver. His face crumpled as he tried hard not to weep

'And you too, Robbie. What a terrible shock for you'.

'No sympathy needed for me either, Connie', said Robbie. 'It's Kitty who needs it. She looked as though she was bleeding out.' He covered his face with his hands. Finally, he said,

'I'll fill you in, Connie, in a minute. Your son has been amazing'.

Connie looked at Peter.

'That doesn't surprise me at all', she said. 'Now let's get you all a cup of tea, and I think something sweet would be the order of the day', she said, relieved that she had a practical task on which to concentrate.

'Bruce has gone up to the hospital, and I think Clara too'. She walked slowly towards the kitchen, only too aware of the wound from her hysterectomy, the dragging of her episiotomy scar from her recent childbirth, and the heaviness of her legs in post-operative fatigue. Oliver noticed.

'Sit down, Con. I'll do it. You look absolutely worn out. What a dreadful homecoming for you'.

'I'll be all-right, Oli. For me, it's nothing that a few days won't put right. For Kitty – well, that's another story'.

'It's a desperate situation, Con', Oliver said, 'We must all pray very, very hard'.

'Kitty may die anyway, whether you pray or not', said Peter matter of factly.

'I know,' replied Oliver quietly. This was *the* dilemma and, in the eyes of some, the absolute folly of faith.

The police entered and took copious notes from Peter and Robbie, going over several points again and again. Oliver and Connie could see that Peter was growing impatient with their repeated questions and dreaded that he would succumb to his instinct of making cutting remarks. He behaved impeccably, however, occasionally restrained by a look from Robbie, and only at the end said,

'Now, do you think you have got that, Officer, or would you like me to repeat it a fourth time?'

'That's it, son. Well done, all of you', said the Officer, wisely ignoring Peter's sarcasm. 'Particularly you, son', he said, turning to Peter, 'Your mum and dad should be proud of you'.

After he had left, Peter sat down and suddenly burst into floods of tears. No-one said a word, but they all quietly drew round him and put their arms round each other's shoulders in a tight circle of love.

xxxxx

Hope arrived at the vicarage with Lucy and her newly discovered mother, Maria Murphy. Maria had already decided that she would leave the family alone for a while. She had a key to Hope's house and, with Hope's agreement, left her with Lucy at the vicarage door and drove down the hill to buy food for when Hope and Lucy went home. It was very clear that Hope was in no fit state to support Connie at the Vicarage, and Maria decided she would take compassionate leave for another two weeks. For the first time in her adult life, she was sure where her priorities lay, as her heart sang a new tune: grab and delight in oceans of time with your newly discovered daughter and granddaughter and leave the paid work to someone else.

Chapter 25

Clara Connors put the kettle on, kicked her shoes off, and picked up the script of 'Me and My Girl' which she had been given at the audition. She decided she would leave Bruce to see the Medics about Kitty and bear the brunt of the first fifteen minutes or so of the visit. She was concerned about Kitty, of course, but knew that Bruce, like his sister, was a prophet of doom as far as medical matters were concerned and had a tendency to blow things out of proportion. She supposed it was because of the things that had happened to them as children. Clara herself knew that she loved Kitty, but motherhood, she also recognised, had never really been for her, which is why she refused to countenance the possibility of having another child, even though Bruce had been persuasive.

A few years back, when Kitty was eight, Clara had found herself pregnant again. She knew without a doubt this time that the baby was Bruce's and was sick, not so much from the early weeks of pregnancy as from the thought of another baby putting her career on hold. She didn't tell Bruce about the pregnancy. At nine weeks, she paid for a private abortion, informing him that she had to go away for a few days for residential auditions. She booked herself into a five-star hotel for three days to recover and then returned home, seemingly without a care in the world, and concocting some story or other about how the auditions were delayed.

She made herself a coffee now, reached for the biscuits, and then curled up on the sofa to read the opening scene of the musical. She became so absorbed that it was forty minutes before she realised the time. Hurriedly reaching for her car keys and packing the script in her leather drawstring bag, she drove as fast as the build-up of traffic would allow, to the hospital.

Bruce had heard the devastating news that the surgeon was in the process this very minute of removing Kitty's right lung, which the switchblade had perforated. What had appeared to be abdominal bleeding was, in fact, coming from a pneumothorax wound, the knife missing the abdomen completely. If it had penetrated the abdominal aorta, Kitty would have bled out within minutes. At least by removing the damaged lung she stood a better chance of survival. However, as the consultant went on to explain, the ongoing risk was that the remaining lung would collapse in shock. It can happen, he had said, adding that if Kitty survived all this, however, her life would be pretty much unaffected in the long run by having only one lung. The remaining lung would, in time, fill the chest cavity and do the work of two.

Kitty was still in the operating theatre when Clara finally arrived.

‘Oh, so sorry, Bruce. I got carried away with the script. What’s happening?’

Bruce explained everything to Clara.

‘Oh no! That’s terrible. Poor Kitty. How exactly did it happen?’

Bruce had gleaned more information from Oliver during a further brief phone call to the vicarage.

‘It was one of Gary Johnson’s gang – Mickey, I think his name was. Kitty was defending Peter’.

‘That wimp of a nephew of yours needs to learn to protect himself! Kitty’s always been ridiculously protective of him’, said Clara scathingly to Bruce. ‘And so has Connie. That’s why he’s got no backbone’.

Bruce did not answer, but inside, he was increasingly shocked by the hardness in his wife, and her seemingly callous attitude was taking its toll on him emotionally. Breaking into his dark thoughts, Clara announced she was going to find the hospital cafeteria as she hadn’t eaten all day.

‘Do you want me to bring you anything, Bruce?’

Bruce wasn’t sure how Clara could eat in a crisis like this but concluded that everyone must react in different ways to bad news.

'Come back soon, Clara. The surgeon will want to talk to us, I'm sure'.

Clara had been gone about ten minutes when, sure enough, the surgeon came out of the operating theatre and headed for Bruce.

'I think we've done a pretty good job, Mr. Connors. Your daughter should be fine, but the next twenty-four hours are critical. She's in the recovery room now, but when she's safely round from the anaesthetic, I'll call you. She's got a chest drain in to combat any pleural effusions. They can be rather uncomfortable'. He paused. 'Are you on your own?'

'No. My wife is having a sandwich in the cafe'.

'I see', said the surgeon, in a way that suggested he glimpsed the kind of situation this might be.

'It will have to be one at a time, just for five minutes each,' explained the surgeon.

Bruce felt a huge relief that Kitty was through the operation safely. It was now a case of hoping fervently for the best. He had asked Oliver and Connie to pray for his daughter, assuming their prayers would reach God more effectively than his, which were only activated in dire emergencies. Clara returned, carrying a takeaway mug of tea.

'Here you are, Brucie. Thought you might like this'. She handed it to him.

'That's nice. Thank you Clara'.

'Actually, I didn't like the milk in it', she said. 'It's plastic stuff. Got myself a hot chocolate instead. Any news?'

Bruce filled her in with the surgeon's report.

'Oh, Bruce. Poor Kitty. Can I go in first?'

Bruce was pleased to see that, at last, it seemed Clara had some feelings flowing through her about the severity of the situation. Then, however, she ruined it by saying,

'Then if she's pulling through, O.K. I'll go back home and learn a bit of the script while the house is quiet. O.K. Brucie?' She paused. Bruce said nothing. 'In fact, maybe it's better if I come back later and see her. I'm not very good in a hospital situation'.

Bruce did not reply. He was in turmoil. His wife's hardness hit him as if he had been struck by a slab of concrete. Finally, he said softly, restraining his feelings,

'Clara, you do realise the next twenty four hours are critical for Kitty, don't you?'

'You'll be here, won't you, though, Bruce? You can phone me if anything goes wrong and I'll be up in a trice. You know I can put my foot down when I need to, and it's not far'. She paused. 'You don't need me here, do you, Brucie?' she said, stroking his cheek. 'You're much better in these situations than I am. You'll be O.K., won't you?'

Bruce wanted to say that he would love nothing more than to have the company of his wife at this critical time, to share the pain if nothing else, but not if she was in this kind of mood, with one foot out of the door already. It was as if gaining the lead in the musical was all that mattered in the world to her.

'You go now, Clara, as long as you know Kitty is not out of the woods yet. Nowhere near'.

'She's a tough cookie, Bruce. She'll be ok. There's nothing really I can do here. You know I've waited a very long time for this part, and I simply *have* to do it. It's not an option to turn it down. I'll see her when she's a bit more compos mentis. Make sure you give her my love'.

Not an option for who? The company? The director? Or – Clara? Bruce was defeated by his wife's apparent lack of feelings for her daughter. She drew the car keys out of her bag and jingled them in front of his nose.

'Remember, Brucie, I can come in a jiffy if you need me', she said, almost coquettishly. She kissed him on the cheek, went to the revolving door and turned and blew another kiss to him. Bruce felt sick. He knew Clara was tough; he knew she was ambitious;

he knew she almost always got her own way in situations; he also knew that motherhood did not come naturally to her. Her attitude now, however, took things to a new level for him both in terms of incredulity and inner loneliness.

Bruce saw Kitty before an hour passed, entering the high dependency unit with butterflies in his stomach and having run to the loo several times with the usual bowel reaction in times of stress. He was awe-struck and terrified in equal measure by the uncanny quietness of the unit, broken only by the generally rhythmic bleeping of the monitors keeping watch over their patients. Kitty was very sleepy, linked up to what seemed like numerous drips and tubes, and still full of the after effects of her anaesthetic. She raised a hand weakly off the bed to Bruce.

'Sorry for the fuss, Dad', she slurred. 'Sorry. Where's Mum?'

'She'll be here very soon', replied Bruce.

Kitty nodded and said sleepily, 'Love you Dad'.

'Love you Kitty - so, so much'.

It was clear that Kitty was drifting off again, so Oliver simply said,

'I'll be nearby if you need me, and Mum too'.

Whether her mother would be or not remained to be seen, but all that mattered to Bruce at this stage was that Kitty must be peaceful. He was quietly reassured by his brief conversation with his daughter and phoned Connie and Oliver to tell them the news.

Bruce stayed at the hospital all night, curled up on an uncomfortable two-seater sofa near the high-dependency unit. He visited Kitty twice more before midnight, and on one occasion, she acknowledged him. On the other, she was asleep. Her breathing was steady, and her vital signs were good, although she frequently clawed at the chest tube drain.

By dawn, Bruce was feeling Kitty must have taken a step towards safety as he had not been called during the night - something which he had dreaded. He actually slept a little before the army of cleaners, scrupulous with their mops, moved around the area like a highly disciplined colony of ants. One of the cleaners, middle-aged and kindly-looking, moved towards his seat.

'My goodness, love, you been there all night? Someone you know is in there; I shouldn't wonder'.

'Yes, my daughter'

'Oh, my giddy aunt! What a strain for you! Must be in agony. They're very good in here, you know', she added reassuringly.

'Yes, I can see that', Bruce replied, running his hands through his hair to smooth it and deflect from the fact that his eyes were filling up with the sudden sympathy.

'Oh, you poor dear. You had anything to eat?'

'No, but I'll get a sandwich soon'.

'Oh, let me get it for you, my duck'. What do you like?'

Bruce agreed gratefully to her help and fished a five-pound note out of his wallet.

'No, no. I'm not taking that. It'd be a shame if I couldn't buy a man a sandwich in his hour of need, wouldn't it?'

Bruce felt like weeping. There seemed to be more genuine compassion and concern in this humble lady than he had seen at all in his wife. The lady soon returned with two packs of sandwiches.

'There we are', she said, putting them on the seat beside him.

'There's an egg and bacon one and a cheese and onion. You may not feel like them now, but just wait until you have good news. You'll feel hungry as a hunter then!'

Bruce thanked her profusely. She moved on. Bruce thought again about a quotation that Oliver had used years ago.

'When angels visit us, we do not hear the rustle of wings, nor feel the feathery touch of the breast of a dove, but we know their presence by the love they create in our hearts'.

Oliver decided he would see Kitty one more time before he ate a sandwich. He entered the high-dependency unit and was met by the ward sister. She was smiling.

'Mr. Connors. If Kitty continues to make this progress, we can move her to a side ward out of the high-dependency unit after forty-eight hours. I thought you'd like to know'.

Bruce could have kissed her.

'Thank you so, so much. That is wonderful. Can I see her?'

'Of course. We'll keep to the five-minute visit for now, though. She's had a major operation'.

The effect of the anaesthetic was wearing off his daughter. She put her hand out.

'Dad. What's the time?' she asked, her speech still a little slurred.

'It's twenty to six in the morning, Kit'.

'Have you been here all night, Dad?'

'Well, yes. I just wanted to know you were out of the woods'.

'They said I was doing well. Dad, I don't know what they have done, but they won't take this tube out, and it's agony,' said Kitty, pulling again at the chest tube drain. Bruce hesitated. If the nurse or surgeon had not told her about the pneumonectomy, then should he?

'Just a minute, Kitty'.

He went quietly up to the nurse and told her the conversation.

'If you want to tell her in simple terms, Mr. Connors, then do, but I'll come with you to see she's all-right and to answer her questions. We didn't tell her before because she was too weak to take the news'.

Kitty seemed to accept the information quite well. She wept a little, asked for a tissue, and mopped up the tears. Bruce waited, holding her hand.

'I guess I'm lucky to be alive', she murmured eventually. Her next questions were more difficult for Bruce to answer.

'Dad, where's Mum? Didn't she stay with you?'

'She's coming very soon, Kit, I promise'.

Kitty's eyes filled with tears, but she said nothing. She knew her mother only too well. A few more seconds elapsed, then,

'How's Pete?'

'I don't know, darling. I'll find out very soon. I'll give Auntie Connie a ring'.

'He was so brave, Dad'.

'Tell your mum that when she comes, Kit' he replied. 'You're going to be fine, my love. They are getting you into a chair tomorrow if you carry on progressing like this. That's really good news, isn't it?'

Kitty nodded weakly. Bruce kissed her lightly and left. His five minutes (and more) were up. He went back to his seat, but still, he could not eat the sandwich. His lack of hunger now was not primarily due to Kitty but to his wife's indifference. Bruce knew in that moment that any excuses he had made for his wife in the past, as was his norm, would now be misplaced. There were no adequate excuses regarding her lack of visits to her daughter and, worse, her apparent absence of any real concern in such a life-threatening situation.

A radical thought took root in his mind. 'I can no longer share my life with a woman who cares so little about everything and everybody else and who has failed her only daughter in her hour of need'. It was as if the scales had finally fallen from Bruce's eyes, and he was seeing for the first time the actual nature of his wife.

The nurse approached him again.

'Mr. Connors...' she said

'Bruce, please,' he said simply.

'Bruce, the police want to talk to your daughter about what happened. I've told them not yet, but they would like to come later in the day. Would you be able to stay? She might be traumatised talking about it'.

'Of course', replied Bruce. I'm not going anywhere until the critical forty-eight hours are up'.

'Kitty's mother?' asked the nurse hesitantly, sensing by now that there might be a problem. 'Could she take over and give you a break?'

'I'll give her a ring and ask her', said Bruce. 'She'll come'. ('Please God', he muttered under his breath). 'She's very tied up with rehearsals at the moment'. It sounded so hollow, so trivial, but Bruce knew Clara's part in this production meant the world to her. He had always encouraged her to pursue her dream, hadn't he? But now?

Bruce could not get hold of her on the phone. He was tired, dishevelled, and badly in need of some clean clothes, or at the very least a shower, and quite frankly, some fresh air. Right on cue, the nurse returned.

'Bruce, I've arranged for you to have a shower in the staff quarters if you'd like'. She laughed, embarrassed. 'I'm not implying anything, but I thought it might be nice for you'.

'Wonderful!' said Bruce, smiling.

'And when you come back, I'll go to the canteen and bring you some breakfast. Full English and a cup of tea?'

Bruce could have hugged her. This was the compassion of the NHS revealed in all aspects in glorious technicolour. He wasn't used to such tenderness. He decided to wait for his shower until he had reached Clara on the phone. At four o'clock in the afternoon, he finally managed to access her.

'Clara, where are you? Kitty is asking for you'.

Clara hesitated.

'Brucie, I'm in Chichester. Once you said she was coming out of intensive care, I knew she would be all-right, and -' Clara used her most well-rehearsed persuasive strategy, '- She's got *you*, Brucie. Who could ask for anyone better? It is so important for me to be here. It's a read-through of the play with....'

'Clara' – Bruce interrupted. 'I know it's important, but Kitty needs you. The police are coming to talk to her this afternoon'.

'You can manage that', replied Clara. 'Give her *all* my love and tell her I will be up first thing tomorrow morning. I'm driving back late tonight, so I'll be tired'.

Bruce put the phone down. He could not bear to hear any more. The nurse directed him to the showers. She had laid out a large clean hospital towel for him, a throwaway shaving kit, and had discreetly put a pair of clean boxer shorts (provided for patients if they needed them) on the bathroom chair. Bruce looked in the mirror. He felt he had aged a hundred years, never mind being fifty next month. Brown, slightly reddish stubble peppered with grey lay in abundance on his face and neck, and his thick brown hair, longish and beginning to fleck with silver, normally wavy but tidy, had already grown tousled and unkempt. He looked, in his dead mother's words, a complete and utter Wreck of the Hesperus.

He let the hot shower water soak him, feeling its cathartic and comforting magic. Just for a moment, he thought about an adult baptism he had been to as a child, where the subject was totally immersed in water. He saw the point that he had missed before: it was a cleansing, purging, purifying act and symbolic of a fresh start and an act of commitment. Bruce now felt a commitment to his fresh and more honest way of thinking about his wife and his determination to change things. He had been at her beck and call for too long. He must reshape the future as best he could.

Invigorated, he towelled himself dry, shaved, and dressed, leaving his outer sweater off so that his olive green tee shirt with its motif saying *'Every Day's a Holiday'* was on display. Kitty had given it to him one Christmas. He ran his hands through his hair to smooth it and examined himself closely in the mirror.

'Marginally better', he said aloud.

The nurse who had offered him the shower saw Bruce a little later. She said nothing but realised what a very striking man he was. He 'scrubbed up well', she thought, recalling her mum's phrase, and wished she had the courage to say it to Bruce.

Bruce's next move was to phone Connie. He knew she would be anxious. She would be praying, and although Bruce did not use Connie's language, he knew that she would have been pleading to God to draw alongside Kitty and save her life.

'Oh, Hi Con'.

'Oh Brucie, I've been so, so worried. What's the news?'

'She's pulling through, Con! She's pulling through! She's stabilised, and the medics are cautiously optimistic that she'll make a full recovery. She's not out of the woods, but it's looking good'.

Connie cried openly down the phone.

'Oh Bruce, that's wonderful news! Darling Kitty! How is she feeling?'

'She's very sore and troubled by the chest drain, but that will come out in a few days. She's taken the news bravely, but, oh Con', Bruce suddenly burst into tears, 'She's got such a hard road ahead for the next few weeks'.

'I know she has, bless her, and it's terrible what has happened', Connie said, 'but she's not alone. We'll all support her and do everything possible to help, and she's a brave and feisty lass'. Connie paused. 'Brucie, is Clara there?'

Bruce swallowed hard. Although he had made a resolution to be honest with himself about Clara, he still found he wanted to defend her.

'Um, she's coming soon, Con'.

There was silence.

'Brucie....?'

'Connie...?'

He knew his sister was a non-judgemental person. He knew what she had noticed about Clara all through his marriage but was loyal and supportive enough to him not to say anything. He also knew that Connie believed wholeheartedly in the sanctity of marriage. How could he tell her his thoughts now? But of course,

Connie was one step ahead and sensed her brother's pain.

'Brucie, you can tell me, you know'.

'I know'. There was silence, and then it was as if a dam of pain and frustration burst inside him, causing a Tsunami of pain and despair to flood through his being. He shared everything with Connie. In the end, she was silent, but eventually she said simply,

'Bruce, you deserve better'.

That was all, but Bruce understood from it that his sister would not judge him harshly if he took the brave step of leaving his wife.

There was another silence. Finally, Bruce said,

'Con, how's that brave boy of yours? Kitty wants to know, and so do I'.

'He's amazing', replied Connie. He surprises us all on a daily basis, particularly over this crisis. I can see he's going to be OK'.

Connie and Oliver had agonised over Peter ever since that day when he was eleven months old and would not stop his constant grizzling. Nothing would pacify him. Connie, desperate to understand her baby son, searched through medical books and documents and finally deduced that Peter's lack of eye contact, his fluctuating sleep patterns, his devastating temper tantrums, and later, his hand flapping were all signs of what the psychiatrist later diagnosed as 'Infant Autism'. It may have been labelled 'Infant', Connie reflected, but Peter's symptoms had become worse during the early teenage years. He had finally learnt some social skills, thanks to Connie's and Oliver's infinite patience and wisdom. Supported by the wisdom and guidance of a skilled psychotherapist, Peter had gradually learnt to control his behaviour. It had been a hard path for them all and, most of all, for Peter himself.

'He'll make his own way in life now, Connie. He's brave and can respond in a crisis. But most of all, he is incredibly kind. You should be proud'.

Connie was – yes, she was very, very proud of her complex and wonderful son. Currently, their anxiety —the endless cross borne by caring parents—had focussed more on Jamie than Peter. Jamie, their eldest son, was desperate to spread his wings, which they knew was normal, but with this desire went a kind of arrogance that both parents found difficult to handle. They never wanted to humiliate him unduly, but they simply could not let him get off scot-free with some of his cutting and high-handed remarks. They saw evidence of his kind heart, but it was as if Jamie was constantly seeking to prove how adult and wise he was, when actually, just at the moment, he was neither.

‘And how are you, Con?’, Bruce asked, drawing Connie back to the here and now.

Connie wanted to say that she had been worried sick by the whole situation, that she knew both Peter and Kitty had possibly avoided death by a whisker, that she ached throughout her body and was more tired than she had ever been in her life; that all she wanted to do was sleep.

Instead, she simply said,

‘I’m O.K., Bro, and the babies are beginning to settle. I’m keeping praying for you all’.

‘Of that, I have no doubt, Sis. Love you’.

‘Love you, Bro’.

Bruce turned his phone off and thanked the powers that be for the unswerving love of his sister.

Chapter 26

Clara arrived the next day at the hospital with a flourish, carrying armfuls of roses and a huge box of chocolates. She met Bruce in the cafeteria as pre-arranged and kissed him extravagantly.

'Brucie! I've missed you so! How is she this morning?'

'She's pulling through, Clara, and she's desperate to see you'.

' But she's had you all the while, hasn't she?'

'Yes, but it's her mum she needs as well'.

'Where is she?' replied Clara, either not noticing or else choosing to ignore the cold tone of Bruce's voice.

Bruce indicated the way to Clara.

'Check first, Clara. It's not always convenient. They do the medical stuff with her in the mornings'.

'I'll just tell them I've come all the way from Chichester to see my daughter', Clara replied.

Bruce sighed inwardly. He had always known that Clara was thrusting when she wanted her own way, but now every statement she made grated on him like a razor scraping on glass. Clara waltzed into the ward to be met by the ward sister, who put a firm arm out in decisive action to barricade the way.

'I'm sorry, Madam, um – I'm not sure who you are?'.

'I'm Kitty Connors' mother, Clara Connors. I want to see my daughter'.

'Yes, of course'. She looked at the roses Clara had brought in.

'I'm afraid we don't allow flowers in the ward, but you could leave them in the reception area for everyone to enjoy. They're beautiful', she said, gazing at the array of bright roses.

'Well, if Kitty isn't allowed to have them, I'll take them home. They're too good simply to leave in the reception area to wilt'.

'Very well', replied the sister icily, gaining the measure of Clara Connors. 'I'll check in the ward to see that no doctors are examining her'.

'Thank you', replied Clara, 'but I'm due back in Chichester in a couple of hours, so I would appreciate a quick response'.

The ward sister said nothing, but her look of disdain, which she quickly suppressed, spoke volumes. She returned in a few moments.

‘That’s fine. Kitty will be delighted to see you. It was touch and go at one point, Mrs. Connors. You know she’s had a lung removed?’

‘I do’, replied Clara. ‘Poor Kitty. Will she need a convalescent home do you think?’

‘She’ll just need the tender loving care of mum and dad, I guess, and we’ll arrange a district nurse to visit her and change her dressings’.

‘Her father’s incredibly capable at this sort of thing. I never signed up to be a Florence Nightingale. I *do* admire you’, Clara said disingenuously, ‘But for me, nursing would have been the last career I’d have chosen. Too messy. Too demanding. I’m simply not cut out for it’.

The ward sister felt the implied put-down but bit her tongue and ignored it.

‘Your daughter tells me you are an actress, Mrs Connors’.

‘That’s right, and I’ve just landed the part of my dreams. The timing couldn’t be worse’, she said, sighing.

‘Mrs. Connors, Kitty will need a lot of support, both physically and psychologically. She has been through a huge ordeal, you know’.

'Yes, I know, and no thanks to my husband's nephew Peter. I understand Kitty was defending him. He's a nice enough lad, but he's autistic, and he gets things wrong. Kitty stepped in and took the brunt of the knife attack, I understand'.

'When the police were here, Mrs. Connors, she wanted me to stay in with her, so I did. Kitty was adamant that Peter was defending a young man – Robbie, I think his name was – from being stabbed, and then they turned the knife on Peter. Kitty said she saw the whole scene'.

'Yes, she defends him to the hilt. It's sweet, really – Peter needs all the friends he can get, but this is the result. My daughter gets hurt in the process. Life's not fair, is it Sister?'

'It certainly is not', she replied, 'and people always have to apportion blame when clearly the young men in the gang are the instigators. Certainly, Kitty has come off worse. She's in a lot of pain, Mrs. Connors'.

'Yes, but is she out of the woods, sister?'

'We like to see three or four days clear before anyone can give that opinion, but yes, she seems to be recovering according to plan. She's young and fit, which is on her side', the sister replied.

'Oh, that's good – mainly for Kitty's sake, of course – but it helps me make my decision' said Clara, tossing back her mane of chestnut hair. ‘Thank you for everything, Sister’, she said sweetly and walked towards Kitty.

Kitty smiled wanly when she saw Clara and then burst into tears.

‘Mum, where’ve you been?’

‘Sorry darling’, replied Clara, ‘but I had this wretched play introduction. I just couldn’t miss it’.

‘Not even for this, Mum?’ she said, pointing to the array of tubes attached to her.

‘Well, Dad was here, wasn’t he? We know he’s omni-competent, don’t we?’ she said in what passed for a smile.

‘It was you I needed as well’, said Kitty softly.

‘I know, darling, I know. I’m so sorry you’ve had all this pain’.

‘I’ve had a lung removed, Mum’.

‘I know that too’, replied Clara, ‘but apparently, your remaining lung will do the work of two and fill the chest cavity, Kitty, so it’s no big deal, darling one. Don’t worry’.

Clara reached for Kitty’s hairbrush and began to brush Kitty’s hair.

‘This is a tangled mess’, she said, ‘and I do believe they haven’t even cleaned the blood off’.

‘That’s nice, Mum’, said Kitty, shutting her eyes as Clara brushed. Clara began to sing softly to her - a song from Kitty’s early childhood years.

‘Hush little baby, don’t say a word, Papa’s gonna buy you a mocking bird’.

‘Oh, Mum, that’s lovely’, whispered Kitty. ‘I’ve missed you. I need you, Mum’.

Bruce had crept into the ward and saw the scene of Clara’s tenderness towards Kitty and Kitty falling into a peaceful sleep. Now, *that* was nice. Suddenly, Clara saw him approaching, stopped singing, and said in a sotto voce voice, ‘Bruce. She’s doing well. I’m going to go back to Chichester for a few days. These rehearsals are absolutely vital. I’ll be back on Sunday. That’s only four days. That’s all-right, isn’t it?’

‘Oh Mum, *no!’* said Kitty, rousing. ‘*Please* don’t go’.

‘Kitty, you know how long I’ve waited for a part like this. Don’t feel sad. It’s a massive opportunity for me. West End next’, she said with a smile. ‘Won’t you be proud to see your mama’s name up in lights!?’

Kitty sighed, acutely aware of the pain in her chest from the draining tube and another kind of pain, far deeper and one of which she had always been aware.

Kitty knew even as a small child that she came some way down on the list of priorities in Clara's life.

'You go, then, Mum,' she finally, resigned to the situation and knowing from experience that her mother was single-minded and obdurate when it came to her theatrical career. 'I've always got my dad', said Kitty weakly, her eyes moist as she held out her hand to her father.

'It's not an easy decision', Clara purred. 'Of course, my *heart* wants to stay with you, darling. But sometimes work must just come first, Clara'.

Clara left for Chichester that evening, leaving Bruce with a heart that was freezing over towards his wife, and a daughter's that felt near breaking point.

Chapter 27

Kitty came home from the hospital after two weeks. Physically, she had made a good recovery, but emotionally, she was at a very low ebb. Post-operative depression was beginning to set in. Clara had visited her twice on two consecutive Sunday afternoons but always left well before official visiting hours were over. Kitty was deeply hurt. One evening soon after her homecoming, she curled up on the sofa, her little cat Tabitha on her lap, and asked Bruce if they could have a frank talk. Bruce cleared away Kitty's meal tray and settled down with her.

As soon as she started talking about Clara, Kitty began to cry and found it impossible to stop. The layers of hurt that she had often felt as a child when Clara was more absent than present in her life were gradually peeling off to reveal an emotionally scarred and bereft young woman at the centre. Bruce's dilemma was that he knew every word Kitty was speaking was the truth and not a distorted memory of childhood. He wanted to support his daughter to the hilt and yet again felt the old familiar tugging of split loyalties. In the end, when Kitty had finally wept herself into exhaustion, she turned to Bruce.

'Dad. Answer me honestly. Have you ever thought of leaving Mum?

Bruce had felt anguished as he listened to Kitty's pain. Kitty didn't deserve this. She had always been a pretty good kid, he thought, and her sweet nature had been remarked upon by many. He felt she deserved the truth.

'Kit, I hadn't until your stabbing, and then, to be honest, I was appalled by her'. He put his arm around Kitty and held her close. 'I don't think she has it in her to reach out to you, and it was as if the scales fell off my eyes, Kitty. I don't know if you understand that? I know I idolised her for years, but now.......' It was his turn to stop and take a tissue from the box on the coffee table.

Kitty nodded. She had felt sad and appalled, too, and refused at first to believe her mother's lack of concern. It now felt as if all the years of watching her mother subtly humiliating Bruce, as if all the care and the love and the support her father had given his wife down the years, counted for nothing. Kitty had not stopped loving her mother – she could not – but her respect for her had gone. She began to weep again.

'Dad, you deserve better', she said, inadvertently echoing the words Connie had said to him on the phone. 'Don't stay for me, Dad. You deserve better', she repeated.

Father and daughter wept in each other's arms. Finally, Bruce said,

‘Kitty, I think I will try to get Mum to come to a marriage guidance counsellor with me. She has a perfect right to her career, and God knows, I have tried to support her and encourage her and I was proud of her. I’m sure I’ve failed her often but have never stood in her way. With hindsight, perhaps I have spoilt her rather. But I had not expected this over your terrible stabbing, my darling’. He kissed her cheek, reached for a tissue, and this time gently wiped the dampness from his daughter’s face.

‘I think it would be good, Kit, if we found someone you can really trust to talk to. You have been through such a trauma, and I am not enough’.

Kitty was silent. Bruce slowly continued.

‘You’ve met Professor Maria Murphy once round at the vicarage, haven’t you? She seems a very nice person -wise, I would say. She’s a Medical Psychotherapist, but don’t let the label put you off. She’s very human’.

Kitty thought about it and finally spoke.

‘If you think it would help me, Dad, I will, but I’ll make a bargain with you. I’ll go to Professor Maria if you promise to go to a marriage guidance counsellor with Mum’.

Bruce nodded. At least a way forward was opening up. Strike while the iron’s hot, he told himself. He looked up Maria Murphy's number there and then picked up the phone and dialled. After quite a long wait, Maria Murphy answered.

'Hello Professor Maria. It's Bruce Connors here'.

'Bruce! Good to hear you. How is Kitty? I've thought about her a lot. Connie told me what had happened. I'm dreadfully sorry about it. By the way, I'm just Maria to you, and anyway, I'm not on duty at the moment', she laughed.

'Ah. That's a moot point', Bruce replied, laughing back nervously.

'Can I help?' replied Maria, sensing a situation developing.

'I wonder if you would consider taking on a little paid private counselling- um - Maria? Just whatever your fee is, I will pay'.

'Bruce, don't let's talk about money at this stage, Bruce. Outline the problem briefly to me?'

Bruce explained as succinctly as he could his assessment of Kitty's needs. He found himself telling Maria more than he intended about his own predicament, too, and how the accident had been the catalyst for his sudden shock and insight about his wife's behaviour.

‘So my Kitty needs some support and to talk things through with a trusted counsellor, and - I thought of you’, he finished.

Maria was quiet for a few seconds, then,

‘Is it just Kitty who needs the support, Bruce?’

It was Bruce’s turn to be silent.

‘Why don’t you come and see me together as a first consultation? I think we must meet on some neutral ground. Tell you what. I’ll book a hotel lounge I sometimes use near Putney. You’re in Richmond, aren’t you? You tell me when you can manage it. I’ve booked myself some more leave for the next two weeks, by the way, so let me know what suits you during that time’.

A date was arranged. Bruce thanked Maria profusely and put the phone down.

‘Now it’s your side of the bargain, Dad. A marriage guidance counsellor’.

‘Yes, I’ll ask around discreetly for a recommendation. Maybe Maria can give me a name. I’ll get hold of Mum and pin her down to a date’.

‘Well, good luck with that!’

When Bruce finally managed to get through to Clara later that evening after Kitty had gone to bed, Clara, as he had predicted to himself, was dismissive of the whole idea, more than dismissive, positively hostile.

‘Bruce! What are you talking about? What’s wrong with our marriage? Just *what*? Nothing! What are you saying? Do you have to derail me just when my rehearsals are underway? That’s really selfish of you’.

‘Clara, I have – um – issues with how we are’.

‘*Issues!’* Clara replied, scandalised. ‘That’s a disgusting word. I thought we were happy!’

‘You may be, Clara, but I’m not, and I think we need help’. He paused. Had he the courage to say what he really felt? Was it fair over the phone? But if not now, when? He tried to remain measured, but as he spoke, his voice and its tone intensified.

‘Clara, Your attitude towards Kitty and her stabbing has opened my eyes. You haven’t visited her much at all, and she really feels it’.

‘Oh, I see’, said Clara sarcastically. ‘All this is because you’re resenting my involvement in the production. I might have guessed that just when I have a breakthrough, you would cause trouble. I’ve waited a long time for this and I thought you always supported me and were proud of me and....’

Bruce interrupted. ‘Clara, I am all those things under normal circumstances, and you know it because

I tell you often enough, but you haven't phoned for four days, nor have you asked me how Kitty is'.

There was a long pause.

'Bruce', said Clara, 'Has something happened?'

'No', replied Bruce, 'but it might well have done for all the interest you've taken in your daughter'.

Clara screamed down the phone.

'You don't realise what these rehearsal processes are like! There is *no* spare time, and by that, I mean *no* spare time. Sometimes we don't even have a break for a sandwich till about three o'clock'.

'Stop shouting, Clara!' Bruce said emphatically. 'I know rehearsals are pressurised, but our daughter nearly died. Does *nothing* get through to you?' Bruce began to match Clara's shouting. 'It's always about you and your needs, isn't it? It always has been. Come to marriage guidance with me or, or – I may have to leave you'. There. He had said it.

'Leave me then', she screamed, 'and take Kitty with you. You don't deserve me, either of you and anyway', she spat out, 'she was never meant to be your child. She should have been *Oliver's!*'

Clara slammed down the receiver.

Hearing her father shouting, Kitty had crept down the stairs in her nightdress. She had heard everything

Clara had screamed down the phone. Unaware of her, Bruce sat and wept. Kitty, shocked and shivering, moved off the bottom step where she had been sitting stiff and rigid and put her arms round him tightly.

'We'll be all-right, Dad, you and me. Mum can just sod off. I never want to see her again'.

'Don't say that, Kit'.

'See! Even now, when she treats you like dirt, Dad, you are standing up for her. Be strong. Let's face it, Mum is a selfish bitch'.

She was right, and Bruce knew it, and he didn't reprimand her either for her language or her opinion of her mother.

'And some time, by the way, Dad, I want to know exactly what she meant about Uncle Oliver'.

Chapter 28

Maria collected her daughter and granddaughter from the hospital two days after her momentous revelation to Hope had taken place. Hope was thankfully making a good recovery apart from deep bruises, residual shock, and soft tissue damage, all of which she was assured would heal in time. She and her newly discovered mother Maria had talked about the future, and both agreed that they wanted to spend as much time as possible with each other in order to catch up on the lost forty years of their history. As yet, they kept their joyful discovery to themselves. Hope invited Maria to stay at her house in Southwark for as long as she could.

Maria now was thoughtful. She was fifty-nine, loved her work, and had planned not to retire at sixty but to work for as long as she was fit and healthy and, as she put it, 'had all her marbles'. She had never had a break from her work and so had accrued a good fat pension. Finding Hope and Lucy had led to a paradigm shift of seismic proportions in her thinking. She realised that through her work, she had not only been able to find her identity but also to express it. Later, when Bruce and Kitty were to unburden themselves about their frustrations over what they saw as Clara's obsessional need to perform, Maria found herself with more than a grain of sympathy for Clara. She, Maria, had been the same over medicine, although, unlike Clara, she had no conflict of loyalties and no living daughter to her knowledge at that stage.

Having realised the pure joy of discovering Hope was alive caused Maria to reflect on the priceless treasure she had found. Acknowledging this led her, for the first time in years, to think about her own mother. She remembered her mother's harsh words and the head tilted in the air in defiance of her daughter, but she also recalled the tight lips, sealed against quivering, and her inability to look at Maria when she flounced out of the house announcing she was going forever. Maria had never wondered what her mother felt at that moment, she herself being so full of anger and hurt and intent on getting away as far as possible. But now, her perspective was different. Had she misread that tight-lipped look and proud tilting of the head? Was her mother, in fact, hiding grief and desperation with her typical defiance and bravado?

Her parents had opened a bank account in their daughter's name and poured a great deal of money into it for Maria's higher education if she ever wanted to take up that opportunity in the future. They had always been proud of her high academic achievements, and somehow giving money to her was a way of allaying some of their unexpressed and buried feelings of failure as parents. Maria had never written to them or acknowledged the money in any way. She always thought it was the least her parents could have done. She had held onto her anger and resentment and knew it but had, up to this point, been disinclined to do anything about it.

Perhaps, Maria wondered now, she had not grasped the enormity of what having a pregnant daughter and subsequently a baby out of wedlock meant to that strict and suffocating catholic community in early twentieth-century Ireland, and especially to her ultra-conservative and religious parents. She saved no energy reflecting on her father's attitude. To her, he would remain cruel, mean, cold, and without love for his only daughter, Erin. Discovering Hope softened Maria's heart and understanding, and she determined to find out more about her mother and see she was still alive. If so, Maria reflected, she would be well into her eighties, probably senile and possibly in a residential home. She assumed her father would have died as he was several years older than her mother. She would follow up her thinking with action.

On another subject, Maria now wondered if she could have done more for Gary Johnson. She had written a report, as requested by Gary's lawyer, on his state of mind and psychiatric needs as she saw them and later had defended him in court. But facts were facts. Gary had led a gang rape, stabbed and nearly killed Robbie Taylor, stolen his own daughter from her home and her mother twice, and most recently had virtually raped Hope, tying her up and leaving her bound and gagged, indifferent as to whether she lived or died. Maria could not, with integrity, put up a strong defence for him. She had emphasised the fact that Gary, in her simple words, had 'never stood a chance' with the animal buggery he was forced to take part in, filmed by his depraved parents. He was the ultimate definition, Maria said, of a 'latchkey kid' except that 'latchkey' indicated access to a home of some kind, which Gary had never had, having been forced to wander the streets while his parents served various prison sentences for their crimes. They would then be released to continue their wicked ways, using and distorting their young son's mind and ruining any chances he might have had of a normal life.

Gary was sentenced to twenty-five years imprisonment in a high-security psychiatric hospital. On the day he was sentenced, Maria thought she had never seen such a sad sight in her life. The lad who had been defiant, angry, and spirited was now broken and utterly crushed, seemingly without a friend in the world. Maria determined she would visit him as soon as she was allowed and was burdened by a recurring feeling that maybe she could have done more for the sad case of Gary Johnson.

Finding her daughter had illuminated so many issues, and at times, Maria was consumed with guilt over aspects of her past, which was an unfamiliar feeling for her. She had always avoided introspection, sub-consciously never being able to face where it might lead. The tender part of her heart had been pretty much barricaded against anyone who might hurt her, and she had done a good job of developing defences against anyone and anything that might try to break down the barricade. Stroking her granddaughter's silky gold hair had allowed her heart to express love, and finding her daughter had made it sing. She was determined to tackle issues she had hitherto shut out: her mother's grief, perhaps, for a start.

When she had been waiting for her baby to be born in that dreadful mother and baby institute which she had hated so much, she met the sweet young girl Cathy Ryan, age twelve, whose baby son Callum was torn away from her at birth. Some years later, she made a phone call to the Mother and Baby home, saying she was a medical psychiatrist and was following up on a patient and please she could have information about Cathy Ryan. She gave an anonymous name for herself and spoke convincingly down the phone. There was a long pause. Finally, the Nun returned from her fact-finding mission.

'Why, how long in God's name is it since you had contact with her? Cathy Ryan left the home when her baby was only twelve days old. She was found in a ditch three miles away. She died from dehydration and exhaustion, silly girl. It need never have happened, to be sure, but it must have been God's will for the poor little sinning waif'.

'Where was her body laid, Sister?'

'Why, in a grave behind the home, with the babies', she had replied.

'Is there a headstone?'

'No, no, the home couldn't afford anything like that,' she said reproachfully, 'But Sister O'Reilly, I remember, made a simple cross with her name on it. She did it for the other mothers, too'.

'Other mothers?'

The Nun was suddenly flustered.

'You're not from the papers, are you? We've had journalists round asking all sorts of ridiculous questions about what they called 'baby disposal'. They were dangerous with their ferreting around.' She paused and suddenly said, 'Tell me, are you writing any of this down?'

'No, I'm not. I needed to follow up with Cathy Ryan, that's all. Thank you for the information. Goodbye'.

Maria put the phone down and wept into her hands. Poor Cathy Ryan, dying loveless and without a friend in the world. Maria had promised to contact her when she had her baby, but her grief at the loss of her own child overwhelmed her. Maria vowed now that she would put flowers on the poor girl's grave as an act of contrition for her own neglect and broken promise to follow her up. She wondered too about Callum, Cathy Ryan's newborn son from whom the poor young mother was so agonizingly parted.

The next day, Maria spoke cautiously to Hope about what was on her mind regarding Gary Johnson. She was very careful how she outlined her thoughts as Hope was one of Gary's prime victims and would almost certainly be relieved and glad that he was finally behind bars and out of harm's way. Maria's instinct and observations, however, led her to understand that her daughter was a very special woman with an incredible facility for understanding and forgiving rather than simply judging. She had already seen those qualities in Hope's actions and conversation, so she spoke cautiously to her daughter, trusting that she would receive what she had to say.

'Hope, I'm thinking of going to visit Gary Johnson in prison. I'd like to see how he is and have further talks with him if he will let me. Twenty-five years is a terrible life sentence for him, and I doubt he will have any visitors ever'.

Hope was silent.

'See, I didn't manage to get his sentence reduced, even though I thought I put up an adequate case for leniency for him'. She paused. 'Hope, you know I have no real understanding of your faith, but' she paused again, choosing her words very carefully, 'Everyone needs support.' What she wanted to say was, 'Everybody needs forgiveness, but that was not her language.'

Finally, Hope replied, 'Everyone needs forgiveness as well as justice, don't they, Maria? That's the essence of the Christian faith, I believe, but it also requires repentance on Gary's part – that's what we are taught as Christians'.

'That's a tall order', said Maria quietly. 'Maybe Gary hasn't got the wherewithal to do that. He sees himself as the victim of his parents' abuse and doesn't – or *can't* - take responsibility for what he's done. It's a thorny issue, but words of regret for his actions have never passed his lips, as far as I know. 'No remorse', the judge remarked'.

Maria paused, then continued.

'No *outward signs* of remorse, I wanted to add to the statement. I suppose we don't know what's going on in his heart now'.

Hope was thoughtful and finally replied very quietly, 'You must go if you need to, Maria. I understand your need'.

Maria looked at her daughter and saw that a tear was slowly trickling down her cheek. Hope continued, brushing the wetness off.

'If I hadn't been raped by Gary, I would never have known the love it is possible to have for a child. My little Lucy is the most precious thing in my life – and now I have two most precious things,' said Hope, touching her mother's hand. 'Lucy is a wonderful gift to me, and ironically it's because of Gary's vicious act'. She gave a slight smile through her tears. 'I'm not sure what my faith says about that! I'll have to ask Oliver', she said, smiling more. 'He'll have an answer. He's so lovely, isn't he, Maria?'

'He is. He's the nearest thing on this earth to a saint, I'd say', replied Maria.

'Yes, absolutely, until the babies cry in the night, or there's another pooey nappy to be changed!' laughed Hope.

Maria laughed, too, and the atmosphere relaxed. Hope hugged her mother.

'Yes, I think you should go. You never know what good it might do for Gary'.

'And for me', replied Maria softly.

Chapter 29

Gary had been taken initially to the St. Bernard's wing of Ealing Hospital for forensic psychiatric analysis before starting his imprisonment at Wandsworth jail. He was told the forensic psychiatrist assesses offenders who have exhibited some violent behaviour. Gary had appeared completely unperturbed by this. He knew about St. Bernard's Hospital, previously known as The Hanwell Pauper Lunatic Asylum. Despite modernisation, both in architecture and philosophy, old die-hard residents living in Hanwell or Southall still referred to it in derogatory terms as 'St. Bernard's Funny Farm', or 'the Loony Bin', or simply 'being sent to Hanwell'. The fact was that there had been a huge turnaround of philosophy accompanying a change of management, and subsequently, the St. Bernard's Wing had become a shining example, both at home and internationally, of sound moral management and a model to aspire to for future psychiatric hospitals.

Gary was housed in the secure unit reserved for those with 'addictive personalities'. The hospital had been required by the judge and his team to use a forensic scientist to delve into Gary's psyche and assess whether he was mentally deranged, potentially violent, thereby needing constant psychiatric support and supervision, or simply lacking in any kind of moral principles and acting on impulse at will, with no regard for the consequences, no signs of any empathy for his victims, and little hope of change.

Maria knew that these cases were never cut and dried. To polarise those statements, in her view, was an indication of a serious lack of insight. Gary would not fit simply and solely into one or even two or three other categories any more than anybody else would. To lock him up for twenty-five years hardly seemed in Maria's view to be addressing him as the needy, deprived, and more sinned against than the sinning young man that she believed he was. Maria also had the wisdom, however, to know that Gary was a menace to society, had to be brought to justice, and constrained from repeating his violent acts.

Gary was in St. Bernard's Psychiatric Wing for a month's assessment, and it was during the last week of this period that Maria drove across London and onto Uxbridge Road. It was two o'clock in the afternoon, but traffic was already building up towards the M40 and M25 motorways. Maria tapped the steering wheel impatiently. She hated waiting in traffic, and furthermore, she found herself strangely nervous about seeing Gary again. She could not banish the feeling that she had let him down.

Gary was led down by a nurse into an airy and light day room. He was wearing his own clothes – a tee shirt of indeterminate white/grey and scruffy jeans, which had unintentionally fallen down to hip level due to his considerable weight loss. These items of clothing would soon disappear for at least two weeks when he entered Wandsworth Jail at what was termed 'Entry-Level'. They would be stored away and exchanged for regulation prison-issue clothes consisting of oversized grey tracksuit bottoms and a grey tee shirt.

'Hi Gary' said Maria. 'How are you doing?'

No answer and no eye contact.

'Sit down, Gary', she said gently.

Gary remained standing. The nurse hovered.

'How are your discussions going with the psychiatrist, Gary?' Maria asked eventually. It was clear that Gary was not going to speak. His eyes looked dull, and Maria wondered if the hospital had prescribed him some strong sedatives.

'Is there anything you need brought to you if I can get permission?'

Silence.

After a few more minutes, the nurse intervened.

'I'm afraid he's like this for most of the time. You know, I don't think you'll get through to him. Gary, are you going to speak to your friend?'.

Gary looked up under hooded eyes.

'Friend? Whatcha talking about? She's a snake - slimy. You think she's on your side, but she ain't'.

Maria gulped. She was afraid Gary might feel like that even if, in the eyes of everyone else, she had done an excellent job defending him in court. She was about to speak up in her defence to Gary but found she had no words. The lad himself looked beaten, finished, abandoned, which was what Maria felt about herself in those few minutes. Her heart ached for him.

Eventually, she said,

'Well, if there's nothing I can do for you, I'll be off'. She paused. 'O.K. Goodbye Gary'. She got up, slinging her brown leather bag over her shoulder, and slowly made her way to the door.

'Wait', murmured Gary. 'I ain't got a photo nor nothing. Can you ask Hope if I can have a photo of me daughter?'.

'What do you think Hope will say to that, Gary?'

Gary thought.

'She's a good 'un, in't she? She'll say yes'.

Maria had a feeling he was right and that Hope would say yes, even if it felt like the most tremendous personal tussle for her.

'And anuvver thing. When I was round at 'Ope's about to do the business, you know,' Gary made the crudest of gestures, 'I took off me belt, didn't I? It' still round at her house. It's not just any old belt, you know. Oh no. It was me dog's lead – Wolfie's – the one I told you about. Thing is, it smells of Wolfie, and I want it. Reminds me of him - plus me jeans are falling down'.

'I'll see what I can do, Gary. You're off to Wandsworth in a couple of days, aren't you? I'll keep in touch with the Warden there. If you do as they say – stick to their rules – I'll be able to bring them in for you. But it won't be allowed for a while. You have to earn privileges'.

As Maria opened the door, Gary said quietly, 'Thanks, M'ria'.

That was all, but it was enough for Maria. As she walked back to the car park, she thanked God for a tiny breakthrough, even if it was because Gary wanted something. At least he had spoken to her. That was progress. She would talk to Hope about the requests.

Chapter 30

When Maria returned to Hope's house, she found Connie had come on a visit. Despite having newborn twins, three other children, and recently recovering from a hysterectomy, she had somehow found time to make Hope a large beef casserole, an apricot crumble, and a wobbly red jelly in the shape of a rabbit to welcome Lucy on her return home after her stay at the vicarage.

Connie had let herself in and found Hope resting. Maria surveyed the scene. She noticed immediately that Connie was looking pale but lovely in a post-operative, new mum kind of way and was perched on the arm of the chair by the side of Hope. Maria exclaimed when she saw the food on the table waiting to be put in the fridge.

'Connie! However, have you had the time and energy to do all *this!'* she said, waving her hand towards the food.

'I'll tell you how,' said Hope, 'It's because my sister here is a miracle worker!'

'No, I am *not*', replied Connie emphatically. 'When you start off by cooking for a family of six – which includes Robbie and his huge appetite - it's no great hassle to make one or two more portions'.

Maria smiled. There was a thread of sheer goodness running through both Connie and her half-sister Hope. They were very alike, even though they had different mothers. From everything Maria knew about their father, Albert Connors (her deceitful lover), it was a surprise to know that both daughters had somehow not only survived but risen above the angry and violent aspects of his personality. She remembered how she had been infatuated by the charming side of him, the kindness and warmth of him at first, his initial tenderness as a lover, but she would never blot out his ugly reaction when she told him she was pregnant. She had no idea he was married and told him so in no uncertain terms, which made him curse and swear in a violent and dangerous rage she had not encountered before. She was sure he was going to strike her or even worse.

His daughters Connie and Hope had triumphed above the inherited genes of their father. Would it be possible for Gary, she mused, to do the same – to rise above the toxic combination of his inherited nature and the learned ways of behaviour indoctrinated by his deprived and depraved childhood and turn himself around eventually to reintegrate into society? Maria had studied the nature/nurture arguments in detail which still dominated much of psychological assessment. She had lectured on it to medical students. With regard to Gary's parents, both nature and nurture seemed to have worked against their son. His parents were clearly deviant by nature and made sure that Gary was nurtured (if it could be called that) in a sick and corrupting environment.

What motivation was there for Gary to work at reintegrating himself into society? He would not be out of prison within about twenty-two years, pending good behaviour. He would be forty-six, with over half his life gone, and with no friends, no money, and limited intellectual skills, although Maria assessed that he had a street savvy and shrewdness about him.

'How was Gary?' asked Hope tentatively, breaking into Maria's thoughts.

Maria searched for the right word. She did not like to use the word 'despairing', although that is what had come across to her through his body language and silence.

'Pretty depressed, I'd say – angry, dark. I hardly got a word out of him until I was about to leave'.

'What did he say then?' asked Hope cautiously. She dreaded that Gary would be full of recriminations and boiling over with anger about his imprisonment. Maria thought hard. On her way home she had decided not to tell Hope about Gary's request until Hope was stronger after her hospitalisation. Now, as both the women looked at her expectantly, it was not so easy to follow through with her decision.

'Maria?' asked Hope again.

Just tell it the way it is, Maria decided.

'Hope, he has asked for two things: his belt that he used as a dog's lead. He said he left it round here, and....' She hesitated.

'And the second?'

A long pause, then,

'A photo of Lucy'.

Hope's eyes filled with tears. She was quiet for a moment, then spoke almost in a whisper.

'Poor Gary. He must feel he hasn't a friend in the world'.

'He probably does think that, but you mustn't feel you have to compensate for that, must you?' said Maria, taking Hope's hand and holding it tightly, worried that her daughter's tender heart would be consumed with misplaced guilt.

'No, I don't. But if a dog's lead and a photo are his only requests, then in God's name, I can't deny him those, can I?'

'You could if you wanted to', replied Maria.

They were all silent.

'I don't want to', Hope finally replied quietly.

'You are a special lady, Hope. Isn't she, Connie?'

'Yes. You know what? I'm so glad and proud to call her my sister and to think we didn't even know each other until Hope found us four years ago!'

Maria was desperate to say, 'And I only found my daughter a few weeks ago', but she didn't. She was actually relishing the fact that it was *their* secret, and just for the time being, it was good to keep it that way. Hope, unseen by Connie, gave Maria a sidelong smile, which she returned. It was a wonderful conspiracy just for the moment. When the time was right, they would share it with the family and have the celebration of a lifetime!

For the next few weeks, it was as if the entire family and even the bricks and mortar of the vicarage had taken a deep breath and let out an enormous and cathartic sigh of relief. It seemed that the crises that had beset them all in the last few months were finally behind them, and they could start to live again. Robbie was more subdued after he had been released from custody with a heavy fine and a warning about withholding information from the police. He threw himself wholeheartedly back into his youth work with renewed energy and commitment and tried to blot out the fact that he had been partly instrumental in Gary's twenty five year prison sentence. Having spent a couple of nights in prison awaiting trial and a further two years of his past locked in a cell for administering grievous bodily harm, Robbie knew what Gary had come to him in Wandsworth Prison.

Connie was now fully recovered. The babies were gaining weight, beginning to smile, and had slotted into a routine, even dropping the one a.m. feed and stretching it to after four a.m. Oliver began to sleep better, and Rosy was her usual ebullient and cheerful self and had become an expert at bottle feeding. Hope was recovering from the trauma of her near-rape and her daughter being taken from her, and little Lucy herself appeared to have few ill effects from her nasty adventure, the only visible change in her behaviour being anxiety about separation from her mother. James was off to university soon – another sigh of relief - and Peter seemed to have visibly grown in self-esteem and stature since his courage in the marketplace had been commended by the police.

Much to Connie's delight, her eldest sister Sadie, now happily settled in Scotland with her partner, had written saying she was coming down soon to be introduced to her new nephews and to see Connie after her recent medical traumas. Connie was relieved to sense that Sadie was happy and making a new life for herself. She had been through such a hard time after her son Jack was killed outside the vicarage door in his faulty wheelchair. Everything, thank God, was beginning to feel on an even footing, and life was returning to something resembling normality.

The one person who was far from happy was Bruce Connors.

Bruce missed his wife Clara badly but knew in his bones that it had been the right thing to have taken her to task about the state of their marriage. Daughter Kitty, thank goodness, was coping well after her pneumonectomy, and as the surgeon had predicted, her remaining lung was busy compensating for the loss of the removed one, her X-rays showing that the chest cavity was already accommodating her healthy lung's expansion.

Clara, meanwhile, had taken huge umbrage at Bruce's frank remarks down the phone to her and had booked herself into a hotel in Chichester. What she felt inside was anyone's guess. If she was hurting and upset, it did not show; neither did she ask Bruce to reconsider, and any kind of apology for letting her daughter down in her hour of need was out of the question. She came home every other Sunday to see Kitty but barely said a word to Bruce despite his frequent requests to try and sort things out and find a way ahead.

'Seeing Kitty' consisted of taking her out for a pizza and a glass of wine (in Clara's case, three glasses of wine) and either not noticing or trying to ignore her daughter's withdrawal of warmth from her. Not once did Clara broach the subject of her lack of visits to her daughter in hospital, nor Bruce's ultimatum about their marriage. It was as if she had either locked away or else simply obliterated all her feelings about what she thought of as ‘the little upset’. Either she was never going to deal with it or had shelved it until after the three-month run of performances of *Me and my Girl* was over. Apparently so wrapped up in her own life was Clara that she barely asked how Kitty was, if she needed anything or how her daughter was feeling without her. It would seem that Clara had few feelings of any kind except for herself. A textbook case of a narcissistic personality, Professor Maria Murphy, was to conclude.

Something had to change.

Chapter 31

Hope sorted out two or three photos of Lucy and was having trouble selecting the most appropriate one for Gary. The first was of Lucy in a paddling pool, laughing and splashing; another was of Lucy in her high chair, laughing as she blew her food out of her mouth, and a third was of Lucy running up to the camera with her white toy rabbit. Hope decided on the one with the toy rabbit. She took a photo of her newborn daughter out of its lightweight frame and replaced it with the one for Gary. At least he could stand it up somewhere in his cell if there was a ledge or a table.

Handling Gary's belt was harder. It was on top of the piano where one of the police officers had quickly put it when Gary was struggling hard to resist arrest. It reminded her of his ugly violence as he had impatiently torn it off in order to pull his jeans round his thighs low enough to rape her. Hope shuddered as she placed it in a carrier bag, holding it disgustedly away from her with two fingers rather like she might a mutilated dead bird found in the kitchen. She wrapped the framed photograph in white tissue paper before she put it in the bag, an unconscious need not to contaminate her little girl's purity with the offending belt.

She decided to visit Gary as soon as his weeks in regulation prison uniform were up. Oliver had told her that she would not be allowed to hand Gary the goods herself, but they would be taken by a warden, scrutinised, and then stored in a locker for him. He could have them at a later date, pending good behaviour.

Hope dreaded visiting Gary, but something burned inside her to treat him as a human being despite his actions against her. When she thought of his evil acts of tying her up and escaping with Lucy while she lay gagged and bound, she found it all too easy to hate both the act and the perpetrator. Dismissing this feeling took a huge amount of willpower and mental discipline, and in her mind, she had to replace that picture with the one of Gary in the dock looking frail and shrunken, pinched and ashen-faced and without a friend in the world. Her strong Christian faith required her to forgive, and she kept saying her favourite verse from the Bible over and over again:

'Be kind to one another, tender-hearted, forgiving one another, as God in Christ forgave you'. (Eph.4, 31 – 32).

Whilst forgiving, Gary was an act of will required of Hope by her faith. It was her tender and forgiving heart that had the upper hand and had the greater influence in this case, so she actually had no choice in the matter. She could not hear of his suffering and simply passed by on the other side.

Hope booked her visit to Gary well in advance, as advised by the prison service. She sorted out her personal identifications required by the prison for access and set off on a bright October morning. She alighted from the train at Wandsworth Common Station and walked the rest of the way, checking several times that the photograph and belt were firmly in her patchwork canvas shoulder bag. Visiting Gary took enormous courage on her part, although she would have dismissed such a comment vehemently. She was just doing what was required of her for the sake of Gary - Gary Johnson, who had raped her twice, stolen her child twice -once as a newborn baby - gagged and bound her, knifed both Robbie, the friend who had first welcomed her to Southwark, and Kitty, her brother's daughter, causing her a near-fatal bleed and a lung removal. Finally, this was Gary Johnson, who had drowned his own mother apparently without any guilt or remorse, justifying every action he took.

Kitty and Robbie, however, would remember it was also the same Gary who dived into the Thames and saved Kitty from drowning after a tragic boat accident on the Thames, and Hope would remember that it was that same young man who efficiently helped her in the top flat of the vicarage during her early stages of labour with Lucy, bringing towels and making himself useful. It was not a clear-cut case of Gary the Bad Boy.

Was it ever?

Oliver tried to persuade Hope that he should go with her to the prison in his capacity both as brother-in-law and Gary's vicar. Maria did the same in her capacity as Hope's (as yet secret) mother and as a Medical Psychiatrist. Hope was adamant, however, that this was something she needed to do on her own. She found a steely determination within her not to condemn but to try from the depth of her being to understand and support Gary. This conviction was underpinned by much prayer, which was the bedrock of her faith.

Everyone thought it remarkably courageous (and perhaps headstrong) of Hope to insist on going it alone, and Connie particularly was worried for her. What Connie had not fully appreciated was that Hope could be as brave as a lion when she needed to be. She had no knowledge of the Hope who had endured the hardship of the children's orphanage in Ireland, nor the strict regime and sheer hard labour of life at the Convent – the hours and hours she had spent digging up potatoes from the frozen earth, or diligently slaving over steaming hot wash tub copper boilers and scrubbing sheets until her hands were red and raw. This was the other side of Hope, the tenacious, unshakeable, tough side of an ex-nun who had endured many things in her forty-three years. And still, she had the capacity to love as few others could.

Hope entered the forbidding Victorian building and presented her credentials to the officer on duty. She also had what she was told was a 'pat down' search. If this proved ambiguous in any way, then the sniffer dogs would be brought in. Her watch and sunglasses were removed, and she was read out a list of rules by the officer who had a particularly monochrome and monotonous voice. He had clearly read the list out a thousand times and unsurprisingly found no poetry in it, but what he did notice was that Hope was a particularly pretty woman. Her fingerprints were taken to be kept on file, which made her feel as though *she* was a criminal. Pictures kept flashing through her mind of how she might feel about going through procedures like this, and many more, and knowing that at the end of them, she would be locked away from society for twenty-five years, as in Gary's case. She could hardly bear to imagine the horror and despair that must enter the heart of the condemned.

Finally, her bag and gifts were taken from her. She was asked about the contents of the parcels for Gary. They sounded harmless enough to her, but unluckily, Hope was in line for one of the random spot security checks, and the parcels were opened there and then.

'Well, he can't have this for a start', said the examining officer. 'No belts allowed. Too risky'.

'Risky?' she queried.

'Suicide'.

'Oh', Hope replied and shivered inwardly.

The Examining Officer opened the picture.

'Who's this then?'

Hope hesitated.

'Um, well' - a pause - 'It's his daughter'.

The Warden looked at it closely.

'Frame's a bit dodgy. Glass?'

'Only a 3 x 5', replied the Officer. And that looks like cheap plastic to me. Not much he can do with that', the warden commented.

'Let the bugger have this, but definitely not the belt. Stanley!' he called, tossing the belt over the counter. 'Put this in storage for when he comes out'.

Hope felt despair on Gary's behalf. Twenty-two years minimum with good behaviour.

'He can have the picture when he's allowed', said the officer.

Hope refrained from asking what Gary had to do or not do in order to be allowed the picture. She was already finding the whole process unspeakably painful and revealing. Eventually, she was shown the way to the Visitor Centre. She waited. A bell sounded, and a variety of prisoners came in, scrutinised the area, and identified, most with some alacrity, their particular visitor. Gary came in towards the end of the group, shuffling and looking down. Hope put up her hand and gave him a small wave as he looked up. He saw her.

'Gary. Come and sit down?'

Gary sat down heavily on the edge of the seat, still looking at the floor.

'Gary, I've brought you the picture you asked for of Lucy. They'll let you have it later'.

A half smile crossed Gary's face then he looked at the floor again.

'Thanks'.

'It's of her running towards the camera holding up her white rabbit, Gary'.

'Nice one,' Gary said without looking up.

'It is', said Hope. 'She looks pretty in it. They said you'd be allowed it'.

There was a prolonged silence. Hope was not sure of what conversation to initiate. 'How are you?'

sounded so feeble; 'What's it like in here?' just plain unacceptable and trite.

It was actually Gary who broke the silence.

'What about me, belt then?'

'I brought it, Gary, but they won't allow you to have it'.

'Bloody hell, why not?'

Hope shrugged her shoulders.

'I'm not sure', she lied.

''S'pose the officer fancied it for 'imself', said Gary.

Hope hardly thought so. Its faded brown leather was cracked with age, water water-stained, and the hole markers were stretched and ragged.

'They said you can have it when you come out, Gary', Hope said tentatively.

'Well, there's something to fuckin' aim for then', replied Gary bitterly.

'Is there anything else you need?' asked Hope eventually, more to break the oppressive silence than anything else

'Like what?'

‘Well, I don’t know. Some chocolate, for example?’

‘Fags more like’, replied Gary. ‘Or drugs’, he said with a faint smile.

Hope didn’t answer. Silence again.

‘Gary, I’m sorry it’s ended like this’ said Hope. ‘I really am’.

Silence.

‘Nearly ‘ad you twice, didn’t I? Don’t worry. I won’t be past it when I get out. I’ll come and find you. You can still have it at sixty, can’t you, *Sister* Hope?’

There was no threatening edge to Gary’s voice, but still, it filled Hope with fear and made her feel sick. For the first time, she felt glad that he was locked up for a very long time. There seemed no repentance in the man.

At that minute, thankfully, the bell marking the end of visiting time rang loudly.

‘Come again, will ya, ‘Ope? I ain’t got no-one else’.

‘I’ll see what I can do,’ said Hope. ‘Try to obey all the rules, Gary, so that they give you your picture’.

Gary said nothing. Hope got up to leave, and Gary suddenly grabbed her arm. A warden moved closer. Gary looked intently at Hope.

'Ope. You're all I've got, you is. Bring the bairn next time? They're allowed'.

Hope smiled slightly and inwardly made a vow that never would Lucy set foot in this place nor know the truth about who her father was and the circumstances of her conception - not if Hope could possibly help it.

She walked to the station with a heavy heart and a feeling of deep despair inside that there seemed to be no sense of remorse in Gary Johnson.

Chapter 32

Clara was halfway through the three-month run of *Me and My Girl'* in Chichester Festival Theatre. At the beginning of December, the musical would transfer to the West End, having been deemed a huge success with rave reviews. Chichester Festival Theatre would soon begin to prepare for the Christmas season. Clara was reckoned by most of the critics to have been an excellent *Sally* and was said to be in line to transfer with the company to London. She barely thought of Bruce but kept visiting Kitty every two or three weeks.

She was glad to see her daughter looking fit again, but the two had lost a huge amount of ground in their relationship as mother and daughter. Kitty was often taciturn and answered pretty monosyllabically during their pizza lunches.

'Are you coming to the show, Kit? If so, I'll get you tickets'.

'Mum, you've got a nerve asking that?'

Clara looked genuinely bewildered.

'A nerve? But you're my daughter! What do you mean?'

'Dad is sad, Mum'.

‘That’s his fault, Kit. In effect, it was *he* who turned *me* out’.

‘He’d have you back if you wanted it’.

‘Well, I don’t want it’, replied Clara emphatically.

What neither Kitty nor Bruce knew was that Clara had embarked on two brief affairs during the two months she had been away. Neither meant very much to her, although she made sure that the sex was good, being an accomplished lover. She had also started drinking too much and relied on two or three whiskeys each night to get her through the shows. Kitty noticed that she regularly ordered red wine with her pizza lunch and had at least three large glasses each time, then would ask the waiter to put a stop in the bottle so that she could take it with her when she drove home. She had, to date, somehow avoided being caught by the police and breathalysed.

Clara may have appeared happy-go-lucky and fulfilled, but her behaviour seemed to tell another story. Apart from parting from Bruce, she had actually never quite managed to stop loving Oliver Lockwood despite the intervening years of satisfactory marriage to her husband.

‘One day I’ll make it impossible for him to resist me’, she promised herself.

xxxxx

Maria returned to work on a part time basis and spent the majority of the rest of the time with her daughter Hope and grandchild Lucy. They were planning a big family party near Christmas when they would announce their newfound discovery. Oliver was actually secretly worried. He had observed before Lucy was born how close Hope had become to Sadie, her freshly discovered half-sister, and Hope had confided in Oliver that Sadie had admitted that her feelings for her were more than purely sisterly. Sadie eventually moved away with her new girlfriend to Scotland and seemed fulfilled and happy if her letters and emails were anything to go by. Was the same thing happening between Hope and Maria now, Oliver surmised?

They were certainly demonstrative, appearing very loving towards each other, and seemed to spend every spare moment together. It had been difficult for Oliver to reconcile the lesbian relationship of his sister-in-law Sadie with the teachings of the Anglican church and, indeed, his understanding of marriage as outlined in the Bible. Was it happening again with Hope and Maria? He was a gracious man and made room in his heart for a generous compromise, but it did not sit happily with him.

Life in the vicarage was busy, noisy, and generally happy. James had been at Cambridge University for nearly a term now reading Politics and was due home on 10th December. Oliver was very proud of him, even though he knew his son had some attitudes that needed modifying. He wasn't sure that Cambridge was the best place to smooth the rough edges off his son, however, and feared the exciting but rarefied atmosphere might even increase James's irritating attitude of superiority.

'Call that working?' his brother Peter had teased down the phone to his brother. 'An eight-week term doesn't even give you time to unpack! S'pose being the cream of the intelligencia you don't need to study for as long or as hard as us *normal* people.'

Peter himself was undecided about his future path. He didn't want to work with people or animals, nor in the medical profession, despite loving science and physics, nor in the catering sector. Oliver worried a lot about his second son, but Connie was more philosophical about him.

'He'll sort himself out, Oli. Maybe he shouldn't apply to University just yet. He needs thinking time. Look how far he's come lately'.

'He's had nearly eighteen years to think about it', replied Oliver, uncharacteristically irritable. 'He'll still be thinking about it in ten years' time left to his own devices'.

Connie sighed. Oliver was over-tired from still sharing most of the four a.m. feeds despite her trying to persuade him that she could manage. He was finding the constant demands of two lively little babies, three older children and the needs of the parish, over which he never stinted, suddenly overwhelming. The babies were a joy, but Oliver confessed he would find them more interesting when they were two years old, and he could teach them to kick a ball around. Rosy seemed to be pure sunshine, and the whole family basked in her sunny disposition.

Chapter 33

Hope's visit to Gary had distinctly unsettled him. She was the only visitor he had had in the three months he had been in prison. There simply was no-one else who cared for him or about him. Oliver now put it as an urgent priority to go and see Gary, as did Maria, but somehow the days were eaten up by a myriad of 'things'. Oliver, however, phoned the prison and arranged a date in ten days' time, and Maria and Hope decided they would go together if allowed.

During that ten-day period, Gary behaved impeccably. He was almost silent. He did not come out of his cell for meals or relax in the day room, which was permitted at certain times. He gave the impression of being unconcerned about his predicament, and even the skilled and wise female chaplain could hardly get a word out of him. Gary's total focus was on behaving well enough to receive the photo of his daughter, and then, after that, it was anyone's guess how things would be.

The door of the cell door clanked unlocked. Two wardens stood outside, each as burly as the other.

'Here you are, Gary. See? Good behaviour pays off, don't it? Here's your package'.

'It's been undone,' murmured Gary scrutinising it in the warden's outstretched hand. 'Who undone my parcel?'

'Well, we have to make sure there's nothing harmful in there'.

'What about me dog's lead then? Why can't I have that? That ain't harmful'.

'We don't want any bad use of things like that', said the other warden.

'More like someone's stolen it', said Gary sullenly.

'Do you want this or not?' said the first warden, holding out the parcel.

Gary took it, and the cell door clanked shut and Gary was left alone with the parcel. He hardly dared open it. It felt so special. At last, someone was actually giving him a gift. Even on birthdays as a child, his parents had given him no more than a chocolate orange, which he had to share with whichever dog he was instructed to seduce.

Holding his breath, he unwrapped the parcel. There was a note attached to the final layer of tissue paper.

'*Dear Daddy Gary. This is from Lucy Grace Erin x'*.

And there she was! Pretty and almost coquettish and holding out her soft white rabbit toy towards the camera as if to Gary. For the first time since his dog

Wolf died, Gary cried. He kissed the little girl in the glass picture frame, and the tears fell onto her image.

'You's a pretty little thing, ain't you? I loves you, little Lucy. When I come out, I'll buy you a big present'.

Suddenly, he sank into a corner of his cell and started sobbing and wailing loudly. This was the first emotion he had expressed since his arrival. The enormity of the situation hit him. Lucy was three now, and he was inside for twenty five years. She would be twenty-eight when he was released, probably married, and more than likely would disown him. It was an utterly hopeless situation. Blackness overwhelmed Gary. Drowning in a flood of bad memories, he remembered sitting outside the London pub on cold winters' nights, waiting for the closing time when his drunken mother and father would stagger out. If it had been a good evening, one or other of them would toss a bag of crisps towards him. If it had been bad, or if they were totally inebriated beyond reason, he would be told to sling his hook and not come home till morning.

He remembered wandering the streets while his parents were locked up inside. It was during one of those times that Gary linked up with a gang of similar outcasts, with nothing better to do than steal for survival and use violence as self-protection and later sexual gratification. His parents never came to find him when they had served their time in prison, and it was by chance that Gary had linked up with his mother at the Church Army Hostel.

The only people who had shown him kindness and given him a home for a few weeks were the people at the vicarage and Robbie, the youth worker. And what had he, Gary, done? He had ruined everything by stabbing Robbie, near-raping Hope, and stealing his daughter from her. He had blown the only chance he had of climbing out of the snake pit he was in.

Oliver Lockwood arrived at Wandsworth Prison. He went in his dog collar, hoping it might give him quicker access to Gary or even a visit in his own cell. In some situations the clerical dog collar was proven to be a powerful tool, giving a sign to the uninitiated of spiritual status and superiority. Oliver hated this kind of reverence to 'the cloth', understanding all too well that priests had feet of clay and stumbled like the rest of humankind. All the same, the symbol of the dog collar had its uses.

On this occasion the symbol did bring about easy access through Security: no fingerprints, no pat search, no questions other than a quick glance at identification papers. He was known at the prison by many. He arrived in the visitors' room fifteen minutes early and had the usual stomach-churning he associated with an empathetic sense of corporate shame that there did not seem to be any fresh or credible answers as to how to treat the misfits and casualties of society other than to lock them away.

Gary had no knowledge that Oliver Lockwood was visiting him that day. Later, Oliver pondered deeply whether, if he had written to Gary telling him he was coming, the day would have had a different outcome.

Inside his cell, Gary took the photo out of its frame, put it close to his heart under his grey shirt, doing up its top button to protect the picture, then purposefully smashed the glass of the frame hard against the metal bed frame. Pondering for no more than a few seconds, he reached out for his pillow and stuffed the corner of it into his mouth to muffle any sounds or inadvertent screams he might make. He then slashed both his wrists deeply several times with a small piece of the jagged glass, severing an artery in each during the process.

The procedure was agonising torture - but Gary made no sound. He wanted no-one to come in until the deed was done and completed absolutely. The blood came slowly trickling out of his wrists at first and onto the floor. He sat there, leaning on the bed, with his daughter's photograph next to his heart. Memories swamped his mind. He remembered the way he had tipped his mother overboard and how her head had popped up above the surface, her eyes wide with shock. He felt no remorse for drowning his terrible, terrible mother. He simply wished he had done it earlier. He remembered, too, his father beating both Gary and the innocent animal when they had failed to perform. Afterwards, he felt a mixture of anger and pity for the creature.

He thought of his daughter Lucy and the precious few hours he had with her on Bankside beach and his joyful discovery of her webbed toes that were just like his. He liked the way the newborn had turned her head inwards to his chest, instinctively looking for milk. He liked her soft, downy blonde hair and the way she smelt. He just liked *her*.

Finally, he thought of Wolfie, his dog, whom he had loved more than anything and anyone in the world. Even he had died in the end. Gary's head began to spin, and the blood pumped out regularly, relentlessly, and then profusely. He did not try to stop it and, after fifteen minutes, became surrounded by an ever-growing pool of red on the hard grey stone floor around him.

He murmured weakly, 'Damn you, mother, damn you, father, fuck you, world'.

Then, with his final halting breaths,

'Love you, Lucy. I'm comin' Wolfie'.

xxxxx

The shrill Visitors' bell sounded. The two wardens came to find Gary to unlock his cell and lead him down to Oliver, his visitor – always two wardens, at least in case Gary chose to be violent, which he never had up till now. The first warden put the huge key in the mortis lock and turned it. He opened the heavy creaking cell door slowly and reeled back, aghast, as he saw Gary sitting with his head slumped on his chest, his body tilted over towards the bed, lifeless in a river of his own blood.

'Fucking hell', the warden gasped, ringing the emergency alarm and causing a cacophony of clashing sounds, 'There'll be some enquiry after this!'

Tragic Gary Johnson, more sinned against than sinning, standing little chance in life, seeing no single star above and drowning on the margins of society in its neglectful blood – 'Ask not for whom the bell tolls; it tolls for thee'.

It was a surprisingly long time – probably ten minutes - before emergency backup guards arrived at the cell. Part of the reason for the delay was the all too frequent misuse of the emergency bell by prisoners. The guards were so used to running to a cell and finding the bell sound was a hoax, and they had become desensitised to it. When they arrived this time, they all stood rooted to the spot at the door.

Meanwhile, Oliver Lockwood had sat himself down in the visitors' area and was waiting for Gary. He reached for his diary in the inside pocket of his faded brown corduroy jacket and thumbed through it, not actually looking at any of the entries – a habit of his when he was on edge. The prolonged ringing of the emergency bell unsettled the visitors, and they began to speculate with each other about the cause.

After a few minutes, three guards came into the waiting room and ushered all the visitors out, explaining that there had been an emergency and to wait in the entrance hall until further notice. Oliver stayed put and went up to one of the guards.

'I need access to Gary Johnson. I'm his pastor', Oliver said authoritatively.

'You a relative or a friend, Father?'

'A friend. I'm his parish priest',

'I'll go and make some enquiries'.

'I'd be grateful', replied Oliver.

The guard returned in a few minutes, ashen-faced.

'What's the matter? Has something happened to Gary?' Oliver enquired.

The guard hesitated.

'The worst, Father, but I'm not free to say.'

'I'd like to pray with him – or for him', he added, sensing this might be the ultimate prison tragedy.

'Too late for the last rites, Father'.

Oliver felt sick at heart.

'Please take me to his cell', said Oliver. 'I am closely connected with him'.

His tone of voice, combined with his priestly appearance, worked. The guard led Oliver through several locked doors and up into the appropriate level of cells. The prisoners had disappeared as if by magic on the urgent orders of the officers, and many would have been shaken by the news of another suicide. They might not show it, but they felt it all-right, and it tapped into the desperation they probably all felt in the dark watches of the night.

Oliver went up to the cell door, which was open. He hovered outside, then, taking a breath to steady himself, took a step inside. The prison doctor was covering Gary up with one of his bed sheets, and two guards were mopping up the pool of blood around him, their clothes saturated in red.

'You're too late', the doctor said matter-of-factly to Oliver, 'This young man died about fifteen minutes ago. He made several slashes in each wrist. He meant business all-right. Severed both arteries'.

Oliver cautiously went up to the body of Gary Johnson and shut his eyes, putting a hand on the shroud.

'Into thy hands oh Lord we commend your servant Gary. May he rest in peace and rise in glory'.

Lying on the floor by the body was the photo of Lucy, which the doctor had removed from Gary's shirt when listening to his chest for any signs of life. The photograph was smeared with blood and had been tossed aside in the emergency of the situation. The innocent child smiled happily up from the photo as she held out the soft white toy. Oliver went to pick up the photo.

'No, sir, don't touch it. We'll need it as evidence at the enquiry'.

Just then, the prison chaplain came quietly into the cell. She acknowledged Oliver with a quick smile and then went straight up to the guards. She put her hands on one of the guard's shoulders,

'Are you all-right, fellas? A nasty shock for you, I'm afraid'.

They acknowledged her briefly.

'Hi Elaine. You're right there, poor bugger'.

The chaplain was clearly a friend to them.

'Never gets easier, does it?' she said.

'He didn't give the impression of being at the end of his tether', said one guard. Mind you, we couldn't get a word out of him most of the time'.

'I couldn't get through to him either when I saw him for our chats. I reported to the Psychiatrist that I thought he was probably deeply depressed, poor fellow. If only he'd *talked',* she sighed, shaking her head. 'Poor fellow', she repeated. 'He'd disappeared inside himself, out of reach'.

What none of them knew was that Gary Johnson had intended to hang himself with his beloved dog's lead immediately after slashing his wrists. That original plan was thwarted by the banning of the lead by the guards before it ever reached his prison cell. Had Gary succeeded, there would have been an even more gruesome trauma for everyone to contend with.

Within minutes, the paramedics arrived with a stretcher, and the body of Gary Johnson, age twenty-three, of no fixed abode, was lifted gently onto it and began its tragic journey to the mortuary.

It gradually impinged on Oliver's consciousness that the emergency bell had not stopped ringing in twenty minutes. How quickly the mind filters our irrelevancies at times of trauma, he thought, and the John Donne phrase became engraved on his mind and was to take up residence there for the next few weeks:

'Ask not for whom the bell tolls; it tolls for thee',

He tried without success to replace it with '*Rest in peace and rise in glory',* but it refused to take root.

Chapter 34

Oliver and the prison chaplain, the Rev'd Elaine Winters, took a simple funeral service in the prison chapel, followed by the briefest of committals at the local crematorium. Oliver found Elaine a compassionate person with a healthy streak of no-nonsense about her, and he ruminated on what a very special calling prison chaplaincy work was. The only people who attended the fifteen-minute service were Maria Murphy, Hope, Robbie, and, at his insistence, Peter, Oliver's son. Needless to say, the entire family had taken the news of Gary's death with sorrowful hearts, and each in his or her particular way felt a guilt and remorse that no-one in the family, and particularly not they themselves, had been able to reach Gary to save him. Both individual and corporate guilt seemed often to be the legacy left after a case of suicide.

Maria Murphy felt this particularly acutely. Having seen Gary in St. Bernard's before he was transferred to Wandsworth prison, she had sensed he was in John Bunyon's 'Slough of Despond': a deep, dark mire of depression and perhaps an utter self-loathing, disguised in Gary's case under a bluff exterior and almost nonchalant manner. She had written an in-depth report about this to the prison psychiatrist, but since Gary had been moved to the prison, she had not followed his progress. So taken up was she with her new daughter and grandchild that she had quite successfully obliterated him from her shorter-than-usual list of anxieties. Now, the guilt was kicking in, and it made her think hard.

Maria returned to her flat in Rotherhithe to have some space and think. She stayed up late, turning events over and over in her mind and weeping inwardly about the sad ending of Gary, whom she felt strongly she had failed to help.

In the vicarage in Southwark, Oliver also stayed up late. Although desperately tired, his head was swirling and images of men mopping up blood with large cloths saturated in red, accompanied by the sound of a bell that rang incessantly. Impinged on his brain was the image of the plywood coffin with a simple spray of white roses sent by the family on top of it and, one small bunch of autumn harebells picked by Hope and Lucy with a tiny pink rosebud in the middle and a label saying 'Love from Lucy x'. Added to this was Oliver's version of a musical earworm - the phrase, 'For whom the bell tolls, It tolls for thee'- slowly driving him to distraction. Oliver prayed long and hard for Gary's soul. He drew out a hymnbook from the overloaded bookshelf and turned to the hymn that always spoke to Him:

There's a wideness in God's mercy like the wideness of the sea.

There's a kindness in God's justice, which is more than liberty.

He scribbled it out on his notepad and fixed it onto the pin board above his desk, and then finally went to bed. The babies were now in their own room. Connie had begun supplementing their ten p.m. feed with a little cereal. It had worked like a dream, and both little boys were finally sleeping most mornings till around six a.m. Oliver finally went to bed, snuggled down on his side with Connie and put one leg over hers. She turned and put her arms round him.

'Oli. What you been doing? Come here, darling'.

She kissed him tenderly, starting with his forehead, then his cheeks, then his lips.

'It's been pretty challenging for you, Oli. I love you so much. I'm so lucky to have you. Thank God we found each other. Would this help you to relax, my love?' she said, stroking his chest gently.

'Oh, Con. You always know. I always said you were an angel.'

He rolled over and kissed her before they gave themselves to each other in love, temporarily blotting out the traumas and replacing them with the delights of healing, tender lovemaking.

Miraculously, the babies were not awake at seven o'clock, and Oliver and Connie lay entwined in each other's arms until then. Finally realising the time, Connie crept out of bed to check on them. Oliver tiptoed after her, and together, arms around each other, they gazed at their beautiful, still-sleeping sons, and thanked God for His goodness.

Maria Murphy had no such comfort.

xxxxx

Since Gary's untimely death, it had felt wrong to Maria to keep the secret that Hope and she shared. Maria was becoming so much part of the family and now, too, uniting with them in their grief. Waiting to announce things at a big family Christmas party somehow no longer felt appropriate. She voiced these feelings to Hope. Hope had been thinking along those lines, too, so the decision was easy. They would let the initial shock of Gary's death pass and then share their news. Peter particularly seemed very distressed by the trauma of the death. He could not yet process it sufficiently to move on but kept talking over and over again to Maria about it. He had also developed something Maria realised was mild Tourette's Syndrome. During patches of acute anxiety, Peter's tendency to shake his hands and wrists in a flapping motion became worse. When Peter heard about Gary's death, albeit gently from Oliver, his initial reaction was disbelief and apparent unconcern, but the following day when he came down to breakfast, he was flapping his hands and asking a myriad of questions very rapidly. In addition, he was jerking his head repetitively. Maria drew alongside him as much as she could, and Peter gradually began to open up to her about his feelings. Maria felt marginally apprehensive about his confidences, as her sensitivities told her that it began to feel to her as though she was intruding into the family territory. The sooner everyone knew she was Hope's mother, the better.

She realised the matter had to be handled delicately; after all, she was the reason that their father had missed several army 'leaves'. When he could have been with his pregnant wife and young son in England, he instead was cavorting and having a full-blooded sexual relationship with a girl of nineteen – Maria – or Erin, as she was then - over in Ireland. She was not proud of this and knew that it would hurt the family deeply when they found out. This was their father she was talking about – warts and all, but still *their* father. She must not rely on their unfailing goodness that she had witnessed again and again. That wasn't fair. That was taking advantage. No. She had to come clean and ask for *their* forgiveness. She realised *she* was the outcast, with no Connors nor Lockwood blood running through her veins and therefore had absolutely no right to expect acceptance automatically; in fact, they might just turn against her.

The more she thought about it, the more difficult and thorny it all seemed to become. She decided initially to talk to Oliver in his role as pastor and spiritual director and seek his advice on how best to approach it with the family. Oliver was curious when Maria asked to see him in his 'professional capacity'. He wondered if it was about her growing relationship with his sister-in-law Hope. Sadie Connors had, by finding a same-sex partner to love, forced him to think deeply about his own views on homosexual relationships. Was he going to have to travel that road again? He hoped not, but he feared so, as the Anglican Church was very clear about its teachings on the subject.

Chapter 35

Maria was welcomed fulsomely by Connie and immediately drawn into the large vicarage kitchen, the hub of the home, where Rosy was drawing, and Ben and Joseph were each in a baby rocker chair, kicking and gurgling happily.

'Cup of tea, Maria? I've been meaning to give you a ring. We are so grateful for your insights into Peter, you know. He really trusts you'.

'He's a great lad', replied Maria. 'How has he been this week?'

'Better, since he opened up to you, Maria. The flapping is slightly more under control'.

Phew. That was something to be very grateful for. It was clear that Connie had nothing but goodwill towards Maria. Maria bent down and talked to each baby, taking their little fists and feeling their fingers curl trustingly round hers. This was something Gary had almost certainly been deprived of from the very beginning. Mother's love was unique and irreplaceable. As little Ben held tightly onto her finger and gazed up at her with trusting blue eyes, smiling and kicking furiously, she thought suddenly of her own mother again. Presumably, she must have held her baby's fist and let her cling onto her finger, and presumably, she had delighted in it. It had all gone so wrong with her parents – long before she had started her affair with Albert Connors. Even now, she could feel a sense of claustrophobia when she thought about her home life.

Breaking into her thoughts, Oliver swung into the kitchen carrying a cricket bat. It was his day off, and he had been with Peter and a friend at Southwark Cricket Club grounds, a stone's throw from the vicarage.

'He cuts quite a dashing figure', thought Maria. 'Good job, he has a nice secure marriage. The ladies of the parish would be vying for him otherwise. Maybe they are anyway,' she thought sardonically.

'Come on, Maria. Bring your tea into my study. Sorry, I'm a bit late.'

She waved his apology aside and followed him.

'Have a seat. I'm just going to get a jug of water. Hot work playing, my son! He's pretty good, in between the expletives and the flapping!' Oliver laughed.

While he was gone, Maria wandered up to the pinboard above the desk. She read,

'There's a wideness in God's mercy like the wideness of the sea,

There's a kindness in God's justice which is more than liberty'.

'I don't know about God—a wideness in the *family's* mercy would do for me just now', she thought.

Oliver returned and placed the jug of water chinking with ice cubes and two glasses next to a box of tissues.

'This is a great quotation, Oliver. Is it from the Bible?'

'No. It's a hymn'.

'It's a very generous view of God', she smiled. 'Not at all like the one I was brought up with. That was about all punishment for sins and, as far as I remember, eternal damnation for non-believers. That would be me done for, for a start!'

Oliver laughed but did not continue the conversation. There would be time enough to have a theological discussion, but at the moment, he was intent on getting to the nub of Maria's request to see him. Sitting opposite him, she smoothed her pale blue cashmere jumper down and ran her fingers nervously through her well-groomed blonde hair.

'I don't know where to start', said Maria, and that was the truth.

'Take your time, Maria. There's no rush'

How often had she longed to say that to her clients, but the NHS was justifiably so often ruled by the clock and anxiety about the next appointment. But Oliver was eating into his precious day off, so she marshalled her thoughts as best she could.

'Oliver. This is going to come as a bit of a shock,' she started.

'Here we go.' thought Oliver, 'Try to keep an open mind'.

Maria had rehearsed various opening sentences, strange for one so fluent, but in the end, she simply blurted out,

'I'm Hope's mother!'

Silence.

Later, Oliver went over his inner reactions. The first, he decided, had been a feeling of sheer relief. The second was a total surprise, and the third was a kind of joy. Yes, joy. This lovely lady, so wise, so compassionate, so warm, so easy, belonged officially to their family!

'Maria', he stumbled finally. 'Now *I* don't know what to say!'

Finally, Maria replied.

'I have to rely on Connie's and Bruce's understanding and forgiveness. And Sadie's, although I haven't met her'.

'Why forgiveness?' replied Oliver, genuinely mystified.

'Don't you see? Their father was – also the father of my Hope. He was....' she spoke in a whisper, '....my lover, and I am the reason he betrayed his family'.

Oliver was a bright man and a wise man, but it took him more than a few seconds for the penny to drop and for him to see the enormity of the situation Maria had just presented him with. Maria continued in a rush, her words tripping over each other.

'I was seventeen. Albert Connors came into my life, made me feel good about myself, seemed to make up in some way for all the negativity I had received from my parents, and,' she paused, holding her emotions in tight check, 'I fell for him. That's what happened, pure and simple: I fell for him. When I found out he was married, I was horrified, but I still went on doing it. It was nice and brought excitement into my life. I enjoyed having a secret. I felt like the scarlet woman, and Oliver, I loved it.

'I don't suppose you've done anything like that, Oliver', she continued, 'but let me tell you, the instinct both to be loved and wanted, hand in hand with the sex drive, is unbearably and irresistibly strong. It was far too strong for me'.

Oliver was silent. He knew exactly what Maria was talking about. He had been totally infatuated with Clara, Bruce's wife, seventeen years ago and, in those moments of self-abandonment and passion, didn't care that she was a married woman; didn't care that he had taken a self-imposed vow of celibacy before God. It was totally irrelevant in the passion of the moment.

Maria looked down and said in a whisper, 'The sex was pretty irresistible, and I didn't care that he was married, and of course, then I found I was pregnant'. She paused, and her lips grew tighter, and her face hardened.

'He became angry, and then he abused me. He was physically violent, and the last time he made love to me if you could call it that, was out of anger and abuse, not love. It was vile. It was more like rape'.

She shuddered at the memory.

'He was a very cruel man, as it turned out. In the process, I ended up with a couple of broken ribs, but that was nothing compared to the sense of shame and abandonment I felt'.

Oliver knew a lot about Albert Connors and how he had abused his family and driven one of his children to suicide with his intense bullying. He knew that the effect of his sexual abuse on his youngest daughter, Connie, had taken years of loving reassurance in the marriage for her to overcome the emotional damage. He had also learned that Sadie's beloved disabled son was the result of her father's sexual abuse of her. Oh yes, he knew about Albert Connors all-right. He had both sensed and witnessed the depths of their emotional resources Connie and her brother had had to plumb in order to forgive him at the end of his life. Sadie had never reached that point.

Oliver leaned over to Maria and put his hand on hers. In that moment, he wanted to tell Maria everything: about his falling from grace, his infatuation with Clara and the pain that followed. Maria had both a natural and a professional empathy that attracted honesty. But this was about Maria, not about him. Another day, he would share everything with her. He knew he would.

She continued, encouraged by his reassuring hand.

'My parents disowned me, disgraced by me, they said, so booked me into a mother and baby home. I was told my baby had died at birth, and in effect, I was thrown out of both the home and by my parents. I haven't seen them since, and I have no desire to', she said.

As she said these last words, she thought again that they were probably dead. Certainly they would both be well into their eighties. She caught her breath. She had never actually thought of them *dead* before. An imperceptible shudder passed through her.

'I moved to England, not knowing a soul. I changed my name from Erin O'Neil to Maria Murphy, undertook a long medical training financed with guilt money from my parents, and in the course of my work, met Gary Johnson, who was in a mess after his dog had died. He gave the game away over Lucy Grace Erin O'Neill, and I followed her up'.

She paused and looked up, smiling through tears.

'Discovering Hope was the best day of my life,' she said quietly, '- beyond my wildest dream. And little Lucy. I thank God every day for them, even though I've never believed in Him.' She smiled wryly up, adding, 'But, I have to tell you, Oliver, that I'm reviewing the situation....'

Oliver was deeply moved. It was he now who needed the tissues. Finally, he said,

'Maria, tell them your story just like you have told me. There is no-one in this family who will not welcome you with open arms. I can promise you that. It's wonderful.' He said quietly. 'It reminds me of a verse I love from the story of the Prodigal Son:

'For this child of mine was dead and is alive again; was lost and is found. And they began to celebrate'.

'We need to celebrate this, Maria, we really do'.

Chapter 36

Maria was intent on following Oliver's advice to the letter. She telephoned Bruce and asked him if he could spare half an hour, and Kitty too if she could manage it. Connie was full of curiosity about it, but Oliver kept Maria's secret although he was burning to share it with his wife.

On the allotted afternoon, Maria, Hope, Connie, Robbie and Oliver were assembled in the sitting room. It suddenly felt very formal as they waited for Bruce and Kitty to arrive. The last time they had been together like this was after Gary's funeral when Connie provided sandwiches and tea to soothe them.

'Here's Uncle Brucie', cried Rosy, who had been on 'lookout' in the front garden on a chilly November day. 'Hi Uncle Brucie – and Kit-eKat!' she shouted. Bruce and Kitty waved back in unison.

They all watched Bruce lock his car and walk up the vicarage steps with Kitty. Connie was shocked at her brother's appearance. He had lost a considerable amount of weight in six weeks, partly from the trauma over Kitty and partly because of Clara. They came to the front door and were bombarded by Rosy.

'Uncle Brucie, Uncle Brucie!' she said, leaping into his outstretched arms.

'Hello, angel face. How are you surviving all your brothers?!'

'Hi, Rosy', said Kitty, ruffling her hair playfully.

Rosy laughed.

'Jamie comes home for the weekend tomorrow. I can't wait to see him. He always plays Cluedo with me, and I'm *much* better than him! Where's Auntie Clara?' she asked, barely taking a breath between the two subjects.

'She's busy with her play, Rosy', he replied.

'Doesn't she do *anything* else?!' asked Rosy, spreading her arms theatrically, hitting the proverbial nail on the head.

Oliver heard the conversation and intercepted.

'Bruce. Kitty. Good to see you. Come in. Cup of tea? Coffee? Beer?'

Bruce and Kitty were greeted by the others, and Connie gave him a special hug. He had always been her soul mate, especially when they were young children arming themselves against their bullying father. Connie surveyed Kitty. She was looking good, almost, she thought, as though she had not had a major operation to remove a lung. The resilience of youth! It was lovely to see her with roses in her cheeks. Robbie moved nearer to Kitty. Theirs was a relationship wrought in the early days when Robbie was newly out of prison, and Kitty was small and coping with the side effects of chemotherapy. It had always been special. Often, lately, Robbie wished it could be something more special. He loved Kitty's kindness and warmth and what he called her 'sparkiness'. He knew, though, with a sixteen-year age gap between them it was never going to happen, and anyway, Kitty had never shown any more signs towards him than a kind of loving brotherly affection. He took her hand and kissed it briefly. She smiled.

'This is all very mysterious', said Bruce. 'I'm burning with curiosity'.

'Maria, do you want to make a start?' asked Oliver.

And so the great unburdening and revelation of Maria Murphy took place. Hope did not interrupt but made sure she sat next to her mother. The family was silent as they absorbed the news. When Maria had finally finished, the silence continued, then, one by one, led by Connie, each went up in their own time to Maria and then Hope and hugged them long and hard. Both Maria and Hope were weeping, and others were not far off.

Finally, Bruce raised his beer glass.

'I'd like to propose a toast. Please raise your cups of tea, beer mug or whatever and toast out wonderful new family member: Maria Murphy. Maria, we are privileged to have you in our midst. 'To Maria and her fantastic daughter Hope''.

They all raised their cups and glasses,

'To Maria and her fantastic daughter Hope!'

Oliver sidled up to Maria.

'What did I tell you, Maria?'.

She smiled at him.

'You were right, Oliver', she whispered, then 'Thank you, thank you, everyone. This is the special family that I could never, in my most extravagant dreams, have ever thought would become a reality.'

Bruce started talking, his face serious and lined.

'Maria, our dad behaved disgracefully towards you. I must say that your affair was not exactly a good thing, but no-one could condone our father's behaviour. Let me tell you something. It is only because of Connie's devotion and forgiveness that our father died in peace. For me, my forgiveness for him came too late, but thanks to Oliver and Robbie here, I became reconciled to my father, but I apologise to you on behalf of him, Maria', he added at the end rather formally.

Maria nodded through her tears, and Hope held her mother's hand.

'And' Bruce continued, 'We would never have had our half-sister Hope, who has brought us all a whole load of joy'.

'Bottle this moment', thought Connie. 'This is very precious'.

Oliver's phone pinged. A text. As it was a working day for him, he went aside and accessed the text:

'Hi Rev. I need to talk to you. Please read the email. Clara'.

Oliver's heart sank, and he groaned inwardly. He did not want to be a go-between counsellor between Bruce and his wife. They all had a history, and it was not good for Oliver to take on this role. Connie was still a bit fragile from the birth of the babies and her emergency hysterectomy – not physically, but she was more emotional than usual, and Clara was definitely not her favourite topic of conversation at the best of times.

After everyone had gone, all having been warmed and gladdened by the news of the expanded family, Oliver helped Connie feed one baby while she fed the other, and then he went to his study. He retrieved Clara's email with some trepidation.

Hi, there Rev,

I need to talk to you. I expect you know all about Bruce's ultimatum to me. Very harsh and unexpected.

I need to talk to my very favourite vicar and counsellor. Book me a slot? Show going OK but they are dumping me for the London run. No idea why. Not good news. Clara.

Oliver wasn't sure how to squeeze out of this one. He felt duty-bound to see Clara in his official capacity and as a friend and member of the family, but Clara always spelt danger in his life, especially when she was needy. He talked to Connie about it at the first opportunity and showed her the email. There must be no secrets whatever between them as far as the subject of Clara Connors was concerned.

'Why would they drop Clara from the London run?' said Connie, baffled. 'She's got rave reviews everywhere'.

'I've no idea, except that Kitty said her mum was drinking far too much'.

'Hmm. You'd better see her, Oli'.

'Are you sure, Clara? I don't want you upset'.

'Oli, of course. We trust each other, don't we? Mind you, I don't trust *her'*, she said with a grimace. 'Remind me to be out when she comes,'

A more worldly wise woman may have said, 'Remind me when she comes to be *in'*......

Oliver replied to Clara giving her a couple of dates to choose from around midday time so that she would have time to drive up and back to Chichester for the evening performance.

Chapter 37

The next day, Connie collected Jamie from King's Cross station. She was desperate to escape from the house for a while, so, having made sure the babies were well fed, with an extra spoonful of cereal in each bottle for good measure, she left them sleeping upstairs with a baby alarm on so that Rosy and Oliver would hear them. Oliver had said he would be in as he had a sermon to prepare.

As Connie drove across to the station, she suddenly burst into tears. She really didn't know why. It was just that life seemed overwhelming. The news of Hope's mother, Maria, was wonderful and terrible at the same time. She had put aside all her feelings of anger towards her father and reacted genuinely joyfully to Maria. Now, though, finally on her own – no babies, no Rosie, no worrying about her son Peter, no Oliver, no parish demands – purely on her own, she had time to think and react uninhibitedly.

She would never forget her father creeping into her room late at night and pulling up her winceyette nightdress to do his disgusting deed when she was just six years old. She remembered the barley sugar afterwards, and being told it was 'their little secret'. Did he even then still have a teenage mistress somewhere in the country whom he visited? And what about her own mother? She thought of her dear, dear mother, far too passive for her own good, tolerating all things to keep a roof over her head for her four children. Her mother was an angel, but a passive one, carved more in alabaster than in fire. Connie's tears flowed. She hardly knew how to cope with the sudden solitude, and the car felt like a soothing cradle as she negotiated it through the London traffic without a qualm. Life was good, life was fulfilled, but my goodness, life was *tiring* and it was complex. A sense of deep fatigue washed over her. She felt she could sleep for a month, given half the chance. She knew she must be very careful not to fall asleep at the wheel.

Now there was Clara rearing her ugly head again in Oliver's life, except it wasn't an ugly head; it was a very, very beautiful head with the most amazing flowing chestnut hair. That was part of the trouble. Connie ran the fingers of one hand through her own hair. It needed a wash, but she simply hadn't had time in the last week to do it. It could do with a bit of brightening. She felt drab, ugly and unlovable. Connie was teetering on the brink of post-natal and post-operative depression.

She arrived at the station, found a parking space relatively easily and walked towards the train from Cambridge platform. Jamie had been away six weeks - not long, but in a completely changed environment. Would he have changed at all? The train was due in ten minutes. Connie bought a takeaway coffee and sat, stemming the tears and remaining in a sad, reflective mood that she could not shake off, waiting to greet her son.

The train was on time, and suddenly, as if a switch had turned inside her head, Connie felt a rush of excitement about seeing her firstborn son. Jamie had become a trifle arrogant and know-all at times, but he was still an easy boy and always had been. She saw a figure in the distance alight from a carriage at the back of the train. She knew it was Jamie because he was so like Oliver! He had the same slightly meandering walk, the same hair on the long side swished into a side parting and looking marginally scruffy. She squashed up to the ticket barrier. Jamie saw her and waved. Connie's heart missed a beat. He was so handsome in a quirky kind of way; so *Oliver!*

They had a wonderful journey home, with Jamie talking nineteen to the dozen about Cambridge life and the friends he had made. He had always been open with his mother and loved her company.

'Ratio of blokes to girls is still a bit poor, Mum'.

Connie laughed.

'Is that your way of saying you need a girlfriend, Jamie?'

'Desperate, Mum!' he laughed.

‘There’ll be someone special for you, Jamie, don’t you fret’, She paused. ‘I’ve never heard you say anything like that before.’

‘Well, the blokes on either side of my room have both got girlfriends, and I hear them groaning away doing you-know-what sometimes. I’m jealous, that’s all’, he laughed. ‘Also, quite a few blokes are gay, so at least they’re out of the competition!’

Connie laughed.

‘My goodness, Jamie, so worldly wise so quickly!’

‘Well, Mum, you must admit Dad is narrow in that respect. You’d have thought that Auntie Sadie’s cavorting with her lady partner would have broadened him out a bit. By the way, how are those little brothers of mine?’

Connie was relieved he had changed the subject. She was intensely loyal always to Oliver, and she too had not found her sister Sadie’s choice of partner easy to come to terms with either, although she delighted in her happiness.

‘They are lovely. You’ll notice a big change in them, Jamie. They are very happy little people, thank goodness’.

‘Then tell me why you’ve been crying, Mum’, Jamie said.

Chapter 38

Oliver had booked to see Clara in his study at four-thirty the following Wednesday afternoon. He had a Finance Meeting at 5.30 in the church office, so that would give him a good cut-off point. Connie was delivering Rosy to a party and then going shopping in Southwark with the babies in their double pram. Peter was doing his holiday job stacking up shelves in B&Q, and Jamie was around and about, enjoying being home for a couple of days, raiding the larder and the 'fridge at frequent intervals and using the washing machine.

Oliver was apprehensive about the meeting with Clara. His loyalties were firmly with his brother-in-law Bruce. Years ago, when Kitty's paternity was in question, Bruce had shown incredible graciousness. He had worked at loving Kitty from the moment she was born, even though she may have been Oliver's daughter, and during the first three years grew to adore her as a natural father.

As fate would have it (or God, Oliver had emphatically said), the results of blood and marrow tests had proved conclusively that, in fact, Bruce was the natural father. The Consultant had told them in plain black and white, no-nonsense terms that despite Bruce's inability to reach an orgasm in the early days when making love to Clara, some sperm had escaped.

Statistically, he had said, it was very rare for a woman to conceive in this way, but certainly not impossible. It felt like a total miracle when Bruce discovered he was Kitty's natural father, although it had left Oliver feeling strangely bereft. He owed a huge debt of gratitude to Bruce for the way he had handled the whole scenario. In the beginning, the two had been distant from each other, but over the years, their relationship had become easier, so that now each would regard the other not only as a brother-in-law but also as a friend.

Despite this regard for Bruce, on a second occasion, Oliver had found himself within a whisker of succumbing to Clara's overt seduction techniques and was only saved in the nick of time by a sudden telephone call informing him that Connie was dangerously ill with an ectopic pregnancy. He learnt quickly from that moment on (as if he had not known it already) that he had feet of clay just as described in the book of Daniel in the Bible, certainly as far as Clara was concerned at the very least.

Now, sitting in his study, he was not at all happy to think the Temptress was about to spend time alone with him, whatever her pretext. Oliver was secure in his total love for Connie and knew he had grown both in maturity and wisdom since the last encounter several years ago. Nevertheless, Clara had remained a source of troublesome enticement to him; the proverbial thorn in his side; his Achilles Heel. He wished she would never darken his door again.

Three rings on the bell. Oliver answered the front door, and there she was: as usual with a slinky black top on that outlined her lovely shape, a colourful flowing gypsy skirt, big silver hoop earrings and ethnic-style thonged sandals. Her glowing hair was caught up at each side with two large tortoiseshell slides, leaving the rest to flow nearly to her waist. It had to be said that she was a vision of loveliness even to the least susceptible pair of eyes.

'Hi Rev', she said, using the name she had cheekily called him when they first met at Richmond Theatre. 'How you doing with your tribe, then?'

'O.K. thanks Clara; fine really'.

'Where's the lovely Connie then?' asked Clara.

'She's out with Rosy and the babies'.

Was that a slight smile that crossed Clara's lips?

'Sit down, Clara. Let's get down to business. What can I do for you?'

'Ooh, very formal, Rev'. she said with a coquettish smile.

'Well, you've come to discuss an issue, haven't you, Clara?'

‘I have. You will have guessed it’s about Bruce. This is the thing. He’s acting totally unreasonably. Doesn’t want me in the house, won’t talk to me, seems to think *I’ve* been the unreasonable one’.

‘Do you think you have, Clara?’

‘What, because I’ve pursued my career? Don’t I have a right after all this time of patiently taking on minor roles? Now I have a lead, he can’t take it! Very much sour grapes, if you ask me’.

‘Wasn’t it about Kitty’s stabbing and your response to it?’ Oliver asked, knowing full well that this was the straw that broke the camel’s back as far as Bruce was concerned.

‘Kitty was in good hands with Bruce, Oliver. It wasn’t as though she had no-one with her at the hospital. I was in a difficult position’.

Oliver was quiet. He could not understand how Clara had not been desperate to be by her daughter’s side when she seemed to be at death’s door, but it was not his place to voice this. This would be questioning her motherhood, and he knew would stir up a hornet’s nest of fury if he tiptoed down that avenue.

‘Surely you see that Oli, surely? You’re a reasonable man, aren’t you’, she said, suddenly coming across the room. ‘I’m relying on the lovely Rev to take my side’. She twisted his ear. ‘You always liked this, didn't you?' she said, caressing the lobe of it. 'I remember, and so do you!'

Now Oliver saw what she had really come for. She had always said there was unfinished business between them.

'No, Clara, if you're going to – um – pursue this avenue, I must ask you to leave'.

''Pursue this avenue – *pursue this avenue!'* she retorted scornfully. 'Don't talk to me like that. You and I are made for each other, and you know it'.

'No', said Oliver quietly. 'That is not true. Connie and I are made for each other'.

'Oh yes, she's *safe* for a man of the cloth', she said. 'She's safe, Oli, but this is what *exciting* is. Who wants *safe?'* she said, sliding onto his knee and beginning to kiss him sensually.

Oliver felt the old fatal urge all right, knew he desired her like he always did, and could smell the familiar smell of apples in her hair, but he quickly twisted himself out of the chair.

'Sorry, Clara, but this is not right for either of us. I don't belong to you, nor you to me. I must ask you to leave'.

Just then, there was a brief knock at the door, and James came in.

'Hi, Auntie Clara. I thought I heard you. How you doing? How's the show?'

Quickly, Oliver seized his opportunity. Implying he had received an urgent message on his mobile phone, he said,

'So sorry, Clara. I must be off. Bit of a parish emergency. I'll leave you two to have a chat. Nice seeing you.'

He pecked Clara on the cheek, feigning normality in front of Jamie, who had come in just seconds after Clara had been sitting on his father's knee. With that, Oliver picked up his keys from his desk and waved them breezily, saying,

'I'm off, Jamie. Enjoy your chat.' He exited rapidly, slamming the front door with relief as he went.

'Wow, that was rather abrupt!' said Jamie. 'Not like Dad at all. What happened? You two had words?'

'No, of course not', replied Clara, 'but your father is always in such a *rush*, isn't he?'

Jamie didn't reply but, feeling he must make up a bit for his father's behaviour, asked Clara if she would like a cup of tea. Clara drew a bottle of red wine out of her bag.

'No, but I'll have a corkscrew, Jamie, and bring two glasses. I want to hear *all* about Cambridge'.

Jamie looked across at Clara. She was in her early forties, but she looked twenty-five, he decided, and very sexy and attractive with it. He had always found her interesting company but, for the first time, looked at her as a woman rather than simply his aunt. Confused by the sudden rush of his feelings, he went to the kitchen and fumbled around in the drawer of ramshackle oversized utensils, and eventually found a corkscrew and returned, brandishing it in the air.

'We shall do the deed, Auntie Clara!'

'We shall indeed,' promised Clara ambiguously.

'My goodness, you are so like your dad!' she continued, 'In fact, I'd say pretty much a split image of him. Nice!'

'You're not the first person to say that', replied Jamie, drawing the cork out of the bottle and relieved that he hadn't messed up the procedure. It had slid out smoothly and in one piece. It was important that Auntie Clara approved of him, and he suddenly wished she would see him as more of a man and less of her gauche student nephew which he knew he was. He poured two glasses and carefully handed one to Clara. They had a convivial fifteen minutes talking about Jamie's first five-week experience of college days and then about Clara's show. Clara downed her red wine quickly and poured herself another. Jamie, not wishing to show her that he was actually quite an inexperienced wine drinker, filled his glass up also and downed it rapidly. He poured another glass and topped Clara's up so that the wine bottle was almost empty. Jamie began to feel very mellow indeed.

'Auntie Clara, you look great,' he said. 'I love the skirt. You are amazingly beautiful, you know,' he said, beginning to slur his words.

'Oh Jamie, that is such a sweet thing to say'. She came across the room to where he was standing.

'Now let's put that glass down', she said, taking it and putting it on the coffee table, 'And come here. I need to teach my nephew a few things in preparation for when he finds a girl.'

She put his hand near her breast.

'Count it as your initiation, Jamie,' she slurred.

She kissed him on the lips and lingered there. Jamie was taken by complete surprise, but his body reacted. He was a virile young man and full of vigour. He did not feel quite in charge of what was going on.

'Auntie Clara, don't, it's not right, I mean, do you think?.....' he said in a croaky voice, but it was too late. Clara was weaving her spell on Jamie, and he felt himself losing control.

'Everyone's out, Jamie. Come on. Don't be afraid. It's easy,' she said and proceeded to use all her female wiles on Jamie, who had no sexual experience to date but was learning fast.

'It's good to have an experienced teacher for your first time – it *is* your first time, isn't it, Jamie?'

Jamie didn't answer, couldn't answer. His mouth and throat were dry, and his heart was thumping wildly. Clara pulled him down onto the sofa, realising that it was the very same sofa that she had made love on with Oliver that first time all those years ago. Now, that was an exciting thought!

Halfway through, Clara murmured in Jamie's ear,

'Like father, like son, oh yes'.

Jamie heard Clara but was too far gone to question her. He was deeply roused. Clara writhed under him, and very soon, sooner than Jamie intended, it happened.

In two minutes, the front door slammed, and Connie called out,

'Hi Oli, Hi Jamie. We're back!'

She left the sleeping boys in the pushchair and came breezing into Oliver's study. She felt quite liberated from having a few hours around the shops and buying one or two little clothes items for the babies. Suddenly, she stopped in her tracks like a car slamming on its brakes and skidding violently before crashing.

'What? WHAT?' she screamed. She raced over to the sofa and pulled Jamie off Clara with all her might.

'GET OFF HER!' she yelled. She put her face very close to Clara's, screaming,

'You're a WHORE. First, my husband, now my son. GET OUT OF MY HOUSE!'

Jamie, acutely embarrassed by his fast-collapsing manhood and being caught in the act by his mother, pulled his trousers up and moved swiftly out of the room. Clara lay spread-eagled on the sofa and began to pull her skirt down from up around her waist, her bikini briefs out of reach across the room where she had tossed them. She sat up and coolly put her top on and finally said to Connie, who was shaking violently,

'Connie, it's time you lived in the real world. It happens all the time, and your boy was needing an initiation into what it's all about. He's a bit too innocent for his own good. Your vicarage has always been an ivory tower, you know. Your boys need to be shown a thing or two', she said, crossing the room to retrieve her bikini briefs.

Connie, reliably sweet-natured, non-violent, non-aggressive, non-confrontational, ready to turn the other cheek in all situations, flew across the room like a tigress and grabbed Clara by the hair, clawing and scratching her face hard.

'You whore! You bitch! Get out of my house and never come back!'

Clara's face started bleeding profusely. She was profoundly shocked by Connie's physical eruption and, picking up her bag, swiftly left the room. As she opened the front door, she sneered through gritted teeth,

'You're nothing but a little Christian mouse, Connie. How on earth can Oliver be satisfied with such a frigid little goody-goody? No wonder he came to me'.

With that, she was gone, leaving Connie curled up in a ball in the hall and sobbing. On her way out, Clara bumped into Oliver as he was coming up the steps to the porch of the vicarage.

'Clara, whatever's happened?' he said, seeing the blood on her face. He drew out a clean handkerchief from his pocket.

'You're bleeding!' he said as he started to dab the scratches

'That ridiculous bitch of a wife of yours! She's mad, Oli. A lunatic. She should be locked up. You'll need a straitjacket for her', Clara screamed.

Oliver left Clara immediately to her own devices and rushed into the house. Both the babies were screaming in their pram. To his horror, he saw Connie curled up on the floor in the hall, rocking and sobbing violently.

'Darling, darling, - whatever's happened?' He cradled her in his arms, kissing her forehead and gently moving her hair out of her eyes strand by strand. She continued sobbing. Jamie was coming slowly down the stairs, white as a ghost and clearly had also been crying.

'It's all my fault, Dad', he said very softly, 'It's me. I've caused this'.

Oliver led Connie into the kitchen. He barked an instruction at Jamie,

'Jamie, see to the babies. Now! Wheel them around or something. We can't have Mum in this state. There are two dummies in the fridge. Mum hates using them, but I can't help that. It's an emergency'.

Still, Connie cried and shook. Jamie acted quickly, doing anything he could to redeem himself even a little. He unceremoniously thrust a dummy in each of the babies' mouths and walked them up and down the hall, still shaking from the trauma of it all.

Finally, Connie calmed down. Oliver fetched some kitchen roll, ran it under the cold tap and gently dabbed her face. He then put the kettle on and went back to Connie, kneeled beside her and put his head in her lap.

'Connie, please tell me what's been going on. Clara was bleeding out there. What's happened'.

Connie gradually took some deep breaths and spoke haltingly between intermittent sobs.

'Clara – Jamie – I found them together – on the sofa'.

At first, Oliver didn't understand, and then the truth dawned on him. *His* son had been seduced by Clara? How dare she? The nerve, the audacity of the woman! Their son, in a sexual encounter with her? It was more than dreadful! Oliver was incandescent with rage.

After a couple of minutes, however, Oliver, being Oliver, activated his sense of justice and began to modify his thinking. He realised that Jamie would have been tempted beyond endurance by Clara just as he had been once (and almost a second time). His son, though, had to take his fair share of responsibility for his behaviour. He could have said no, just as he himself could have done. He also knew how impossible that seemed when the passion of the moment took over and how totally alluring Clara was.

Jamie left the babies, now temporarily pacified, and crept up to Connie and Oliver, kneeling beside them. He tentatively took his mother's hand, but she pulled it away.

'Go away, James. 'Don't come near me', she said, turning her face away from him. He looked at his Dad with pleading eyes.

'Dad. Sorry. It just seemed to happen. I couldn't do anything else. Clara is overwhelming'.

Oliver knew that. He briefly touched his son's hand.

'Go for a walk to cool off, Jamie, and don't come back for an hour', he said authoritatively. 'There's some complicated unravelling to be done here'.

Chapter 39

Clara staggered down the vicarage steps, fumbled for her keys, unlocked her car, lurched into the driver's seat, turned the ignition, stalled the engine, turned it again, looked in her mirror, saw the scratches and cried angrily.

She sat outside the vicarage for many minutes, thinking that Oliver would come and find her after he had comforted that whimpish wife of his, but he did not. Maybe Jamie would have the grace and courage to take her side and see how she was? He did not come out either. She suddenly thought of Bruce. Feeling an urgent need for his all-enveloping, comforting arms, she wondered if she should head to their home in Richmond to see him, but she was due in Chichester in two hours' time for the warm-up and notes before the evening performance. She knew she was drunk, but was in such a devil-may-care mood that she eventually drove off and somehow, more by luck than judgement, reached the A3. She did actually drive very slowly, knowing that if she was breathalysed she would fail miserably and be banned from driving for at least a year.

Clara acknowledged to herself that what she had done was unwise and foolish, to say the least. She had badly wanted Oliver, but clearly, he was out of reach, so in order to punish him, she turned to Jamie and blatantly seduced him. She had hoped that it would be Oliver who had come in and found them in the act, but it had to be Connie, didn't it? Clara had for years been jealous of Connie. Oliver belonged to Connie, not to her, and what's more, was devoted to his wife, even if he had slipped up with Clara herself some years previously. As far as she was concerned, it was definitely unfinished business. She knew that if she caught him in the right mood – vulnerable, stressed, needy – he would be hers, if only for half an hour. She would *not* give up; she announced to herself as she was picking up speed on the A27 and hitting seventy. She saw a police car behind with its blue lights flashing and held her breath, but it went steaming past her on the outside lane to some emergency or other.

Clara reached the theatre, parked the car and slightly swayed through the stage door. She was late. The warm-up had begun. Clara always found these physical and vocal warm-ups the height of tedium. Could she slip in without being seen? Of course, she couldn't. She was the female lead. Her absence would already have been noted and would be causing some consternation.

The company director, youngish, tense, wiry, volatile, with long, prematurely greying hair tied back, saw her hovering in the wings.

'Clara Connors! You're *late!'* he barked over the sound of the vocal exercises. The performers would not have heard him, but Clara did. She went over.

'I'm sorry, Hugo. The traffic was dreadful'.

He looked hard at her.

'NO more warnings, Clara. And how much have you consumed tonight already? You'd better make this the performance of a lifetime'.

'Don't I always?' said Clara, looking him fully in the eye and feigning coquettishness. It seemed not to work this time on Hugo, although he and Clara had briefly been lovers.

'Get up there and warm up', he said sternly, but as she turned, he flicked her bottom with his notebook. It seemed no-one could quite resist Clara, however angry she might make them.

The first half went well, with Clara on form. During the interval, she slipped into her dressing room and took out the bottle of whisky that was hidden amongst the hairpieces. As she drew it out, it dawned on her for the first time that her dependency on alcohol had become a problem. She poured herself a very generous double whiskey, then another, then a third, and put the bottle back, vowing to herself that she would do something about it - tomorrow.

She started the second half, and it very quickly became clear that Clara was inebriated; clear to the cast, to the company manager, to the musical director and to the audience. Having had two gins with tonic before her encounter with Oliver, then well over half a bottle of red wine with Jamie and finally three generous double whiskeys before the second half of the musical had made her very much the worse for wear. A little into the second half and the beginning of her appropriately titled song '*Don't be Silly, Sally'* found 'Sally' staggering towards the very edge of the stage area, falling, tripping down the shallow steps into the auditorium and straight into the arms of an unsuspecting elderly gentleman. Two members of the stage management team rushed on, quickly pulled Clara back up the steps, and half carried her out. Amidst the consternation of cast, audience and elderly gentleman alike, the company director rapidly ordered a blackout of the lights and was within a few seconds picked out in a bright follow spot as he walked briskly into the centre of the stage and addressed the audience:

'Ladies and Gentlemen, I'm afraid our lead cast member, as you saw, has been taken ill.' (Were they jeers from the audience?). 'The part of Sally Smith will now be taken by Miss Cheryl Sinclair. The second half will commence in ten minutes. We apologise for the inconvenience'.

In the wings, Clara was flustered and confused.

'Sorry, I'm so sorry. I'm OK. It's all-right. I just felt a bit, er, dizzy', she slurred. 'Let the show continue', she pronounced grandly, with a sweep of her hand vaguely in the direction of the stage.

'Go home! You're a disgrace! What's more, you're fired, Miss Clara Connors, prima donna *extraordinaire!*' Hugo, the Company Manager, said, curling his lips. He marched her backstage and into her dressing room.

'Get changed and don't come back. I'll pay you up to last night. Don't darken these doors again. Get yourself to an A.A. group or something. You sure have some thinking to do about your life, Clara. You're a waste of space at the moment. Let's hope there are no critics tonight. I'll explain it all to the director in the morning.'

He slammed the door shut, leaving Clara in a state of shock.

She sat on her stool in the dressing room and stared at her highly made-up face in the mirror, illuminated vividly in the harsh lighting. It dawned on her how grotesque she looked. 'You've done it now', she said aloud to her image. 'That's the end of your career, darling. Hey ho, so that's the way the cookie crumbles!'

Clara packed her bags, spent a few minutes longer gathering her belongings, making sure she took the hidden bottle of whiskey with her, then stumbled through the Green Room and out of the stage door to the street. Normally, after every performance, there would be a crowd brandishing autograph books, programmes, even tee shirts, and thrusting them for autographs under the noses of the still adrenaline-fuelled actors exit-ting the theatre. Not so now for Clara. There was no-one around. She sat herself down on the pavement and had a swig of the whiskey.

'Definitely a problem, Clara Connors', she said, waving the bottle. 'Not such a good outcome today, all things considered'. She walked out to the main road to find herself a strong coffee and mingled into the crowd, soon finding herself a corner seat in a bustling cafeteria selling burgers, sandwiches and drinks. She twirled her high stool to face the pavement so that no-one in the cafeteria could see her face. It was not the time to seek celebrity status, that was for sure.

She owed rent. She had found a decent Bed and Breakfast near the theatre and hired it for three months for the run of the show. She had paid one month up front and now had the surplus of rent still to pay. What to do now? The answer was simple: find a job. Fortuitously, there was an advertisement on the door of the cafeteria asking for waitress help. She lurched up to the till.

‘I’ve come about the job, sweetheart’, she said to the wide-eyed young girl behind the counter. ‘I’m interested’.

The girl eyed her but said nothing. Clara still had her stage makeup on and smelt strongly of alcohol. Within a minute, the proprietor came out. He took one look at Clara.

‘Sorry, love. The post has been filled’.

‘Take your bloody advert down then’, slurred Clara. ‘Anything else going?’

‘No’, said the proprietor and as Clara moved away from the counter, the proprietor turned to the assistant.

‘Over my dead body’ he said, he said to the girl behind the counter, ‘Don’t serve her again. We want her out of here quickly before she’s sick all over the place’.

As if the proprietor had planted the idea in Clara’s mind, she promptly vomited as she reached the door. She was hustled out, and the door promptly locked behind her, with the ‘Open’ sign turned firmly to ‘Closed’. She sat down on the pavement, recovering.

‘My God, what a mess of a life’, she thought, and suddenly needed Bruce. She thought too of her daughter Kitty, and her whole being ached for them. Up till now she had not given either of them very much thought, but the vision of both of them – Kitty, so gentle, so spirited, so kind, and Bruce, so strong, so steady, so uncomplaining, filled her mind. Suddenly, she longed for them with a passion. Tears tumbled down her face. Passers-by saw her and hurried by, but not before they had taken in the sight of a woman whose thick stage make-up was becoming increasingly streaked and smudged, more and more resembling a grotesque clown's face; a woman who was clearly very drunk and weeping piteously.

Someone put a five-pound note by her side.

'Have that, girl. Get something to eat - mop up the damage'.

Clara swayed to the kerb with the bottle and tipped the remaining contents of it down the drain. Several people watched her. One or two commented wryly on the waste it was, but most observed with a mixture of pity and disgust.

Her next port of call was at the Employment Office in Southgate. Usually, she loved wandering around beautiful Chichester, with its colourful quirky shops and warmly lit and inviting cafeterias, but today, with a fine drizzle setting in, today was anything but positive. On arrival, she stared in the window of the Employment Office, not mainly to read the advertisements but to scrutinise her own reflection. Her chestnut hair still had long hair slides in it for the part of Sally, and she realised that she hadn't taken the orange beret off that was tilted at a raunchier angle than originally intended for the part. Briefly, she stood there and wistfully sang on the spot a few lines of '*Me and my Girl' to* her reflection. An elderly couple saw her.

'You're not, are you? No, you can't be! Oh, we love that musical! We're seeing it again tomorrow. Could say we're sort of addicted to it. 'Groupies', I think we're called. You look a bit like the girl that was playing Sally last week. She was *marvellous.* Reminds me of you, now I come to think of it. You should audition - you're a good dancer, aren't you? Look at those feet! Why don't you have a go, love? Just clean yourself up a bit and have a go. They may need an understudy one of these days'.

Clara smiled wanly at them and went into the Employment Office. She looked at the boards with their strings of advertisements for 'Posts Vacant': secretaries, typists, long-distance lorry drivers, shop assistants, dog walkers, cleaners, hotel receptionists, caretakers, odd-job men or women required, and the likes. There seemed to be a wide variety of posts vacant. She was just about to join the queue of people waiting to talk to the earnest young man behind a desk when a middle-aged man sidled up to her. He surreptitiously pulled an embossed white envelope from his pocket. He spoke softly to her in a smooth, well-educated English accent, leaning forward intimately, invading her space.

'I've got just the job for you, my dear. You look to me as though underneath all that,' he pointed to her theatrical makeup, 'you have all the credentials. Excellent pay, evenings out, everything paid for, wine, theatre, weekends away, the lot. There's no better job for a high-class lady like you. Think about it. The phone number is on there if you're interested'.

He left as quickly as he seemed to have arrived. Clara opened the envelope and pulled out a folded invitation. It had gilt edging around it, and the writing on the front was in large italic gold type:

High-Class Escort Service

Female Escorts required for Chichester and the surrounding area.

Must be smart, clever, alluring, refined, sophisticated, and adventurous with the ability to entertain and enjoy male company.

Chapter 40

Clara was intrigued.

'This could be describing me on a good day,' she surmised, summoning up the last shreds of self-respect from her bleakness.

'I qualify for this, whatever it is'.

She flicked the leaflet open and was shocked to see glossy photographs of a bevy of beautiful girls in provocative poses. A phone number invited her to apply. The pay from the agency was astounding. After a little hesitation, Clara made up her mind that it looked too good to resist. She went back to her flat, cleaned herself up, drank two strong coffees and two glasses of cold water, and telephoned the number on the invitation.

'Oh yes, Madame. I think we would like to interview you', answered a woman who was attempting to speak in a BBC accent and giving herself away by dropping 'Ts' and 'Gs all over the place.

'You sound refined, educated, classy - you know what I mean? The clients we have like someone with a bit of grey matter between their ears - a Madame who can talk as well as care for her customer's - needs'.

She proceeded to ask Clara a series of questions, which Clara either answered frankly or replied to obliquely, fabricating the truth somewhat, including her age.

'Are you married, Madame?'

Clara hesitated because denying her family's existence felt like blasphemy.

'I – I have been'.

'That's fine, Madame. As long as your marriage is 'past tense'. A lot of our escorts have been married. It's better, really. Means they have experience'.

She laughed slightly and paused.

'I have to ask this, Madame. Are you familiar with more than one man in an intimate settin' – coping with partners who come in all shapes and sizes, so to speak?'

There was that laugh again.

'I am, yes', Clara replied quietly, suddenly feeling ashamed.

'You sound embarrassed, Madame. Don't be. That's all to the good if you've had a variety of partners. If you had just confined yourself to your husband, I'd be worried. Experience is everythin' in this work', she added.

‘Now. Terms and Conditions’.

The voice at the end of the telephone assumed a tone resembling an automated answerphone, reeling off information without so much as a whiff of inflection in her vocal monologue.

‘Come in this afternoon at three p.m., and we’ll go through everythin’ again to be sure’, the voice said, in vocal tones resembling a human being once more.

Clara thanked her, put the phone down, and felt sick. What was she doing? Was she degrading herself or using a talent in a desperate situation? No-one she had approached had ever found her resistible; no-one, that is, except Oliver Lockwood this last time. She angrily blamed him in her mind for her downfall and that wretched Connie Lockwood, so good, so ‘moral’, so annoyingly pretty and pure, and having the one man who she, Clara, wanted. Their son, Jamie Lockwood, strong, urgent, vigorous, was good, he really was, but not a patch on the real thing. She vowed there and then to have another go at seducing Oliver at a later stage.

What she had not understood was that Oliver was not now, no longer, not ever, for turning.

Clara began her work as a female escort, shutting her mind to what her husband and daughter, let alone Oliver and Connie, might think if they found out. She would make sure they never did.

On her first job, having taken the agency's advice on the matter, she dressed in a low-cut cut, seductive black top sporting an abundance of cleavage and curves, with a glittery jacket slung open over it and slinky black leather trousers with red high-heeled shoes. She applied her make-up very carefully so as not to look in any way too cheap or 'available'. As promised, she was taken to the theatre, wined and dined by a gentleman at least twenty-five years her senior, very polite, very gracious, highly educated and suffering, he confessed later, from problems of impotence. Clara sighed inwardly as she took him back to her boudoir bedroom. Unfortunately for her, she had considerable experience of this particular problem. She worked with patience on her client and, in the end, got something of a result. He asked, very politely, with an almost pleading tone, if he could come to Clara on a weekly basis 'to get back in trim'. Oh well, she thought, the money was incredible, and the evening out made a change, so on balance, it was worth the effort. She had to grit her teeth every time, endure the smell of his highly pungent and probably expensive after-shave, and simply think of England whilst going through the motions.

XXXXX

A week passed. Kitty Connors missed her mother. She was very angry with her, and one part of her mind never wanted to see her again ever, but paradoxically, the other longed for her. She decided to book herself into an evening performance of *Me and My Girl* in Chichester and managed to get one of the three remaining unsold seats in the theatre. She wouldn't tell either her mother or her father but would see at the time whether she felt confident and positive enough to wait at the stage door for her mum or if it was enough at this stage simply to see her onstage, catch a glimpse of her, and leave.

As she walked from the car park to the Festival Theatre, a man approached her, holding out an embossed white envelope. He spoke in soft, highly educated tones:

'I wonder if you would be interested in supporting out cause, Ma'am? We are not asking for money; simply your expertise. In fact, *we* pay *you.* Should you be interested, you will find the number to phone on the inside of the invitation'.

Kitty took it simply because he was so gracious, and she felt it might appear churlish to refuse. The gentleman left her and threaded his way through the theatre goers, and she saw him choose someone else to whom to give an invitation. Kitty, curious, opened the envelope. Inside, she saw the embossed flyer with its invitation to apply to become a female escort. Kitty involuntarily shuddered but opened the flyer. She stared. There, taking up the central space amongst the other photographs, was her mother – *her Mother!* Underneath, in italic gold letters, it read,

'*Meet the beautiful, talented, intelligent addition to our team: Just ask for*

Chloe'.

Her mother was clearly using a different name from her real one, but it was absolutely, definitely her - smiling, pouting, flirting provocatively with the camera. Kitty felt sick. She had no idea at all what to do with this information. She folded up the leaflet, replaced it in the envelope, turned and headed swiftly back to her car. Once inside, she wept silently for a long time as her belief in the world and its essential goodness had been ripped apart.

Chapter 41

Meanwhile, Oliver had been extremely careful as to how he handled the aftermath of the event with Clara and Jamie that Connie had stumbled upon. After her angry, violent outburst, followed by her almost inconsolable sobbing, Connie had scooped both babies up and, holding them very close, walked silently upstairs and shut the door firmly, locking it behind her. (Peter had gone through a stage of barging into their bedroom, and the lock had been a last but necessary resort). Connie placed the still-sleeping boys in their respective cots and lay on the bed staring at the ceiling. She was shaken by her violent reaction but could not come to terms with the actions of her son, let alone unspeakable Clara.

Oliver knew he must reach Connie and console her somehow. Previously, he had always been able to do this, no matter what the situation. He knew that when he took her in his arms, she usually sank into them and listened to him as he spoke gently and rationally about the problems she had or the issues she feared. This time, it felt different. He must find Jamie and talk with him, but how could *he,* who had succumbed to Clara's fatal attraction, say anything other than the truth: *'I know how it was. I've been there'?*

He left Connie for an hour, assuming she needed time to simmer down. Frankly, he had never known her this violent. He had heard that her father, Albert Connors, possessed a vicious temper, and Albert's son, Bruce, when provoked, was said to become enraged swiftly and violently. Peter also. Oliver himself did not lose his temper but knew he could turn silent, taciturn, morose even when his patience was sorely challenged, or he was incensed by events. Sometimes, Oliver felt it was more honest and straightforward to have a good old shout and stomp around like Peter than to refuse to communicate and become sullen and surly. Oliver knew his moods appeared manipulative, but when they happened as a result of a deep vexation or an infuriating situation, it seemed he could not help falling into his comfortingly dark pit and becoming unreachable. He understood that neither could Connie help this sudden temper when she had been so grievously shocked. She had caught her son inflagrante with Clara Connors, who she had always regarded as unscrupulous, and that was the understatement of the year in Connie's eyes. Add to the mix that this was her beloved brother Bruce's wife Clara committing adultery with his own nephew James, and the result became a potent, poisonous, toxic brew bubbling dangerously in Connie's mind.

Jamie left the house in embarrassment, shock and anger. He was angry with his mother for bursting in on the scene just at the very point where he had reached the peak of his pleasure. He was angry with Clara for seducing him so blatantly, but he was most angry with himself for hurting his mother or, putting it more honestly, for being *caught* by his mother. It was his first sexual experience with anyone, and it had overwhelmed him. He certainly could have done with a few minutes to enjoy its aftermath with Clara without his mother cutting that short.

He wandered round the market, looking at the stalls but not seeing and hearing people talking or processing their words as his thoughts were tangled and muddled. He, like his father, was not sure how to play the next few hours of his life. His sexual instincts told him he had a tremendous hunger to repeat the experience with Clara. She had been so sensual, so expert, so accomplished at it somehow. Jamie knew that a repeat would be out of the question now, although the very thought of it – the one linear thought that kept recurring – still stirred him. He was glad it was with such a beautifully accomplished woman that he had lost his virginity and relieved that he would return to Cambridge with some sexual history at last. Many of the students talked about their conquests, including his flatmates next door. By the side of them, Jamie had always felt naive and inadequate. He had regarded himself as an Innocent in a city full of the Experienced - a mamby-pamby from a Christian home whose values were somehow different from most of his peer group's, and that, in a way, set him apart. He looked back with a mixture of intense gratitude on the one hand and deep frustration on the other for his vicarage upbringing. It hadn't been sheltered, but it definitely had been loving and safe, and maybe, Jamie surmised, he had been over-protected emotionally.

Somehow, he had to make peace with his mother before he returned to Cambridge. Under normal circumstances, she was the one he would always turn to if he had any troubles. He had picked up from his mother, in between her sobs, that his father had previously had an encounter with Clara. What was his mother talking about? He definitely needed to know about *that.*

He stopped at a flower stall, not knowing that it was at this exact spot that his brother Peter had become involved with the notorious 'gang', resulting in the stabbing of his cousin Kitty. Jamie looked at the myriad of colourful flowers and could not decide whether his mother would appreciate the gesture or throw the flowers back in his face, saying it was patronising of him to think she could forgive him just because of a peace offering in the form of a bunch of roses. He thought of the nature of his mother, however, and realised she, of all people, knew how to forgive and to bring about reconciliation, whether it was in the parish or in her family. Her middle name *was* Forgiveness, which he had discovered long ago.

He bought the roses, saying a silent prayer over them, asking his mother to forgive him, but almost immediately, a rebellious, angry voice rose up inside him. What had it got to do with his mother? He was nineteen, for God's sake! He was a man with natural urges. What right had his mother to act in the way she had? 'Be cross with Clara if you must, Mum, but not me! You can't mother *me* any more! Get on with the babies you have. They need it. *I don't'*.

In his mind, he was shouting vehemently at her. He threw the roses angrily into a nearby bin and, clenching his fist and defiantly thrusting out his chin, he moved on into the crowd.

xxxxx

Oliver, bracing himself, went up to the bedroom to see what kind of a state Connie was in. She had locked herself in the room for nearly two hours now, and Oliver was beginning to feel anxious. He entered the bedroom carefully, his feet silent on the faded blue carpet, to find Connie huddled in the cream duvet with only her tousled fair hair showing. The babies were asleep finally, Connie having fed them for the best part of an hour, partly for her own comfort.

Oliver sat on his side of the bed next to her and leant his head back against the headrest. What to do? Wake her? Leave her? Come back later? An answer was provided by Connie stirring, pushing the duvet down and sitting up suddenly, looking dishevelled and spaced out, eyes staring as if startled by a nightmare.

'Con. Good, you had a sleep, darling'. He paused. There was no response. 'Let's talk when you've woken up properly, shall we?' he ventured.

Connie immediately pulled the duvet back up around her, covering her face and burying her reactions. Oliver eased the duvet down under her chin.

'Don't do that, Con. It doesn't solve anything. We must decide what to do about Jamie – how to approach things – you know'.

'I don't want to talk about it. Let go!' she shouted, dragging the duvet out of Oliver's hands and pulling it for a third time over her face.

'Connie!' Oliver said loudly. 'Stop it! You've got to break through this. I know it's been a shock, but no-one's hurt and no-one's dead. Keep it in proportion!' he finally shouted, desperate to reach her.

'Don't you care that our son has committed adultery?' Connie suddenly said back through gritted teeth.

'That's not strictly true, Connie. Clara has, but the law would say that Jamie is a 'Fornicator' – a horrible word - but *not* an adulterer'. Connie shuddered.

'A rose by any other name.' she replied. 'You have to be so accurate, don't you?' she said witheringly. 'You're so pedantic'.

She turned her head away.

Oliver took her hand. 'Con, this isn't getting us anywhere. Jamie needs our understanding. What do you think he is feeling now? Wretched and humiliated, I expect'.

'I can't cope with the image of it all, Oliver. It was such a terrible shock', replied Connie, calming down a little.

'Connie, would it help to talk to someone else?' asked Oliver.

Connie was silent for a minute.

'It might', replied Connie, 'as *you* are rather too – 'involved' – aren't you?'

Oliver knew exactly what she was implying. Connie had had the grace and understanding not to talk about Oliver's sexual encounter with Clara when he was a young unmarried chaplain. He had broken his self-imposed vows of celibacy with a married woman Clara causing her, as he thought, to become pregnant. Once more, he went over in his mind's eye that traumatic time when he and Clara both assumed Kitty was *his* daughter until the vital bone marrow test revealed differently.

Connie watched Oliver's reaction.

'Oliver. Answer me honestly. Do you still hanker after Clara – you know –' Connie almost whispered, hurting beyond measure to even voice such a thought. 'Do you hanker after her - physically?'

'It is you I love, body, mind and spirit, Connie. You know I adore you. There is no-one else for me – ever', Oliver replied sincerely.

'But that wasn't the question', said Connie scowling. ' I said, do you hanker after her *physically?'*

'NO!' replied Oliver, pushing aside a small voice that questioned, 'Are you sure?'

'No', he repeated, 'I do not hanker after Clara Connors, and I never will', he stated. 'It is you only that I love, Connie. You only'.

Joseph stirred and started grizzling in his cot. Connie immediately went to reach him.

'Leave him for a minute or two, Con. This is too important to shelve'.

'I don't want to talk', replied Connie, pushing his hand out of the way and reaching the baby. She latched him onto her breast.

'You know what's happened now, Oli, from all this?' she said angrily. 'My milk's drying up, and it's all that woman's fault!'.

‘Not Clara’s alone’, replied Oliver.

‘See? You’re defending her!’.

Oliver gave up. There was no talking to her. He sat on the edge of the bed as he watched his little son searching for milk and whimpering with dissatisfaction.

‘Never mind, Con. You’ve done wonderfully well. Both of them have had three months of you. It doesn’t matter now really, does it?’

Connie picked up her glass of water and threw it hard at Oliver, wetting his hair. The glass bounced on the wall.

‘Get out! Get out now! You haven’t got a clue, have you?’ Connie spat out at Oliver.

Oliver beat a hasty retreat and sat on the stairs in despair. Never in twenty-one years of marriage had he ever seen his wife like this. It was as if she had changed her personality before his very eyes. He sat for five minutes in a kind of daze, then began to think about her history. He was convinced this was not just about Clara and Jamie, traumatic as it was for Connie. The legacy of her dreadful childhood had something to do with it, Oliver was sure. He remembered her halting and broken description to him of her father forcing himself on her as a young child, about Sadie, her sister conceiving from her father’s disgusting violation;

about her father's bullying that was hugely instrumental in both her brother's and her mother's death. Oliver reflected that Connie had given herself wholeheartedly in every way in the early years of their marriage, but Oliver had always had to be very gentle and reassuring, always keeping guard that he respected her past and her subsequent sensitivities. Their intimate life now was possibly the best and richest it had ever been. He hoped to God Connie would not be affected by this long-term.

He also reflected on Connie's enormous capacity to forgive. He remembered how she had nursed her dying father so tenderly, forgiving him in her heart for all his abuse of her as a young child. She was not one to bear malice or resentment. He had seen the light of faith shine out of her. He felt calmer as he reflected on Connie's essential goodness.

But Oliver knew he was not the one to help her now. His own dalliance with Clara in the past precluded that both for him and for her.

He picked up the phone. He needed help, and he knew who might come to rescue them.

Chapter 42

Maria Murphy did not waste any time before heading up to the Vicarage. She was with Hope and Lucy and professionally knew what Oliver had shared with her over the telephone was a confidential and highly sensitive matter. On a personal level, she wanted nothing more than to share the information with Hope and see what her reflections were on her half-sister Connie's reaction to the shock. Of course, her sense of professionalism won, and Maria did not say a word, simply explaining to Hope that she had been 'called away on a medical matter'. Hope was now used to her mother's comings and goings. She treasured every second of her mother's company but was equally happy to be on her own with lively little Lucy, who kept Hope permanently happy, totally fulfilled and ridiculously tired in roughly equal proportions.

Oliver had painted the picture fully to Maria, pausing occasionally to hold back his emotion, especially when he described his wife's refusal to discuss the issue with him. He explained that he and Connie had always been soul mates and shared everything except parish confidences and how shocked he was to experience his wife's emotional rejection and dismissal.

Maria arrived at the vicarage an hour after Oliver's conversation on the bed with Connie. He subsequently took her a cup of tea and received a grudging thank you and no eye contact. Oliver started giving more explanations of events, but Maria stopped him.

'Oliver. I'd like to hear it in Connie's own words. It might unbutton her a bit. Don't worry. I will be sensitive'.

'I know you will, Maria. I trust you implicitly'.

Maria knocked on the bedroom door. She received no answer, so she tentatively cracked the door ajar and peeped in. Connie was sitting on the bed weeping over tiny Ben while he searched for milk at her breast as Joseph had done.

'Hello, Connie. Can I help at all?'

'Yes, please, Maria', Connie replied quickly. 'Can you go down and ask Oliver to make up two bottles of Formula for the babies? My milk has disappeared', she sobbed.

Maria returned very soon with two bottles, having watched Oliver expertly make up the powdered milk, which involved measuring accurately, shaking vigorously, and finally squeezing a drop from the teat of one of the bottles onto the back of his hand to test the temperature. Maria was impressed. Oliver, she decided, was a man of many parts.

Connie took one of the bottles gratefully.

'Maria, could I ask you to feed Joseph while I do Ben?' They are both ravenous'.

And so it was that, while the two babies tugged at the teats of the bottles vigorously, finally making contented sounds, Connie and Maria talked deeply and intimately. Connie's anger was subsiding and leaving her vulnerable. The conversation was to change the course of Maria's life.

Connie described the shock and horror of finding her son on top of Clara in the middle of having sex with her - a woman of double his age and who was his aunt. Maria listened intently. Feeding the babies had turned out to be very cathartic as the action reduced the intensity of what Connie was sharing in a wholly helpful way. Eye contact happened naturally as both women looked down regularly to adjust the level of the bottles, broke off halfway through their feeds to put the babies on their shoulders to wind them, afterwards continued to feed them, then finally, putting the bottles down, nursed the replete babies.

Connie gradually became more peaceful during the conversation. When she knew Connie was really trusting her, Maria asked,

'Connie, can you share anything of your childhood with me?'

Maria partially knew the answer, but she wanted to hear it from Connie. At first, Connie was silent. Then, gradually, she began to speak, haltingly, sadly, gaining momentum as she went along.

'My father used to come into my bedroom about three times a week. I remember hearing his feet as he crossed the landing from my mother's room. The sound always made my stomach turn over inside. The first thing he did was to go to the cupboard and get a large golden twist of barley sugar out of a tall jar. The barley sugar was my reward, waiting for me on the top of the chest of drawers. Then he used to clamber on top of me. I remember his elbows always dug into my sides and hurt me, but whenever I made a sound, he would cup his hand over my mouth. I learnt to just wait and go floppy. I used to count the times he moved up and down. It was usually about twenty, sometimes less, sometimes more. Afterwards he would take a pillowcase off and dry himself. I couldn't look. It was disgusting, but the tempting barley sugar waited on the dark oak chest of drawers as my reward. My mum used to ask me why the pillowcase was sticky, and I used to say I stole a barley sugar in the night and fell asleep with it in my hand'.

Connie paused. She was no longer crying, but her face was full of the agony of the memory of it.

'I don't think she believed me because she looked so sad, but she never said anything'.

'He used to do it to my older sister Sadie too, but I didn't know it until on the day of my father's funeral, Sadie turned up with a child in a pushchair. It was *his* child – twisted, severely disabled, very deformed- none of those words describe how bad he was – but he was as bright as a button, fantastically articulate and beautiful all in our eyes. Sadie adored him. We all did.'

'So the sex act caused great of heartache in your family, didn't it, Connie?'

'Yes', Connie replied softly, and finally, her face lightened.

'When Oliver asked me to marry him, I was secretly rather scared of our wedding night, but he was so – so gentle and beautiful and so patient that he completely cured me of my anxiety over it all'.

Maria saw the breakthrough in Connie's mood when she talked about Oliver. She homed in on it.

'Connie, how was Oliver when he found Clara and Jamie together?'

'He didn't exactly find them, but he saw the aftermath – my anger and Clara's face torn and bleeding'. Connie lowered her head, momentarily ashamed of her violence. 'I can tell he is bewildered and probably hurting like me, but Oli never puts himself first – well, almost never'.

Connie wondered whether to share with Maria the 'dalliance' as she called it, that Oliver had previously had with Clara and its subsequent fallout, but then remembered she had promised solemnly to Oliver years ago that her lips would be sealed forever over it.

'Who were you more angry with, Connie? Clara or James?'

'Both of them', replied Connie swiftly. 'This was my son, Maria'.

'And your son needs you', Maria said softly. 'He needs to know that your love goes way beyond his sexual indiscretion. He is a normal young man who has acted out of temptation but acted *normally* as far as his instincts are concerned. You still love him, don't you?'

'Yes, of course, I do', Connie replied without hesitation.

'Then he is a lucky lad'. Maria paused, then

'I wasn't so lucky'.

Connie looked at Maria. She realised that she had been totally wrapped up in her own hurt and suddenly perceived that Maria herself was bearing an emotional burden that was painful.

'Can you tell me, Maria?'

Maria told Connie her story of how her parents could not come to terms with her own sexual infidelity and threw her out of her home and virtually onto the streets. In the mother and baby home, she felt utterly abandoned, a scarlet woman, rejected and despised by the very people she should have been able to rely upon, lean upon in her hour of need. She was also very frightened.

'Have you made peace with your parents now?' asked Connie, 'and I should say, have your parents made peace with *you?'*

'Not at all on either side', replied Maria. 'I left for England, and I have never contacted them again. I don't know whether they are alive or dead'.

Connie gasped. To her, that was a tragedy of immense proportions, having given birth to five children and knowing how completely precious they were. She realised how terrible it would be if Jamie decided to reject her and never darkened their door again because of how her reactions had been.

'Maria. You must find your parents', said Connie. 'Go and make peace with them if it is not too late. They will have been hurting deeply ever since you left'.

Maria was about to say how very much they *didn't* care about her and then stopped in her tracks. How did she know anything about their feelings if she had not contacted them at all and had no idea whether they were alive or dead?

'Go and find them, Maria', Connie repeated with urgency. You must,' she said emphatically. She held Maria's hand tightly.

'Please, Maria. This is bigger than your pain. *God* is bigger than your pain'.

There was a soft knock at the door.

'Shall I open it?' asked Maria.

'Yes, please. I expect it's Oli not wanting to interrupt'.

There in the doorway stood Jamie, red-faced and tear-stained. Connie looked at him, got off the bed, moved towards him and opened her arms wide. Jamie flew into them, and the two held each other tightly.

'Mum, Mum, I'm sorry. It was such a shock for you, I know'.

'Jamie. You are nineteen. You are an adult. I haven't respected the fact. Please forgive me for that'.

Jamie was silent and weeping.

'Mum, please forgive me for being stupid with Auntie Clara'.

'All I would say, Jamie, is just try, if you can, to wait so that a union with the woman you choose can be made sacred in the sight of God. It matters'.

Maria thought about how times were changing, how most of the youngsters she knew were very happy and relaxed about making love outside of marriage. She respected Connie for her views, although she wasn't sure she agreed with them, but she was relieved, quietly happy and extremely moved by the transformation in Connie from an angry, vitriolic woman back into a loving, forgiving, reasonable mother once more.

Oliver came in, and seeing Connie's face, with Jamie's head resting on her chest, he went up to them both and kissed them gently on the forehead. Then he moved to Maria and tentatively did the same to her.

'Thank you, Maria, thank you.'

'Don't thank *me*', she replied. 'It is *I* who should be thanking Connie,' she said enigmatically.

xxxxx

Maria moved unobtrusively to the front door of the vicarage, daring to think that her mission for the time being might have been accomplished. She was moved by everything about Connie. They would all leave working out how to handle the Clara aspect of it for later. That was a far less straightforward problem.

She heard Oliver running down the stairs to catch her up and turned to see him with his arms outstretched towards her. He caught up and enfolded her in an enormous bear hug.

'Maria, I am going to call you our Family Miracle Worker!' he said.

Maria laughed, suddenly embarrassed by Oliver's fulsome compliment.

'It wasn't me, Oliver. Connie's heart softened. She turned herself around and transformed her anger into a much more powerful emotion.'

'Reconciling love,' Oliver replied.

'Yes'.

They were both quiet. Finally, Oliver said,

'Maria, I believe God has sent you to this family. Just look at what you've dealt with since you arrived: crisis after crisis, and in every case, we have leant on you. I've seen Him working in you, Maria, whether you acknowledge it or not'.

Previously, Maria might have made a throwaway comment, embarrassed by the suggestion, or she might have secretly been resentful that this God always seemed to get all the credit when things went well. However, she simply replied,

'Thank you, Oliver. In that case, I must have let Him in', she smiled. 'And now', she said with a smile, 'I know what true holiness is, Oliver. It encompasses you – whether you acknowledge it or not. It is part of the fabric that makes you *you.'*

She kissed him quickly on the cheek and swiftly left.

Once down the vicarage steps, she took her mobile phone out of her bag and rang Hope's number. There was no answer, so she left her a message.

'Hi Hope. It's me. I'm going to visit Ireland. Will you come with me?'

Chapter 43

In a few days' time, Connie took Maria, Hope and Lucy to Heathrow airport to board the flight to Dublin. It had been an easy decision for Hope to make when Maria explained that she had a deep desire now to visit her parents or at least to see what had become of them.

'Take care, you three,' Connie said as she unloaded Lucy's pushchair from the boot. 'I'll be thinking prayerfully about you. I might even get out my rosary!' she half-joked.

'That's not very Anglican,' Maria laughed.

'Ah, but remember my roots!' she smiled back. She kissed Hope and Maria warmly, held them close in a hug, and then blew a kiss to sleeping Lucy.

'God be with you all. Come back safely'.

She watched them as they made their way to the check-in desk and felt a pang of loss. Maria had been her light in a dark place.

xxxxx

Maria, Hope and Lucy arrived at Dublin airport in the mist. The plane had been delayed for half an hour before take-off due to 'adverse weather conditions'. The mist had been very dense at Heathrow. The plane seemed to wait endlessly at the end of the tarmac for clearance from Air Traffic Control, and Lucy became restless, but much to Hope's relief, as soon as the plane was airborne (finally), she snuggled down on Hope's lap and slept throughout the short flight.

It was strange for the women to be landing at Dublin airport. They had both left Ireland under dramatic circumstances, the pregnant Hope having been scooped up by her newly discovered half-sister Sadie. Maria had not been so fortunate. She had boarded the flight to England entirely alone three weeks after having been told her baby had died at birth. Her parents did not want to know her but gave her a huge financial lump sum, which Maria was sure was more to ease their guilt than anything else. Nevertheless, it had stood her in good stead for her long medical training.

'Just look at my family now!' Maria thought gratefully. Here were a mother, daughter, and a child in a pushchair, swinging out of the airport about to board a train for Galway. From a takeaway stall, Hope bought two Irish brown bread sandwiches stuffed with chicken, two cardboard cups full of steaming tea, an unhealthy crisps sandwich in white bread and a carton of orange squash for Lucy, which she had requested and subsequently devoured eagerly, then asked for more.

The journey lasted well over two hours, the train rambling through the exquisite green countryside and finally reaching the characteristic farmlands and lowlands on the outskirts of Galway. Both Maria and Hope, at different times during the journey, experienced pangs of the deepest longings and feelings - the soul's 'inarticulate groanings' - that no words could adequately express. This was *their* country, *their* beloved Ireland. They had been so long away: Maria for forty years and Hope for nearly five.

Maria's plan was, first and foremost, to visit the makeshift cemetery attached to St.Brigid's Hostel for Fallen Girls. On hearing from the Sister there what had happened to Cathy Ryan – found dead in a ditch and subsequently buried in an unmarked grave, apart from a small wooden cross with her name on it – Maria had now put it at the top of her list of priorities to visit her bodily remains there. She would look for a florist and buy her flowers, preferably cornflowers, which she remembered Cathy had told her she loved. Poor Cathy, age twelve, had been fantasising to Maria about the future and her wedding with whoever that might be, and Maria clearly remembered Cathy saying she would carry the biggest bunch of cornflowers she could 'ever, ever, ever, buy'. Cathy's dreams were not to be realised. Maria was never to forget the sound of Cathy's keening wails when her newborn baby son was taken for adoption, nor the catatonic depression she had subsequently fallen into afterwards.

Maria had booked Lucy, Hope and herself into a hotel nearby, and they would use that as their base. After visiting the grave, Maria intended to find out everything she could about her parents, firstly visiting their home two or three miles away to see if she could glean any information from whoever the occupants might be now. She presumed both her parents were dead, her father being in his nineties and her mother at least in her mid-eighties.

The train arrived at Galway (*Ceannt station*), and the trio took a taxi to their modest hotel on the outskirts of the town centre. Maria left Hope and Lucy in their room almost immediately and went in search of cornflowers. She found a large florist in town and was told in no uncertain terms that the latest she could have hoped to buy cornflowers was mid-October. Seeing Maria's crestfallen face, the assistant added that she could have them flown in within twenty-four hours, but it would cost. With a knowing smile and a broad Irish accent, she quoted an old Irish proverb that so many had used to seduce folk into handing over money for good causes or street beggars relied upon to cajole the more soft-hearted passers-by amongst the crowd to part with some of their cash:
'Money is like muck – no good till spread'

Maria ordered a copious number of cornflowers, much to the satisfaction of the assistant, who assured

Maria she would phone through the order this minute and have them in by eleven a.m. the following day.

True to her word, the florist had the bright blue flowers, hand-tied in raffia, ready for her customer the next morning. Maria parted with an excessive amount of cash.

'For someone special, obviously', said the Florist.

'Someone I've let down', replied Maria frankly.

'Honest to God', the assistant replied, 'I can't believe a lovely lady like you would let anyone down! It's usually the Irish Micks that do that', she said witheringly. 'Can't trust any of 'em, to be sure'.

Maria smiled. She loved hearing the broad Irish accents again and the stock-in-trade phrases. It was good to be back.

'Holy Mary, it's a devil of a day, now isn't it? Now, would you be wanting a card for the flowers?' she asked, without taking a breath between the two thoughts.

'Thank you', answered Maria and used the assistant's biro to write:

Dear Cathy

I'm very, very sorry

Much love, Maria Murphy

Then, her arms full of cornflowers, Maria made her way to the graveyard at the back of the 'Hostel for Fallen Women'. Her legs turned to jelly as she approached the hostel. So many memories! There had been a strong and ever-present undercurrent of sadness and an overwhelming Tsunami of sorrow within those walls. She hurried past, averting her eyes as her tears welled up, and she thought of poor Cathy Ryan and then of the grief of losing her own baby, which had weighed her down for forty years. She edged along by the long grey walls to the hostel's small and neat garden and then through a wrought iron gate which creaked and clanged as she shut it behind her and arrived at the higgledy-piggledy graveyard.

It felt a surreal place in the swirling mist, taking on a dreamlike quality as though a delicate white gauze had been cast over every blade of grass and mound of earth. Maria shivered. She started to peer closely at the half-broken and bizarrely crooked crosses that had been poked down through the grass into the earth in what appeared to be a random and uncaring way. There was something overwhelmingly poignant and desolate about the place. She was overcome by a deep, dark sorrow for the suffering the graveyard silently represented. She came to a freshly dug grave a little larger than the size of a newborn infant and knew that soon, that tiny dead person would be laid to rest in this God-forsaken place, or that was how the graveyard seemed to Maria at that moment.

What was it Oliver had said? 'Faith in God is hope and assurance about what we do not see'. It felt like a tall order, but nevertheless, she paused to reflect and offer prayers to the God whom she had been beginning to know and acknowledge despite all the perceived contradictions of faith. Paradoxically, the sorrow of this place militated against her belief in a God of love, and it upset her deeply.

Quite suddenly, coming from nowhere, she remembered a line from a hymn she used to sing in secondary school assemblies that had always resonated with her:

'God unknown, He alone

Calls my soul to be His own'

She had always liked and felt comforted by the 'unknown' bit. It had implied to her that it was acceptable to live with the mystery of it all rather than seek answers to every apparent paradox and contradiction.

Alternating between bending low or kneeling on the ground, Maria began to read the names on the crosses of the mounds, hoping that the name Cathy Ryan might leap out at her. The whole place and experience was making her shudder. She thought of Cathy being abandoned in what felt, she had to admit, like a place of hopelessness despite the tiny crosses implying otherwise. So fragile were the crosses that

Maria wondered if they had been made out of abandoned ice lolly sticks, which would have needed to be replaced frequently because of their fragility. Maybe school children had collected them as a project for the Hostel, perhaps not knowing that the Nuns would tie them in the shape of a cross and place them in the cold, cold earth to mark the graves of innocent babies and abandoned mothers. There were several very tiny mounds of grass, presumably cradling the newborn babies who had emerged unsuccessfully from their mothers' wombs into this world.

She moved slowly on, inching carefully around the haphazard graves, and as she emerged through another ten yards or so of mist, she noticed a couple of other people in the graveyard. One was a young woman bent over a tiny mound. She could only guess at the woman's tragic situation. The other, standing a little further on, was a man of short stature wearing a beige anorak and a tweed brown cap over what was clearly a mop of curly greying hair. He was slightly bent, and Maria saw he had a white stick. He was peering intensely at a grave and obviously trying to see the name on the cross.

Maria hovered. Her instinct was to help the man, but she did not want to appear intrusive or patronising. He turned when she was near to him.

'Hello?'

Maria backed off a little.

'It's all-right. No need to go'. He paused, and Maria moved a little closer.

'I come here frequently, but I always need to check I'm at the correct grave. I don't want to squander my tears on the wrong person!' He laughed with self-deprecating humour.

Maria moved closer.

'Shall I read out the name so you're sure?'

'Now that *would* be kind'.

Maria bent down. She caught her breath and felt herself sway a little.

'It's – Cathy – Cathy Ryan. Is that right?'

'That's right,' replied the man.

Maria was stunned.

'This is such a coincidence as I'm looking for her grave too'.

'*Really!'* the man exclaimed.

There was silence. Finally, Maria replied carefully,

'I was in the hostel with her. I knew her a little. She was the youngest person in there. Twelve years old'.

'She was my mother', he said softly.

Maria gasped.

'No!' She paused. 'May I ask what your name is?'

'Yes. I'm Callum Ryan. Pleased to meet you'. He held out his hand in her direction in greeting. Maria shook it, trembling inside.

'Callum, I was in bed next to your mother, Cathy Ryan. I knew she had given birth to a son, but I believed he was put up for adoption'.

'Well, here I am!' he said, saluting with one hand and twirling his white stick a little in the other. 'The one and only Callum Ryan!' he laughed.

'So you live locally?' asked Maria, smiling and warming to this quirky, appealing man.

'Now *that* is a long story, full of tangles. By the way, may I ask *your* name also?'

'I'm Maria, Maria Murphy', she replied, suddenly aware that this was an unknown name for her in Ireland.

'I live locally now', Callum replied. 'But I started life in Dublin, adopted by a couple who had plenty of money but nothing much else. At the age of three, I started to lose my sight – infantile glaucoma –blinding if not discovered and treated rapidly. My adoptive parents were in denial. They assumed I was just clumsy'.

'I know of Infantile Glaucoma,' said Maria. 'It's a congenital condition'.

'Yes, it is. The family who adopted me couldn't cope with an imperfect child...' he paused, and it was clear that Callum still felt the pain of rejection.

'... so they asked the Covent attached to the hostel to have me back and get me into another family'.

'And they did?'

'Eventually, yes, but no-one really wants a blind child, do they?'

'Someone did from the sound of it'.

'Yes, thank God for that. I was adopted by a widow. Her husband had died suddenly, and she was lonely. The hostel wasn't officially allowed to let a single or widowed person adopt, but this lady had lots of money and offered a king's ransom for me'. He laughed. 'At last, I was worth something! You know what the Nuns fear most? They are always afraid of being shut down by the bishop, so extra funds keep them afloat for a wee while longer than they otherwise might. You can't blame them. They couldn't resist, of course. The person who adopted me wasn't at all worried that I was blind. She said it was God giving her a second chance to love'.

'That's beautiful,' replied Maria, 'and it has all worked out reasonably for you?'

'Yes, really it has, honest to God. She does 'mother' me and over-protect me, but I suppose I can see why. She's wonderful, really. She told me she turned her own daughter out - abandoned her – when the unmarried daughter told her she was pregnant.' He paused before continuing.

'Now, what kind of parents would do that? Then, after the daughter's baby had died, the daughter walked out and was never seen again'. He shook his head. 'Very sad, very sad. You could say the punishment didn't fit the crime. Two wrongs don't make a right, do they, Miss –um - Maria? I guess adopting me was her kind of penance – she told me I was worth more than a thousand Hail Mary's, so I really did have a value on my head!'

He laughed out loud again, and suddenly, Maria caught a flash of Cathy in his expression.

'It's a fascinating story', said Maria thoughtfully. 'So you're local now, are you?'

'Just a bus ride away. Albert Street'.

Very gradually, the penny began to drop. Maria could feel herself turning the colour of alabaster. She was glad Callum could not see her.

'I know someone who lives in Albert Street. What number are you?'

'Forty One'.

Forty-One. Her parents' house. The house she grew up in.

'Callum. Have you time for a cuppa? There's a nice little place five minutes from here. I think there's a lot to catch up on'.

'Yes, I know it. 'Tara's Tea Shop.' I often go there. I'd like that. You can tell me more about my mother – please? All I know about her is that she was twelve years old and was then found dead in a ditch. Not much of a life, was it? –and not much to tell people when they ask about my 'real' mother. I don't even know what she looked like'.

'No', replied Maria sadly. 'I can fill you in with that a little, Callum'. After a pause, she asked quietly,

'Callum, do you need a hand negotiating the graves back to the gates?'

'I come here quite often', replied Callum. 'I'm used to them, but I do have an occasional trip up and land on some unsuspecting mother or baby! Once, I landed in a freshly dug grave.' He roared with laughter. 'You have to keep a sense of humour, don't you?'

'Absolutely you do.' replied Maria, although falling into a freshly dug grave did not chime with her particular brand.

'Were you leaving those cornflowers for my mother's grave then?'

Maria laughed in embarrassment realising she had been so overtaken by her discovery that she had forgotten the very purpose which brought her here.

'Yes, yes. I'm all over the place meeting you', she laughed. 'But tell me, how did you – did you know – that – that they were cornflowers when I'm blind and can't see them?' 'Good question! Put your nose in the flowers and breathe deeply. See? There's a spicy fragrance - kind of earthy, peppery. Very distinctive, isn't it? I can smell cornflowers a mile off even though their scent isn't strong'.

'That's remarkable', said Maria. 'You are a man of many talents, to be sure, Callum Ryan', she laughed. 'Your mother would be so proud of you'.

She turned, bent over the mound of earth that marked the spot where Cathy was buried, kissed her own fingers, then placed them gently on the broken-down cross.

'Rest in peace, Cathy', she said softly.

'And rise in glory', Callum added. 'Don't forget the important bit'.

Maria liked him enormously. He was fun, brave, quirky, perhaps a little strange, and clearly a man of faith. She wondered what her own straight-laced mother thought of him. She must have changed. She *had* changed, she concluded.

They picked their way around the mounds of earth back towards the gate, where Maria, through the clearing mist, discerned Hope wheeling Lucy's pushchair. Hope, in turn, peered at the sight of the short man wearing a beige anorak and a tweed cap, feeling his way with his white stick as he negotiated the route past haphazard graves to the gate. He was holding the arm of her mother, Maria. What was going on? Her mother hadn't told her anything about this man! Was he a secret of her past? she asked herself curiously.

'Hmm. The plot thickens'. Hope said out loud.

'Plot, plot, plot, plot, plot!' repeated Lucy, laughing, enjoying the sound of the word and bouncing up and down in her pushchair.

Maria waved as she approached.

'Hope, this is Callum Ryan', she said as she kissed her daughter and granddaughter. 'I came here to find Cathy Ryan's grave and met her son! Isn't that amazing? Come with us to Tara's for a cup of tea? We have a lot of unravelling of this tangled tapestry of our past lives to be done!'

The little cafe was warm and inviting. The square tablecloths were a colourful emerald green and white check and a fire burned in a small black grate. They sat themselves in a corner, grateful that there were only a few other customers. A pert young waitress came bustling up immediately. They ordered three cups of tea and a small strawberry milk shake for Lucy.

'Now. Where to begin?' asked Maria, knowing that this would be another of those momentous conversations. 'Shall I tell you first about everything I remember about your mother, Callum?' she asked, answering her own question.

Before Callum could answer, the teas arrived. Hope gave the delighted Lucy her milk shake.

'Ah. Yes. Now let me buy you all one of Tara's specialities: a jam and cream doughnut covered in thick dark chocolate. Delicious! TA-RA!' he shouted jokily, 'Three Specials please'.

'Now you'll be looking like a doughnut soon, Mr. Callum, to be sure!' she said, laughing and left, wiggling to fetch the order.

Chapter 44

Maria began to tell Callum everything she could remember about Cathy Ryan: the clothes she wore, how her longish brown hair was always clipped back with two pink hair slides, her peaches and cream complexion, which Maria had always admired, and the way she would put her hand on her very large pregnancy bump and talk soothingly to the baby cocooned inside. Maria spoke of the chats they had, Cathy's hopes and dreams, her description of her abusive uncle and her longing to leave the home when her baby was born. Finally, she described, sparing the finer detail, how Cathy had come back to the ward after Callum was born, how he had been more or less snatched from her within minutes of the birth, and that Cathy had been determined to stay close to him, wherever that might be.

No-one noticed the plate of doughnuts quietly placed on the table in front of them, nor that Lucy had fallen asleep and dropped her carton of milk shake onto the floor. All Maria saw were the tears flowing down Callum's face as his hands clung to hers. Hope was moved to tears, too and gently put her hands over the two of them.

'Thank you, Father, thank you Father', she muttered under her breath.

‘Thank you for telling me, Miss Maria. She sounds like a lovely woman – or girl, I should say. My mother just twelve years old! She was found in a ditch, you know, trying to escape from that terrible home. Have I said that already?’ he asked, suddenly anxious.

‘I was told by one of the Nuns’, replied Maria.

‘But she’s alive, isn’t she?’ Callum suddenly said, his face brightening.

‘I believe her spirit is’, said Maria, and meant it. ‘Rest in peace and *rise in glory’*. That’s what we said, wasn’t it?’

Hope said not a word, but a warmth spread within her and around her at Maria’s simple statement of faith.

As if a switch had suddenly gone off inside Callum, he said,

‘Now come on! You’ve never tasted such doughnuts in your life!’

They ate for a few minutes, and then Maria turned to Callum,

‘Now I’d like to know more about my mother and father, please, Callum’.

‘Did you know your father had died?’

Maria suddenly felt ashamed.

‘No, actually, no. I had no contact at all with them’.

'Your mother and the priest tried to track you down, but no-one known as Erin O'Neill seemed ever to have existed', he said.

'No. I covered my tracks completely'.

There was silence. Callum looked sad. Maria felt more ashamed.

'Tell me more if you can, Callum'.

'Yes, of course. What do you want to know?'

'When did my father die, and what did he die of?'

'Apparently, he had a fatal heart attack about a year after you left'.

Maria thought back to her father. Whenever he became even slightly agitated, his face reddened with the onset of his inevitable aggression. She had often thought he was heart attack material or ripe for a 'myocardial infarction' as her medical colleagues would describe it. But a year after she left? Shock? Maybe. Grief? No. Anger? Certainly, yes, unless Maria had never understood him accurately.

Maria felt ashamed for a third time during their conversations at the timing of his death, but felt nothing at all in terms of grief or sadness. Now, she urgently wanted to know more about her mother.

'I was told your mother went into a decline after your father died; however, once she told me that she felt liberated when she bought a packet of biscuits because, for the first time since she was married, she bought *chocolate* ones instead of Rich Tea, without fear of your father accusing her of extravagance!'

Maria thought back. Her father had been very frugal, even though he had well in excess of a million pounds in the bank at the time, plus a six-bedroom house.

'I was bought for a huge price – your mother never told me how much – and she gave me the chance of a good life'. He paused and laughed. 'Yes, it was good, and it still is, although she *is* quite a strict taskmaster! 'Have you shaved?' 'That tie doesn't match that shirt!' 'Put the T's on the ends of your words else they'll think you've been dragged up in the gutter!' 'Wipe the mud off the carpet!' 'Clean your shoes!' 'Have you evacuated your bowel today?'

Maria laughed out loud at last at the last question.

'Yes, she used to say that to me, even when I was little. The only 'evacuation' I knew was of all the little children in the war. I never had any idea what she meant!'.

They all laughed.

'But the point is', continued Callum, 'she loves me, and I loved her. You can't beat that, can you?'

‘No, you can’t’, said Hope quietly and put her hands on her mother’s clasped ones.

Lucy stirred, turned her blonde curly head the other way in her pushchair, put her thumb comfortingly in her mouth, and continued sleeping.

‘This little one ran herself ragged in the park, so she’s catching up, thank goodness’, said Hope, pulling the blanket up higher round her sleeping daughter.

‘My mother, Callum? Can you carry on?’

He sat there running his fingers round the chocolaty plate, rather as a child would.

‘Nice, aren’t they?’

‘Delicious’, replied Maria, longing for the conversation to continue.

‘I think your mother was an unhappy woman. She rattled around in their huge house. It was too much for her, but your father had forbidden her to have cleaning help. One of the first things she did after he died (apart from buying chocolate biscuits) was to employ a cleaner’.

Callum suddenly looked very serious.

‘Miss Maria, I don’t think she ever got over losing you. She used to sit and rock sometimes in a dark corner of the sitting room. ‘What’s the matter, Ma?’ I used to say, but I knew, I knew. Sometimes, she might reply simply, 'I miss my girl'.

Now, it was time for the tears to run down Maria's cheeks.

'She would say that it was shame that made your father turn you out, and fear was the reason she did. She was held in the grip of the strict rules of the Priests of the Roman Catholic Church at that time, you see. Not healthy, not healthy', Callum said, shaking his head. 'I've got no time for Priests. Only God.'

Maria thought of Oliver the Priest, so measured, so loving, so open. Now *he* was a man of God, she thought, along with Connie, his soul mate, partner and woman of God. What a gift it was to have met them! She suddenly wanted Callum to meet them, too.

'She wanted to wrap me in cotton wool, me being blind and so on', Callum continued. 'She took me to Braille classes and Lip Reading classes, and little by little, just by seeing how I coped, she – not sure how to describe it-'

'Released her grip and let you fly?'

'Oh beautiful, beautiful. Poetic,' replied Callum, 'Yes, that was it'. He paused and then looked earnestly up at Maria.

'Miss Maria, come with me to see her?'

‘I will’, replied Maria without hesitation. She paused, then smiled across at Callum.

‘You realize this makes you my adopted half-brother, Callum?

He got up from his chair and gave her a little kiss on the cheek.

‘How nice!’ he replied quaintly, giving her a little bow.

‘And you are my step-uncle, Callum, and Lucy’s great-uncle!’ smiled Hope.

He suddenly picked his white stick up and jigged around the table.

‘I’ve acquired a family!’ he laughed, ‘All in the space of about half an hour. You wait till Mother knows about you! CA-RA!’ he suddenly shouted, ‘The bill please, and buy yourself a jam and cream doughnut with dark chocolate on the top and put the usual in the bag for Mother!’

Chapter 45

In the cafe, the three of them had decided that Callum would go into his house first and fill the old lady in very gently with the news of her daughter's return. Callum sat in the front of the car, giving travel directions to Maria. Maria recognised everything around her but confessed she would not have found her way home on her own. Lucy and Hope sang nursery rhymes in the back of the car. Lucy was wide awake, and Hope prayed she could contain her child's energy during the trauma that was to follow.

As Maria drove up the wide road towards her old home, she could barely contain her nerves. How could she begin a conversation with the mother she had not seen for over forty years? Her mother would be eighty-seven now - an old lady. She wondered if she would even recognise her, and certainly, her mother would not know who she, her daughter, was. Maria felt twisted like a coiled-up wire inside: ashamed, fearful, embarrassed, excited.

Callum was worried for his mother that the bus he normally caught from outside Cara's Cafe had long since gone, so deep in conversation had they all been. When they were a few yards away from the house, he guessed that his mother had tottered out to the front gate to anxiously look for him.

'Is Mother there?' asked Callum. 'Oh dear. I'm sure she hasn't got her walking stick with her. It doesn't matter how many times....' His voice trailed off as he felt Maria's tremble.

Maria stared out of the window fearfully. There she was, her diminutive mother, even smaller than she remembered, with snowy white hair replacing the fair hair of the past. She looked frail and, yes, old, but still completely recognisable. Maria's stomach flipped. She wanted to run as fast as she could away from the scene that was to follow: anger, recrimination, endless explanations, tears, guilt.

Her mother tottered out to the kerb as the car came to a standstill. Peering in, then holding onto the bonnet, she walked slowly round and tapped on the passenger window at Maria.

'Now, Erin O'Neill, what kept you so long?' she said, 'I knew you'd come back one day'.

It was as easy as that. No recriminations, no explanations, no tears and no guilt required. Her mother took Maria by the hand as she stepped out of the car and very slowly led her up the path to the front door. Maria gasped as they entered the huge hall. She remembered it being a dull fawn to the halfway point down the walls and then with brown lincrustre lining the bottom half 'to prevent the filthy fingerprints of the child', her father had said. Now, it had gentle cream floral wallpaper from top to bottom.

'Now. Would you be wanting tea or coffee, Erin? I know you college types prefer coffee nowadays, wouldn't you know?'

'Tea, please, actually – Ma'. There. She had said it. Her mother turned and, without a word, kissed the top of Erin's head.

'I'm sorry for everything, child'.

'And I am too', replied Maria, her lip trembling.

'Shall we leave it at that then, Erin?'

'Not quite,' replied Maria. 'Are you ready for another surprise?'

For the first time, her mother looked bewildered and flustered.

'Aren't you enough for one day, Erin? Give an old lady a chance!'

But Maria took her mother's hand and led her once more towards the car.

'Look in the back seat, Ma', Maria instructed.

Her mother peered in.

'Now she's a bonnie wee girl, isn't she just? Who would she be belonging to, then?' she said in her soft lilting accent.

'Ma. She's mine. She's my granddaughter.'

Now, it was finally time for Emily O'Neill to shed a tear. Hope opened the car door and, sensing the mood, whispered, 'Hello Granny. I'm your grandchild. Hope,' to Maria's mother. Not a word was spoken between them, but the four generations of that little family stood on the pavement, hugged each other and let their tears fall. Finally, Lucy broke the mood.

' Garden, please? Now, please?'

'Why I have one as big as a field!' replied Emily O'Neill. 'Take my hand, and I'll show you, but first, all of you, have any of you met my son?'

'We have', replied Maria, sensing the first signs of mental slippage in her mother. 'He drove us here, didn't he?'

'So he did, to be sure. This head is getting addled, don't you know?'

Emily O'Neill went up to Callum and put her arms around him.

'He's my boy, my little lad. The good Lord gave him to me. Recompense for losing you,' she said without guile.

'He gave us to one another', replied Callum, and took his mother's hand, kissed it, bowed, and danced briefly with her, his mother suddenly laughing coyly,

'See what it is to have a son!' she said.

'Second only to a daughter', replied Callum again without a shred of resentment as he bowed and kissed Maria's hand merrily.

They spent the evening catching up on each other's history. Emily O'Neill was flabbergasted to find that Hope was her daughter Erin's baby, who had been presumed dead at birth; flabbergasted and overwhelmed with the beauty and relief of the revelation.

Before the three of them left for their hotel, Maria drew her mother gently aside.

'Ma, I've got something precious I'd like you to have.'

'Now, what in God's name would that be, I'm wondering', Emily said, looking at her daughter quizzically. Maria put her hand into the open neck of her silk blouse and drew out the tiny Swan Vesta matchbox wrapped in a fresh wadge of soft white lint.

'I want you to have this, Ma'.

Emily slowly unwrapped the lint, winding it round her old fingers neatly before sliding it out of the matchbox. When she saw a little blonde-gold curl tied up with a thin pink ribbon, a tear fell down her cheek.

'Well, well now. This is surely one of your curls, Erin?'

'No, Ma. It's one of your grandaughter's. I pleaded with the nurse to cut one off for me to keep. I thought my baby was dead'. Maria found herself welling up, too.

'Would you keep it for me, Mammy? You've missed out on so many years. I'd like you to have it. Please'.

'I will, Erin, I will'. Emily held it in the palm of her hand as if it were as fragile as a bird's egg. 'Now, this is a rare and wonderful gift, sure it is.'

Quite suddenly, she dried her tears and said briskly,

'Now be off with all of you. That's quite enough surprises for one day for an old lady. I'll be having a heart attack next, yes, I will, you know!' she laughed happily.

Maria, Hope and Lucy began to leave for their hotel with glad and wondering hearts at the miracle that had taken place. As they were getting into the car, Emily O'Neill tottered down the path, closely watched by Callum, to wave them off. As she kissed Erin goodbye, she whispered,

‘I knew you’d come. Yes, I did. I prayed every night that you would. He heard me. Bless you, my darling girl. I can die in peace now’.

‘Not yet, Ma-’ replied Maria. ‘Not when I’ve just found you!’ She smiled and waved at her mother until they were out of sight.

XXXXX

Emily O’Neill died that night. She slipped away peacefully with a look of serenity on her smoothed-out face. In her hand, she held the matchbox, which cocooned the precious blonde-gold curl.

At the moment of her death, it seemed as if only the thinnest of lines separated heaven from earth.

Chapter 46

Kitty hadn't intended to show Bruce the shocking invitation she had received from the suave gentlemen outside Chichester Festival Theatre. The picture of her mother had appalled her, and she had afterwards cried herself to sleep on several nights. Bruce was worried about Kitty. Having been looking increasingly healthy after her lung removal, she had slipped back into a pallid state again. Bruce frequently asked her how she was feeling and fretted around her to such an extent that Kitty felt she owed him an explanation. She was unsure of how her father would react. She had only rarely seen him when his temper was in full flight, but when it was, it was terrifying as he became out of control and could act violently and irrationally.

The next evening, when Bruce was bringing her nightly hot chocolate up to her bedroom (something he insisted on doing whether Kitty actually wanted it or not!) Kitty held out her hand to him.

'Sit on the bed, Dad. I want to talk to you'.

Bruce thought her sentence had an ominous ring and sat down without question. Kitty had planned all sorts of introductory lines about her mother's new 'career', but now it came to the crunch, she simply took the invitation out of her bedside table drawer and placed it on the bed in front of Bruce. She watched her father as he read the contents of the card. He went from his normal colour to red, then to alabaster white. Of all the incongruous and unwelcome thoughts that came unbidden to Kitty at that moment was the title of the song she used to love, '*A Whiter Shade of Pale'*.

She took her father's hand as his face slowly turned from its ghostly pallor back to florid, which usually heralded a loss of his temper. He got up from the bed, paced the room, banged his head violently against the wall several times and finally shouted in agony,

'The bitch, the bitch! The bitch!'

'Dad. STOP! You're frightening me'.

With a marathon effort, Bruce stopped in his tracks, looked at his beloved daughter, pulled her to him and sobbed.

'I know, Dad. I know. I feel the same'. She paused. 'What can we do to rescue Mum?'

'Rescue her?' he sobbed. 'She's beyond 'rescue', and I DO NOT WANT HER ANYWAY! She has abandoned us - walked out, and who wants a wife who is a *Prostitute?'* he spat out.

He let go of Kitty.

'I must go and think, Kitty'. He began to calm down.

'It was brave of you to tell me, Kit. *My* wife and *your* mother!' he said bitterly as he banged the door behind him. 'How *dare* she?' Kitty heard him saying repeatedly as he went downstairs.

By the next morning, he had hatched a plan. He spent some time on the phone and then set off the following afternoon for Chichester with his grey pinstripe suit over his arm and a silver tie in his pocket. He looked broken and sad but was still a handsome and striking man. Kitty, surveying him, was both baffled and fearful as to what form his visit might take. She badly needed to talk to someone but knew it was unwise to put yet more burdens on her beloved aunt and uncle, Connie and Oliver. Maria and Hope, she reflected with some regret, were in Ireland.

She phoned Robbie, her lifelong pal. Robbie acted fast on Kitty's call and asked Oliver to find a substitute for his youth club meeting that evening, citing, to the intrigue of Oliver, 'a very urgent matter outside the parish that can't wait', and went to Richmond at Kitty's request. He immediately put his arms round her as she opened the door. It was clear she had been crying, and, bad as the situation clearly was for Kitty, Robbie could not help a secret tingling of pleasure that, at last, perhaps she needed him and might even 'reckon' him.

Kitty shared everything with Robbie as they sat together on the sofa. During a pause, he asked Kitty for a candle that they would light and put on the coffee table. All the while, Bruce was in Chichester so they could think prayerfully of him. Kitty readily agreed, and then, Robbie, turning Kitty's face towards him, murmured, 'And Clara too'.

Kitty paused. It was a tussle. Eventually, she replied,

'And Clara too'.

Chapter 47

Bruce had found out about the agency Clara was working for. It was clearly what was termed by the receptionist 'a high-class business giving high-class service'. He gave a false name, fabricated many details on his application form, given his age as younger than he was and said he was 'not very experienced' sexually. Clients were requested to meet in the foyer of a large and anonymous hotel where a room was booked. The Proprietor himself always met new clients, and his escort, 'Chloe', who the client had requested, would be there with him.

Bruce had not perfected the art of deception; in fact, he was a decent and honest individual, and lying was, on the whole, not part of his nature. He was determined, however, as Kitty had asked, to try to bring her mother home by any means possible. Although he and Clara had parted bitterly and had minimal contact ever since, on reflection, Bruce was appalled and saddened in equal measure to think about what she was doing now. He tussled with the discussion inside himself that Escort Ladies were giving a valuable service and, perhaps, in some measure, fulfilled the role of counsellor for some of their more needy clients. But this job was not for *his* wife. No. In his eyes, she was a talented actress, a mother and a wife, *not* a 'High-End Escort.'

Bruce arrived at a five-star hotel about ten miles out of Chichester. Having parked the car, he walked with increasing trepidation to the revolving door of the entrance. His aim was to talk calmly to Clara and invite her to come home and eventually try to draw a line under everything that had gone before. He would apologise for his part in not understanding Clara's needs and take the blame for being heavy-handed over protecting Kitty's needs when she was ill. Clara would see sense and come home that evening, and they would go to counselling to see what they could repair in their marriage. He tried to banish a stanza that kept repeating itself inside his head incessantly. It came from a poem his teacher insisted her pupils learnt by heart:

'*The best laid schemes of mice and men go oft awry*

And leave us only grief for promised joy.'

Bruce looked around the ornate foyer. There was no sign of Clara. As he hesitated, a refined-looking gentleman with oily and shiny black hair and of smallish stature but with a distinguished and suave manner casually strolled up to him.

'Good Evening, sir. You are very welcome'. He shook Bruce's hand. 'May I enquire – are you Mr. John Hadley by any chance?'

Bruce hesitated before he answered.

‘Um – yes, yes I am’.

‘And you are due to meet someone by the name of Chloe?’

‘I am. Yes’.

‘I am the Proprietor here. Cyril Seddon. May I direct you to her, Sir?’ the oily man asked, bowing his head obsequiously.

‘Thank you. Yes’.

Bruce’s stomach churned, and he wanted to rush to the loo. But he kept following the little gentleman.

‘I’ll just let her know you are here’.

He disappeared for a few seconds and came out, with Clara following. Bruce immediately saw that she was heavily made up but looked tired and drawn under the thick foundation. Wearing a black leather jacket over a low-cut pale silk blouse, tight silk black trousers and very high-heeled red shoes, Bruce could not believe the transformation in her appearance.

He gasped. Yes, she was transformed, but not by any stretch of the imagination, in his opinion, for the better; in fact, he concluded in those few seconds, she hardly looked like his wife at all – very glamorous, yes, but somehow her natural beauty had been eclipsed, or, at the very least reduced, diluted, camouflaged, dulled almost beyond recognition.

Clara saw him and gasped,

‘Bruce!’

‘Clara!’

Suddenly, it was as if a wild cat had been let out of its cage. She flew over to him and beat him ferociously on the chest.

‘How dare you come here? How *dare* you, how *dare* you, how bloody *dare you*? This is *my* life now, and it has *nothing* to do with you’. She spat the words out with venom.

‘Get him out, Cyril’, she ordered the oily man who was trying to calm her by repeating over and over,

‘There, there, Chloe, there, there’.

‘And don’t ‘There there’ me! Just throw him out. NOW’.

Bruce had held onto his temper until that moment. Then, as Mr. Cyril Seddon approached him to take his arm and steer him out, Bruce knocked him violently away. The oily man lost his balance and fell to the floor.

‘What are you doing, Clara? You are a whore and a prostitute! How dare you treat Kitty like this, never mind about me’, Bruce shouted fiercely.

The oily man slowly rose to his feet, clearly shaken.

'I'll have you know', he said, finding his courage, 'that this is a high-class business, and we offer a high-class service. We only take ladies of quality and high calibre, yes, high calibre', he said, stroking Clara's arm to comfort her. Are you Chloe's partner?'

'I am her HUSBAND!'

'You have a lot to learn about this business, sir', he replied shakily, 'We offer a service – a kind, thoughtful, helpful service. Often men who come here simply want someone to talk to, who will listen'.

'But that's not all you offer, is it?' Bruce sneered. 'You are trading with my wife's body'.

The oily man spoke very softly.

'I suggest you examine your own attitude, sir. Maybe Chloe does not want to live with a bully of a man any more'.

Bruce went up to Clara and took her roughly by the arm.

'Clara, this life is not for you. Kitty needs you. She *pines* for you*!'*

Clara suddenly looked as though she was going to burst out crying; but instead of tears, there cascaded a torrent of abuse from her lips.

'You've made sure that Kitty belongs to *you* and not *me,* haven't you? Always. You are besotted with her. You have done nothing but take her away from me', she shouted. 'GO AWAY, BRUCE. I AM NEVER COMING HOME!'

Bruce suddenly turned to the man and shouted in his face,

'See what you've done? See what you've done with your tawdry business and your oily words?'

Bruce struck out wildly at the proprietor, landing his fist heavily on the smallish man's chin. He cried out and reeled back, holding his jaw. Clara took her shoes off and ran to the desk.

'Call Security! Now! A client is running amok. Quickly! I said *Quickly! Now*!'

She need not have gone up, for two burly men from the hotel's security had seen what was happening and had virtually picked Bruce up already and were manhandling him out of the hotel. They marched him out and, by a whisker, refrained from actually throwing Bruce onto the pavement. He remained crouched down in shock for several minutes.

Holding his jaw, Mr. Cyril Seddon looked disparagingly at Clara.

'What a man! No wonder you wanted out. Well, you *are* out, I'm afraid, Miss Chloe. I am letting you go', he said, using the favourite cowardly euphemism. 'We cannot have clients' husbands rampaging into our business. It's shocking for our reputation. I'm sorry to see you go, but this has been humiliating beyond belief'.

Clara stared at him.

'I can't believe you are 'letting me go' as you so 'kindly' put it. I've done nothing wrong'. She shook her head and began to cry. 'I've bought clients *in.* Please Cyril'. Let me stay'.

'Your earnings will be at Reception in the morning. I cannot risk another visit from that – that disgusting - *ruffian*! I will cancel all your further customers and also the fee you were due today'.

He turned quickly and headed to his office, shutting the door firmly behind him. Clara wept silently. As she sat there, Mr. Cyril Seddon reappeared, poking his head round the door and calling out to her,

'Your husband has no right at all to come here, no right at all. I think he might have broken my jaw, vicious man! You're welcome to the brute,' and slammed the door shut again with him inside.

Clara packed up her glitzy costumes, discarded the contents of her ashtray, and poured herself a very large whisky from the concealed bottle in one of the drawers. She headed back in the car towards her Bed and

Breakfast in Chichester, vacillating between white fury and abject misery.

She drove recklessly and was fairly soon stopped by a police car that had been following her and monitoring her haphazard braking and erratic lane control. Clara was breathalysed and found to be three times over the limit. The police eventually removed her driving license for one year and fined her heftily.

She was now without her own transport, without her own home, and furthermore, she knew her money would not last long. But of one thing she was certain: she was never going back to Bruce. Not ever. That was definitely a past chapter of her life, not to be revisited. Bruce had humiliated her beyond endurance.

There was one problem: what to do about her daughter Kitty?

Clara's drinking had become slightly more moderate of late since becoming an Escort, but it was about to take a turn for the worst, leaving Clara in an extremely vulnerable and dangerous state.

Chapter 48

It was now five weeks since the fateful day when Clara washed her hands completely of her family. Neither husband nor daughter had set eyes on her again, nor had she communicated with them in any way. When Bruce returned to Kitty in deep distress, the two of them eventually discussed the shape of their future without Clara. Bruce, in a despairing mood, announced to Kitty that he had wanted to sell their large three-storey Victorian townhouse in Richmond, banish all traces of his wife and move to something more modest. He asked for Kitty's opinion on the matter, but, as Kitty speculated, her opinion would not have made any difference to Bruce, so dark was his mental state. Her heart ached to see her father so torn apart, and the ache deepened whenever she thought of her mother (which was a great deal of the time).

Now, to crown it all, Bruce was suggesting they leave her beloved childhood home. This felt like the final blow, converting the profound ache back into its raw, open, gaping wound in her heart. Despite the abhorrent suggestion on the part of her father, Kitty vowed inwardly that she would never leave him now, whatever the future may hold. He would be her priority. She felt she could never, would never, allow herself to fall in love with anyone. No, she would not be that disloyal to him, so great was his suffering. It would feel like another betrayal.

What Kitty had not taken into account was the fact that Robbie had increasingly become her confidante and soul mate, and Robbie's lifelong affection for Kitty had metamorphosed into deepening love. He realised it; she did not – yet.

Robbie visited the house the day after Bruce had dropped the bombshell about selling up. Kitty shared the news with Robbie, suddenly needing her Anam Cara – her soul friend – urgently. Robbie's reaction was immediate and positive.

'Tell you what, Kit, before that we must 'ave a party! This past year, we've got a heck of a lot to celebrate, ain't we?' He quickly corrected himself, '*Haven't* we? First of all, you recover from your lung thing, Hope finds her lost little'un and all that palaver, then before you know it, Maria meets her long lost muvver - mo*th*er -, and what's more, your runaway Sadie says she's coming home with her partner. All the loose ends are being sort of – tied, aren't they? Then, to crown it all, those two cool little'uns are born and Jamie, clever clogs, lands 'imself a place at Cambridge! As for Peter, well, he's taking on the world suddenly isn't he ...?'

Kitty interrupted him, uncharacteristically negative.

‘Yes, and Mum becomes an alcoholic and a prostitute, Gary commits suicide, Dad has his heart broken, Connie has a major operation, and me? - well, I lose a lung just for starters.....’

Robbie grabbed her.

‘Kit, Kit, I know, I know’. He brushed her cheek with his lips, tasting the salt of her tears that were slowly trickling down her cheeks as she folded into his arms.

‘I’m sorry, Robbie. It’s just that it’s been a dreadful year in some ways, and it’s not over yet. I get this permanent feeling of foreboding now.’

‘It has been a rotten year in some ways, Kit, it has, but not in others,’ Robbie replied.

Finally, after months of wanting to, he found his courage and kissed her gently on the lips. Kitty did not resist, and they both lingered there, the kiss growing in strength and passion. Finally, he moved away. Neither said a word, overwhelmed by the moment.

Suddenly, Robbie clapped his hands joyfully,

‘Now Kit. Let’s think about what we’re going to do for this party. I’ve got quite a bit of savings, so we’ll kill the fatted calf and do Christmas lunch for everyone – lamb, pork, turkey, whatever. Con and Oli could do with a rest, for a start. You and me both will organise some silly party games. Hey, but you know what?

We've got to move fast - two weeks to get everything organised! Can we have it here? Will your dad be up for it?'

'Yes, we'll be up for it!' she replied, shocked and suddenly delighted by what was happening between the two of them.

'Right. Let me get paper and a pen. We must make a list. By the way, Kit, I've been wanting to do this for a long time. Can I have another one?

Kitty did not reply but took his face in her hands, and the two of them kissed tenderly and with increasing intensity.

Chapter 49

In Ireland, Emily O'Neill's funeral had been that unique blend of sadness, laughter, memories and tears, mingling and blending to make a potent mix. There was profound relief that Callum's adopted mother had died so peacefully and had met her daughter, granddaughter and great-granddaughter the previous day. It felt something of a miracle and a blessing to them all.

Callum had some serious thinking to do. In her will, his mother had halved her legacy between himself and Erin O'Neill, the daughter she had prayed at length would come home one day. Maria, deeply touched by the generosity of her mother's unrequited love, immediately announced that Callum must have both the house and the financial legacy. Once Maria had made up her mind on matters, there was rarely any moving her. She and Hope knew they were both longing to go back to England to see the family for Christmas, so Maria decided she would return to Ireland on her own soon afterwards to sort out all her mother's affairs with Callum. There was the matter of her name change for a start.

It was clear that, although Callum had many friends, he was bereft of that profound level of love and caring that only Emily, his adopted mother, had given him during her life. Sensing this, Hope suggested that he come back to her house with them, at least for Christmas. At first, Callum could not envisage leaving the vicinity of either his birth mother's grave or his adopted mother's freshly dug one. With his mothers' bodies nearby, he said, he somehow felt safe and that they were near to him in spirit.

During the days after the funeral, however, Callum changed his mind. He was rattling around in the huge house and feeling increasingly lonely without the mother who had wrapped her love around him and kept him warm inside and out. He, therefore, agreed to travel to England with them – the first time he had left Galway, let alone Ireland.

xxxxx

James returned from the end of the Michaelmas term in Cambridge. At first, he was quieter than usual at home but, as Oliver observed, somehow more mature and thoughtful. The agony of falling out with his beloved mother, in particular, had affected him at a deep level, and he was not sure how she would take his next piece of news. Two evenings after his arrival home, Connie was in the kitchen, having taken up her favourite position: elbows on the kitchen table, chin resting on hands, reading the newspaper. Ben and Joc had turned a corner development-wise and were now sleeping without interruption at night from early evening onwards and smiling brightly and winsomely to anyone who talked to them. Rosy was watching the film *Beauty and the Beast,* and Peter was upstairs on his newly acquired and obsessively loved computer.

'Mum, can I tell you something, Mum?'

Connie looked up. She saw her firstborn looking uncharacteristically awkward.

'What's up, Jamie? Problem?'

'No, Mum, definitely not, but I want to know how you'll feel about it'.

Connie held her breath. Things were beginning to settle down, and the home had returned to something resembling normality now, the babies had moved out of the familiar three-month colic scenario. Did her eldest want to leave Cambridge? Had he been asked to leave, even turned out? Or had he made a girl pregnant? Her imagination moved rapidly over the rush of thoughts that felt like fireworks igniting in her brain.

'I'm sure I'll be happy, Jamie', she said brightly, praying hard that it would be so.

'I've got a girlfriend, Mum. I think I'm in love! She's - Susannah'.

Connie immediately stood up, pushed the chair back so that it fell over and gave him a long hug.

'That's lovely, Jamie. I'm *delighted!* So will Dad be - and of course, I need a full description, please,' she joked, 'and perhaps Susannah could come here at Christmas, and we'll show her how just how welcome she is!'.

'Steady on, Mum! You'll be asking me when the wedding is next!' Jamie replied, relieved and happy. He hugged Connie, then looked serious.

'Mum, I really need to know,' he hesitated, 'How's Clara after – after - you know?'

Connie hesitated.

'*Mum,* tell me.'

'Clara's – well - Clara is not around at the moment'.

Jamie knew Connie was concealing the truth and pressed her to tell. Reluctantly, she gave Jamie the bare bones of what Bruce had told her. At the end, Jamie was silent. Eventually, he said,

'Mum, I wouldn't want to bring Susie home if Clara is back. She's – she's....' His speech trailed off.

'Don't say anything, Jamie. I know, I know', Connie said quietly. 'You don't need to put it into words.'

She wanted to complete Jamie's sentence by saying, 'She's a dangerous woman!', but instead, she held her tongue, finally saying,

'Maybe you could say a prayer or two for Clara? I think she's in rather a bad way'.

Jamie shrugged and turned away, totally uninterested in the state of Clara's soul. The very thought of Clara now made him feel sick as if he had betrayed his new love. Connie had an idea of what her son was feeling.

'It's in the past, Jamie. Leave it there', she said, and purposefully went back to reading her newspaper.

Chapter 50

Connie was delighted to welcome her older sister Sadie back into the bosom of the family. Sadie was looking radiant – dark hair shining, and the figure returned to its generous state (as Peter later pointed out with his usual directness). Sadie introduced her partner Morag, who was quiet, shy and very charming, and Oliver and Connie, despite their personal misgivings of same-sex relationships, made them both feel easy and relaxed. Sadie, although not baby-minded by nature like Connie, surveyed the four month-old twins with joy.

‘I swear they look like Jack!’ she laughed. ‘Look at their little noses, Con, and the way they smile’.

Connie secretly failed to see it. She thought they were the image of Oliver.

‘Yes, you may be right, Con. But they’re like their dad too’.

‘No, they are definitely the split image of Jack’.

Connie smiled indulgently at her sister. It was *so good* to see her looking happy after years of mourning her son Jack’s tragic death.

‘They’ll be handsome little fellows then!’ replied Connie diplomatically.

Connie had written a long letter to Sadie the previous week, filling her in about Clara's disappearance and her brother Bruce's heartache. Sadie had always been close to her brother, and they had remained united, struggling through a sea of troubles during their childhood. Sadie never forgot how they had clung together the night they had found their oldest sibling, poor tormented James, hanging lifeless in his room; how they had been battered and bullied by their father; how their mother had loved and protected them, but to their exasperation as children had failed to stand up for them against their father's brutality. She and Bruce had survived, but both had carried the wounds of their childhood into adulthood. Bruce was afflicted for many years by impotence, and Sadie by an unwanted and embarrassing pregnancy, the result of her father's adultery.

Sadie was anxious to see Hope and to introduce Morag to her. Hope was living in the house in Southwark that Sadie had bought, and at one stage, Sadie knew she had feelings for Hope beyond those of a half-sister. Now she was happily settled, Sadie wanted to hug Hope, look into her eyes and make sure that any difficulties between them were well and truly in the past.

Sadie had brought joy and laughter into the vicarage simply through her ebullient presence. Her son Jack had inherited her positivity and had been a breath of fresh air, coping with his disabilities with good-natured humour and clever jokes that left everyone amazed. He was the 'rhyming couplet' comedian of the family, and everyone adored him, especially Jamie, Peter and Rosy.

'And Robbie?' Sadie asked Connie.

'Robbie is preparing everything for us with Kitty. They are very close still,' replied Connie, and turned away to hide a secret smile and suspicion that there was a relationship developing there, much to her delight.

Christmas day arrived with its usual mix in the vicarage of present unwrapping, exclamations, full English breakfast and the hustle and bustle of getting ready for the morning service – finding shoes, forgetting keys, last minute teeth cleaning, Rosy scraping around to find coins for the collection, and this year giving a last minute top up of milk to the babies before finally strapping them into their pram. The entire family crossed the road to Oliver's church 'St. Luke's', Ben and Joseph, once inside, were duly unstrapped and held delightedly by Sadie and Morag. There were always protests about church on Christmas Day from James, Peter and Rosy. These followed a well-worn annual ritual of dragging of heels and arguments as to *why* they had to go, but in the end, the children, without fail, loved the upbeat and joyful service and carol singing that Oliver and his curate masterminded every year.

Oliver looked down the church at his entire family sitting together in one pew and felt a huge swelling of pride and gratitude. God was good, even though He tested you to the limits and put you through the mill at times.

'To whom much is given, much is required', Oliver thought, somewhat ruefully.

Chapter 51

Kitty and Robbie prepared Christmas lunch with a spring in their step. Kitty was gradually realising that she was falling in love with Robbie, who was sixteen years her senior. He still seemed the Robbie she had always known but with a new dimension of allurement and fascination. She saw her father, brave Bruce, making a huge effort to appear in good spirits as he laid the table, folded the napkins, whistled, emptied the bins and washed pots and pans. The numbers coming to lunch had now risen to fifteen, including the new addition to the gathering, Callum from Ireland.

Bruce put the place names round. He had made them himself out of small log-shaped pieces of wood and carved individual names on each one. As he placed them in front of each set of cutlery, he thought of Clara. Her absence was eating into him, and the factor that prevented him from searching for her was a quiet despair that had taken up residence in his heart. He was still shocked to the core at how she had betrayed him, as he saw it, by selling her body. He doubted he would ever truly recover inside from that.

Everyone arrived: first, the Lockwood family en masse, with one of the babies crying, Rosy leaping around joyously, and Jamie and Peter suddenly looking like mature and fully grown men. They had quite taken Sadie's breath away when she first saw the two handsome six feet something adults who had replaced the rather lanky adolescents she had left behind two years previously.

As soon as Oliver arrived back from church, his first action was to pull his dog collar off and throw it with relief onto the sideboard, immediately opening his grey collarless shirt at the neck with abandon. His Christmas was now well and truly beginning!

Maria, Hope, Lucy and Callum arrived. Callum was introduced to the family, and to each member, he gave a little bow, and to Rosy, he twirled his white stick skilfully, much to her delight. He gave it to her for a minute and told her to 'Do a twirl', winning the hearts immediately of everyone there. Sadie opened her arms to Hope, and the two remained in a bear hug for longer than a few seconds. Sadie then introduced her partner Morag, who was given a similar welcome. Mulled wine and fruit juices were served by Robbie and Kitty, and Bruce appeared from the kitchen, drying his hands on his blue and white butcher's apron.

'Lunch is ready!' he announced, with a sudden feeling of good cheer. It was impossible not to have his spirits lifted by the sight of his precious family and most especially Sadie, returned briefly to the fold.

The carved place names were admired, festive red napkins were unfolded, drinks were refilled, too many peanuts and crisps devoured, and finally, Kitty and Robbie reappeared with a huge turkey and a smaller ham, many vegetables and a large tureen of steaming gravy. While Robbie was carving the turkey, Bruce excused himself for a few seconds to take yet another binful of rubbish to the dustbin outside in order to make room inside for after-lunch food scraps and general Christmas debris.

The freezing air hit Bruce as he opened the front door. He saw his breath steam in the cold. It had been a particularly hard frost during the night, and he was aware of the very slippery surface of the path leading to the dustbin. He realised that even in the short space of time that he had been out with his previous bin load, the dustbin lid had frozen up again. It had to be minus four, thought Bruce. As he was pulling the lid off, he idly glanced right and down the hill. He stopped.

There, slowly, so slowly, climbing the hill carrying two bags and staggering in high-heeled shoes that were broken down and giving little protection against the frozen pavement, trudged a woman veering from side to side on the pavement. She was wearing a long black coat resembling a Dickens' pauper from a period drama workhouse.

Bruce stared hard and kept staring, mesmerised. As the figure moved slowly up the hill towards him, he dropped the dustbin lid, sending it clattering to the ground, and, mindless of the icy pavements, ran as hard as he could towards the woman. When he reached her, he flung his arms wide open.

'Clara, my Clara! You've come home!'

Clara sank to the ground.

'I'm sorry, Brucie. So sorry. So sorry. So so sorry. Forgive me please'.

'Come here', said Bruce, gently easing her to her feet. He wiped her tears with his hands.

'You've come home', he repeated incredulously, kissing her cheek.

'Yes, Brucie. I know I can't live without you. Can you ever forgive me?'

'Yes', Bruce replied simply, then enfolded her in his arms and added, 'With all my heart, I can, Clara.'

He took both her bags in one hand and steered her carefully forward with the other. He could tell from her emaciated face that she was incredibly thin and wasted, obviously from hunger and clearly freezing cold.

'I've been – on – the streets, walking and walking,' muttered Clara, her voice croaky and worn as she struggled up the hill with Bruce.

‘You’re home now, Clara. Tell me later, but I’m *never* letting you go again,’ said Bruce as they reached the house.

‘I never ever want to go again’, replied Clara softly.

‘Is Kitty here?’ she whispered after a few seconds.

‘I’ll fetch her in a minute’, replied Bruce. as he led her into the sitting room. Clara could hear the merriment in the dining room and looked up questioningly.

‘The whole family is here, Clara’.

‘Oh no!’ replied Clara, I can’t face them, I can’t, I can’t’.

‘You don’t need to’, replied Bruce.

‘Just Kitty, please’.

‘Just Kitty’.

Bruce left Clara for a minute, his heart singing, and whispered to Kitty,

‘Kit, it’s important you come for a minute’.

Connie and Oliver looked up questioningly. Bruce’s face was shining.

‘I’ll explain in a minute’, he said. ‘Carry on without me’.

He held Kitty's hand and led her into the sitting room. There were no words exchanged, but it felt to Bruce as though the room was charged with light. Kitty said nothing but took her mother's freezing hands and held them.

Eventually, Bruce whispered in Kitty's ear,

''That which was lost is found, Kit.''

Kitty nodded.

Bruce left Kitty and her mother and went to Connie, who was about to begin her lunch.

'Con, leave it just for a minute. A bit of a miracle has taken place.'

Connie hesitated at first when she saw Clara, and then, being the loving, generous, kind person that she was and realising Clara's pathetic state, went towards her with her arms open.

'Clara, welcome home', she said.

Clara whispered, 'Sorry for the hurt, Connie. Sorry, I'm so sorry. I've been a terrible woman'.

Connie held Clara tightly, finally saying,

'Clara, when you're ready, come and have some lunch? I'll lay a place for you'.

Clara smiled wanly. She wasn't sure if she was up to meeting a large gathering, but she was extremely hungry. She had been sleeping rough in bus shelters for over three weeks, had managed with a marathon effort (and aided by a lack of money) to ditch the alcohol, but had found very little food. With her car and her money gone, she was bereft. Her deep longing for home drove her to trudge and hitch lifts little by little by little from Chichester to Richmond–upon-Thames. Reaching rock bottom, she had nearly thrown herself under a bus more than once. The thought of Kitty and of Bruce drove her onwards.

Deep inside herself, however, despite all her failings towards them, she knew she could rely on their forgiveness. Such was the dear nature of their hearts.

While Clara was briefly attempting to tidy herself up in the bathroom, Bruce slipped upstairs and came down carrying a small item wrapped in soft felt. After half an hour, Clara ventured out of the safety of the sitting room with Bruce to the dining room. There were quiet gasps as the family took in both the suddenness of Clara's arrival, even her appearance, which had descended from one of considerable beauty to diminished frailty. Jamie turned pale and excused himself from the table for a few minutes in order to recover from his extreme shock.

Bruce discreetly unwrapped the felt item and put the carved wooden place name marked 'Clara' on the table by the knife and fork that Connie had hastily laid for her. As he was engraving her name in the wood,

Bruce had not dared to believe he would ever be able to use the place name, but here she was in the flesh – Clara - his wife.

Clara ate a small meal quietly, and everyone continued their conversation, although muted and less overtly light-hearted and jovial. Oliver leapt up after the main course to help collect the dinner plates. Maria and Hope followed likewise and brought them into the kitchen. As Hope returned to gather more plates, Maria turned to Oliver,

'Oliver, What a huge relief about Clara'.

Oliver agreed without reserve. He had been devastated by the sight of her so diminished, so tragic. Maria continued slowly as she began to load the dishwasher,

'I'm beginning to see, you know, after so many traumas in our lives this last year, that there must be some master plan behind everything'.

Oliver nodded but said nothing as he bent down to help Maria load the dishwasher. While continuing to stack the messy plates and cutlery, which the dog was now licking with relish, she continued,

'When you think about it, Oliver, every one of us this last year has coped with rogue strands - twisted threads - in our lives that have needed unravelling, haven't we? I was thinking - it's almost as if a master weaver has been gathering the strands and shaping them into patterns that make sense of our lives'.

She hesitated. Oliver waited. Maria continued slowly, thinking hard about every word.

'Perhaps these gathered strands are intertwining to become part of a beautiful tapestry woven out of our failures, our sufferings, and...' Maria paused again, choosing her next words with great care,

'.....and out of our guilt and our need to forgive both others and ourselves'.

She stood up and looked Oliver straight in the eye.

'Oliver', she said, 'It's God who is Master Weaver, isn't it?'

'I believe with my whole heart it is', replied Oliver, facing her.

Maria replied slowly,

'You know, all my adult life, I have been involved in supporting people as they fathom out how to find ways through their pain to reach some kind of wholeness.' She paused again.

'He's the one, though, who ultimately mends our frailties, isn't He?' she said.

'He is. I believe He's the one', replied Oliver, 'who teaches us about forgiveness and reconciliation and walks alongside us in our darkest times, whether we know it or not'.

'Yes', replied Maria quietly.

'And most of all', Oliver continued, 'He's about Love'.

Maria nodded.

'About Love,' she affirmed. There were tears in her eyes. 'It's an intoxicating mix, isn't it, Oliver?'

'Yes,' replied Oliver quietly. 'It's overwhelming'.

They were quiet for a minute, then suddenly Maria wiped her eyes on a tea towel, clapped her hands and reached the dessert bowls from the dresser.

'And now for the Christmas Pudding! Coming, Oliver?'

'In a second', he replied with a smile.

'There's more than one miracle happening this Christmas', Oliver thought as he poured a generous amount of brandy over the pudding he had made for them all. He lit a match and watched the brandy ignite and the dancing blue and yellow flames begin to leap until the pudding briefly became surrounded by fire.

After all the challenges of the past year, thought Oliver, it was turning out to be rather a wonderful Christmas.

‘Well, Halleluia!’ he said out loud as he carried the blazing pudding in. ‘Tuck in everyone! It’s time to celebrate!’

THE END

Printed in Great Britain
by Amazon

37142559R00249